illy wasn't laughing any more. His face was set. He was working himself up for something. 'So, am I not addressin' Master Joe Rat' – his face was almost touching Joe's now – 'the stinkin' little mudlark?'

'Ain't no mudlark.'

The words came out automatically between fiercely gritted teeth. Joe hadn't meant to speak, but he wouldn't be called a mudlark. He'd just been seven hours in the sewers today like any other day, picking through filth for something worth selling, but he was no mudlark. He was a tosher . . .

JOE RAT

❧❧❦❧❧

MARK BARRATT

RED
FOX

JOE RAT

A RED FOX BOOK 978 1 862 30218 1

First published in Great Britain by Red Fox,
an imprint of Random House Children's Books,
in association with The Bodley Head
A Random House Group Company

This edition published 2008

1 3 5 7 9 10 8 6 4 2

Text copyright © Mark Barratt, 2008
Illustrations copyright © Chris Priestley, 2008

The Random House Group Limited supports the Forest Stewardship Council (FSC),
the leading international forest certification organization. All our titles that
are printed on Greenpeace-approved FSC-certified paper carry the FSC
logo. Our paper procurement policy can be found at
www.randomhouse.co.uk/environment

Set in 11.5/14pt Adobe Garamond by
Falcon Oast Graphic Art Ltd.

Red Fox Books are published by Random House Children's Books,
61–63 Uxbridge Road, London W5 5SA

www.kidsatrandomhouse.co.uk
www.rbooks.co.uk

Addresses for companies within The Random House Group Limited
can be found at: www.randomhouse.co.uk/offices.htm

THE RANDOM HOUSE GROUP Limited Reg. No. 954009

A CIP catalogue record for this book is available from the British Library.

Printed in the UK by CPI Bookmarque, Croydon, CR0 4TD

For Patricia

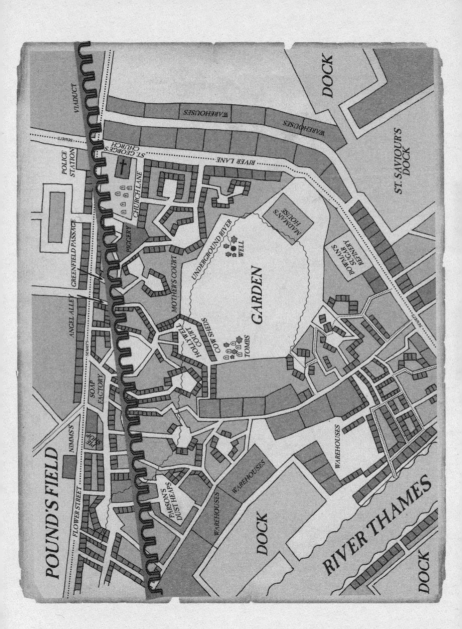

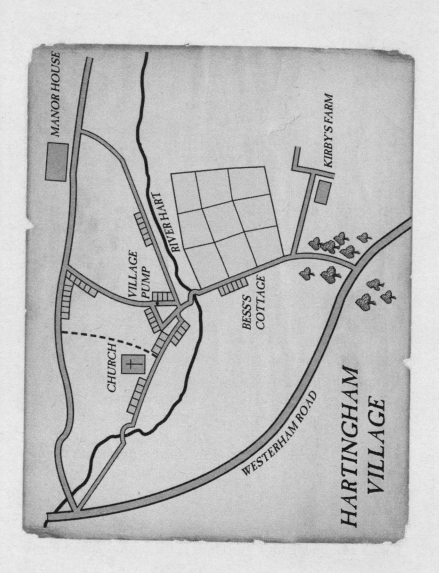

MANOR HOUSE

KIRBY'S FARM

RIVER HART

VILLAGE PUMP

BESS'S COTTAGE

CHURCH

WESTERHAM ROAD

HARTINGHAM VILLAGE

Chapter 1
THE RAT

Up the road the flaring gas jets over Nimms's gin shop lit up the gloom of the November evening. Down the road a single streetlamp flickered and the tramp of the night patrol echoed on the cobblestones. One, two, three . . . eight uniformed figures set out from the safety of the police station. The crushers travelled in groups around Pound's Field, and even then there were parts they didn't visit after dark if they could help it. The tinkle of an out-of-tune piano seeped out into the night. There was damp in the air – not quite rain, not quite fog. Then, in the darkness halfway between Nimms's gaslights and the police station's glimmering lamp, in the gutter where the filthy roadway ended, the ground shifted sideways.

Darker than the dirt of the street, a creature emerged, dripping. Crouched, cowering on all fours, its head swayed this way and that, checking up and down the street, listening as the sound of the police patrol faded down River Lane and away towards St Saviour's Docks. It could have been a dog. It was too big for a cat. Then, as the creature straightened

1

up, the whites of its eyes caught the light. It was a boy.

From his size he might have been eight. From his narrow, wary eyes he could have been eighteen. His feet were bare, but so caked in mud that he looked as if he was wearing long, black boots. Rags clung wetly to his slight frame. Only the eyes shone bright, nervous, alert.

A man and a woman came staggering down the road, voices raised in argument: 'I had it when I went in there!' 'You callin' me a thief?' Nothing seemed to move in the darkness except the whites of those quick eyes, as the boy slid the grating quickly back into place in the roadway and merged with the sooty brickwork of a warehouse. His right hand clutched a little more tightly to the dark canvas bag it held and his left fist closed a little more fiercely over its four brown ha'pennies. The couple passed within touching distance. 'Well I haven't got it now!' 'You sailors is all the same!' The boy could have been invisible.

A pair of costermongers, pushing empty barrows, came up the street on their way home. The boy watched them pass, slipped quickly across the road, ran still half-crouched up the other side of Flower Street as far as the entrance to a narrow alley, and hesitated. He hadn't eaten that day. Just past the soap factory and almost opposite Nimms's place was a cookshop, but the long, bare frontage of the factory was exposed – dangerous. The boy looked into the comforting darkness of the alley. Mother would be waiting. To be safe he needed to go now. His stomach had other ideas.

The canvas bag out of sight under his short, ragged jacket, he walked rapidly up the street, shoulders hunched, arms rigid at his side. Men were suddenly streaming out of the factory. That was good. Amongst the crowd he was hidden. Some of the men crossed the road to Nimms's. Last night there'd been ratting contests in there – dogs killing rats in a ring and crowds of men betting a week's wages on the outcome – but tonight the place was quiet. A few of the factory workers stopped at the cookshop. Most headed on, probably going straight home. It was Monday, and pockets were empty after a long weekend in the taproom.

The boy stood, comfortably ignored, in the centre of a group, eyeing the food through the steamy shop window – great slabs of pease pudding, pie-crust in ha'penny and penny squares, baked potatoes and gravy, flat chunks of dough swimming in grease, bowls of faggots and trays of freshly baked pies. He fingered the ha'pennies in his hand. He stood too long.

'Hey, Joe! Joe Rat!'

'Hey, Ratboy! You smell, you filthy tosher!'

'Hey, how come someone round here smells like they bin down the sewers all day?'

'What's your name, Ratboy? Eh? Oi, I'm talkin' to you.' It was the leader of the gang – a brawny sixteen-year-old named Billy.

Joe made no move to run. His mouth went tight. The men standing around him had moved on, and he'd been so intent on the food he hadn't noticed. It had been a stupid mistake; the kind a complete novice might have made. He should have gone into the shop or gone straight to Mother, but he didn't waste time thinking about that now. His eyes flicked sideways, scanning the figures that surrounded him. There were seven of them. Sometimes it was six; sometimes as many as twelve. Seven gave him a better chance. Not to fight. He was too small for a fighter. But he was quick, quicker than Billy if it came to a chase, and the other boys needed Billy with them to attack.

Billy took a step forward. He was in no hurry. He rolled the sleeves of his shirt tighter over the thick muscles of his arms. Winter or summer Billy wore that shirt – no collar, no kerchief, no coat.

'What you doin' here, Joe Rat?' Billy was enjoying himself, using the rest of the gang as an audience. 'Your family's all round the back in the rubbish.' The gang laughed dutifully. Joe said nothing, gritting his teeth a little tighter. Billy took another step towards him.

''Cept you ain't got no family, have you, Joe? Poor little Joe!' Billy's voice was low, almost gentle. 'I think I smelled your ma last Sunday, Joe. In St George's churchyard. She smelled worse than you do. But then she's bin dead a while, ain't she?'

Another gale of laughter. But Billy wasn't laughing any more. His face was set. He was working himself up for something. 'So, am I not addressin' Master Joe Rat' – his face was almost touching Joe's now – 'the stinkin' little mudlark?'

'Ain't no mudlark.'

The words came out automatically between fiercely gritted teeth. Joe hadn't meant to speak, but he wouldn't be called a mudlark. He'd just been seven hours in the sewers today like any other day, picking through filth for something worth selling, but he was no mudlark. He was a tosher, and every tosher despised the miserable kids and old women who haunted the muddy riverbank at low tide.

The smaller boy's determined face seemed to enrage Billy. Suddenly he was shouting. 'What's your name, Ratboy?' Joe stooped a little lower. His eyes flickered sideways again. The gang was mostly to Billy's left, blocking off the route to Mother and safety. Joe backed the other way. He was almost past the corner of the cookshop. A couple of men stood in the doorway eating pies, enjoying the spectacle.

'Come on, Billy,' said one. 'What you waitin' for? Scared or somethin'?'

'Go on! Clear off out of it, the lot of you!'

It was the shopkeeper, red-faced in a dirty apron. The fracas was obstructing the doorway, spoiling trade. Just for an instant Billy's eyes were off Joe. He ducked and backed and side-stepped in one movement and was past the slow-footed boy on his left and away down the dark passage between the cookshop and the next house before anyone else had moved.

Joe ran. He'd spent his whole life in the maze of alleys and courtyards and lanes they called Pound's Field, and he knew this square mile of East London as well as anyone. He also knew that now they'd spotted him with his toshing bag, Billy and the gang wouldn't give up until he was safe in Mother's Court. Sometimes they caught him; sometimes he got away. It was a game Joe played out twice, sometimes three times a week. But it was a game that had ended in cracked ribs more than once, and working the sewers with a cracked rib was no joke.

Joe dodged left through a narrow passage. A gaslight flickered on his right. Not that way. Blind alley. On down the passage he ran, behind Parson's dust heaps, where men and women picked endlessly over the rubbish of the district. After that there was less light and his bare feet were almost silent on the filthy ground, but that didn't mean they weren't still behind him. He sprinted the length of Sweetwater Lane, following the high warehouse walls. He could hear running footsteps at his heels. Joe was fast, but he tired quickly. He was never going to outrun them. He needed a crowd to disappear into.

He cut down another alley, past men and women idling under gas lamps, jeering at the chase as it passed. It didn't occur to him to ask anyone for help. Out on busy River Lane he turned left, up past Bowman's, the massive sugar refinery, then across the road, dodging amongst cabs and porters' wagons. 'Oi! Mind out, you little ramper!' They were still unloading on the docks, dragging heavy wagons across to the refinery. The roadway was sticky with raw sugar under his feet.

He'd found the crowd he wanted, but two of the gang were very close now – almost close enough to grab him. Joe ran on desperately, fighting for breath, feeling the strength beginning to drain from his legs. Outside the dockyard gates the heavy-set figure of the Watchman stood, impassive as ever. He heard the big man's voice boom out as he passed: 'I'll have the crushers on the whole pack of yer!' The Watchman made no move to stop the boy, but when Joe glanced behind him again, it seemed that perhaps he had delayed his pursuers for a moment, because now there was a gap between them which gave Joe just a trace of hope.

He ran on past high walls and locked gates, past shops stuffed with brass ship's instruments he didn't know the names of. He ducked into Church Lane. They said his brothers were buried in St George's churchyard along with his mother, but he didn't really know. Poor folk who died of the cholera didn't get marked graves. There were so many they just threw them in a pit and covered them over. Billy's jibe about his mother came back to him, and his anger gave him another burst of energy. He sprinted flat out for the low wall that blocked the end of the lane, and vaulted it without breaking stride, skidding through a great pile of rotting cabbage leaves where the costermongers trimmed their vegetables under the railway arch. Through here and he'd be back almost to where he'd started on Flower Street and then it wasn't more than a hundred yards to Mother's.

Down an alley so narrow he could touch both walls Joe came out onto Flower Street, lungs bursting, gasping for air. And suddenly he was lost. The archway – the way to Mother's – it simply wasn't there. A man with a monkey perched on his shoulder was working a barrel organ. A crowd had gathered – men from the gin shop, drunk and laughing, and next to the cart half a dozen ragged children dancing in the light of the organ-grinder's lamp. Confused by the noise and the light and exhausted from the chase, Joe looked around stupidly. Where was the alley? Then he saw it – or thought he did.

He hadn't taken a dozen steps before he knew he'd made a mistake. The organ-grinder must have been blocking the way to Mother's. This wasn't Greenfield Passage. This was the way to Holywell Court and his own lodging house, and since they built the new warehouses on Sweetwater Lane a few years back, there was only one other way out of here, and he wasn't going to show Billy and the gang that. Better to take the beating and lose his tosh.

Joe ran straight past his own house, on to where a blank wall blocked the old alleyway that had lost its name, and stopped, leaning against the bricks. Two stupid mistakes – first standing outside the cookshop, then the wrong alley! But there was no use in thinking about that now. It was only a beating. It wasn't the first, and like as not it wouldn't be the last.

The darkness was almost complete under the towering wall of the warehouse, but not complete enough. Joe heard the running feet of his pursuers, saw them stop at the sight of the warehouse wall. He could see them, so they could see him.

It was two junior members of the gang – both probably younger than him. They stopped at a distance, bent double, getting their own breath back, eyeing him warily, as if now they had caught him they weren't sure who had cornered whom. For a moment Joe thought of charging them, getting his own blows in first for once. But he knew it wouldn't change anything.

He hadn't long to wait. Billy and the rest of the gang came hurtling round the corner, knocking the two younger boys flying. 'What you two doin'?' Billy gasped roughly, pulling the two boys to their feet. Then he caught sight of Joe, and in the dimness Joe could see him smile.

'Well, now, if it ain't Joe. Caught like a rat in a trap, eh, Joe?' Joe held the canvas bag in front of his stomach for protection. There was no way out of here. There were seven of them, but they probably wouldn't all attack. Some of them only liked to come in for a final kick or two when he was on the ground. He knew where the first blow was coming from. It was part of being gang leader – like getting first share of any food.

Billy walked slowly up to him, his breath still coming fast from the chase. Or was it excitement now? He ripped the bag from Joe's grasp and flung it behind him without looking to see who caught it. Joe watched the older boy's eyes run up and down his body. He saw him register the closed fist.

'Shake then, Joe.' Billy's voice was soft. He liked this part more than the punching and the kicking. 'Shake on it just to show there's no hard feelin's, eh?'

Joe had watched a cat play with a mouse like this. Then he had watched some of these same boys catch the cat, hang the screaming, writhing animal by its tail and gouge out its eyes with sticks. Well, they hadn't got him strung up yet! With a quick movement he threw his four ha'pennies full into the older boy's face. He knew it would make the beating worse, but he was glad he'd done it.

Billy dashed the back of his hand across his face, mouth hanging open in stupid astonishment. Joe almost laughed. Then Billy's eyes went blank. He was ready. Joe saw the first blow coming. There was no use in dodging it, but he did it anyway. Billy shouted with anger and was on him like a bear – knees, fists, boots. Once Joe was on the ground, Billy stepped back and let the rest of the gang have their turn. Most of them were barefoot like Joe, and their kicks did less damage, but their fists and knees were hard. Joe forgot where he was. The brick-work of the warehouse was below him now. The sky was at his feet. There was a roaring in his ears above the shouting and cursing of the gang.

'All right, that's enough. I said that's enough!' The gang stepped back at Billy's command. 'Don't want to hurt him too much, do we? A tosher ain't no good if he can't go down the sewers, is he? Are you, Ratboy? Eh? Joe Rat?' There was some-thing almost anxious in Billy's voice, as if he feared he might have gone too far this time. Then the boy stirred and groaned, holding his guts where the worst kicks had landed. 'That's it, Joe. You ain't so bad, are yer? Now let's see what we got. Where's the bag?'

Joe struggled for breath, trying to raise himself onto his hands. The roaring in his ears had subsided, but there was no strength in his arms and legs.

'Pick him up.' It was Billy's voice again. Two of the gang lifted Joe into a sitting position, and propped him against the wall. Billy had the bag open now. 'Stinks! Your tosh stinks, Joe Rat. And you got what?' His voice was heavy with sarcasm. 'Oh, look, boys! Joe's bin scavengin' the sewers all day and he's got a lovely bit of old rope. And what's this here?' Billy passed each item, still dripping sewer water, to another boy to hold. 'Another bit of old rope! That's a wonder, Joe. Two bits of old rope. That's a good day's work for you, Ratboy.' Billy put his face down close to Joe's. 'You got blood on your face, Joe.' He wiped his own sleeve hard across Joe's cut face. Joe moaned. He tried not to, but he couldn't stop himself. Billy liked this part too.

Billy pulled the items from Joe's canvas bag, mocking each in turn: several more short lengths of wet, mud-encrusted rope; maybe two dozen copper nails, all from under the same grating down on River Lane – seeing them, Joe could feel his fingers groping in the mud and slime again, and the chill, oozing filth washing around his legs. Billy drew out an old shawl, too foul to tell the colour. And last . . .

The sky had cleared and there was a glimmer of moon now, as Billy pulled the last item slowly from the dark canvas bag and held it aloft. It gleamed a moment, before the clouds covered the open patch of sky once more. A silver watch chain. Someone had dropped it down the grating and into the sewer, or maybe a dipper had thieved it off a gentleman and dumped it when the crushers got too near. It was the kind of thing a tosher dreamed of finding. You could go weeks, months, without anything worth a quarter as much. Even Mother would have given him a shilling for it. Joe watched the chain slip out of sight into the pocket of Billy's trousers. He felt nothing. It was gone and that was an end of it.

The youngest of the gang was on his hands and knees, searching the alley for the four ha'pennies Joe had thrown at Billy. Finally he presented them to the gang leader.

'Search him,' snapped Billy. 'Four browns is nothin'. Little rat's probably got a sackful of chink hidden in them rags.' The boy, who had looked so proud of the four coins, hung back. 'Go on! What you waitin' for? He ain't gonna do nothin'. Are you, Ratboy?'

Two boys searched every crevice of the rags which covered

Joe's body. He lay still, allowing their search, making no attempt to resist. There was nothing in the big pockets, sewn specially into the inside of his jacket, but in the right pocket of his breeches, screwed up in a twist of damp paper, they found a penny.

'All right. That's it, boys.' Billy was satisfied. 'See yer soon, Joe.' He threw the empty canvas bag back at Joe. And they were gone.

Joe lay still as the gang's laughter faded into the night. A train steamed heavily across the viaduct, making the ground tremble under him. From the clank of the trucks it was probably a goods train, heading into Aldgate Station. Shouting came from Holywell Court. The clock in St George's struck six.

The boy lifted himself to a standing position, testing legs and feet, flexing each finger in turn. There was nothing broken, but the left knee felt bad and his guts ached. He moved to where the shadows were deepest, and for the first time since he came out of the ground on Flower Street his teeth unclenched. He bent double, hand to mouth, stomach working painfully, retching, coughing, holding his sides. But he wasn't throwing up.

From his mouth Joe drew a long, fine, silk thread inch by inch, finally coughing a tiny leather drawstring bag into his cupped hands. He opened the bag and tipped its contents onto the palm of his left hand. A trace of a smile was on his bruised lip. A joey. A single silver groat. Four pence. Mother might have given him a ha'penny for it. He dropped the coin back into the bag, stowed it in his pocket and made his way slowly back down the alley to Holywell Court.

Chapter 2

A Rat's Secret

Close to thirty houses were crammed together around the narrow yard called Holywell Court where Joe lived. His was one of twenty, identical, yellow-brick buildings, which had been put up no more than ten years ago, but were already crusted with coal soot. These made up three sides of the court. On the fourth side stood a group of much older, wooden structures that looked as if they had once been stables. The inhabitants of the brick houses called the old buildings cow sheds and those who lived there cattle. It started a fight at least once a week. Rents were lower in the cow sheds, but Mother collected there, just as she did in Joe's lodging house and nine of the other brick-built houses.

Joe had been sleeping at number 16 Holywell Court for nearly four years. He didn't call it home – he couldn't remember ever having called anywhere home – but it was a sight better than sleeping rough. Back when he was first out on his own, before Mother found him and sent him toshing down the sewers, there had been many a night when he didn't have a penny for his lodging and he'd skippered out in doorways on the Whitechapel Road. Joe still thought about those days sometimes. But he never thought back further than that if he could help it, because back there was a place with towering, whitewashed walls and rows and rows of barred windows, a place he called childhood, a place he was never going back to no matter what.

The front door to number 16 was open, and Joe made his way straight up the creaking staircase, stepping easily over the broken treads. There was no light and no banister, but he was used to finding his way in the dark. On the second floor he pushed open a door, and a familiar airless fug enveloped him. He felt his way past the uncurtained window, past sleeping figures which lay stretched out in beds and on the floor between the beds. People came and went at 16 Holywell Court, but, as his eyes grew accustomed to the darkness, he reckoned there were probably a dozen people in the room tonight. Sticking close to the wall, he made it to the far side, where a boy a little bigger than Joe lay curled up on a bundle of rags on the floor.

'Hey, Plucky Jack.' Joe's voice was a whisper. The huddled figure on the floor stirred.

'Smell you comin', Joe boy.' It was Jack's usual greeting. 'Six already, is it?'

'Past six. I got held up.' Joe knelt on the bare floorboards and couldn't suppress a groan of pain. There was already a swelling coming up on his left knee.

'You all right?' Jack's voice was concerned. 'Billy didn't catch you again, did he?'

15

'I'm OK.'

'You got pluck, Joe Rat. I'll give you that.'

Joe didn't mind when Plucky Jack called him Joe Rat. He didn't mind when he told him he smelled bad. Jack had matted black hair that stuck up almost straight on his head and a grin that showed where a front tooth was missing. Out on the streets he sold oranges, lemons, nuts, chestnuts, onions, salt, watercress, boot laces, coat studs, steel pens – in fact, anything he could lay his hands on. Though where he got his gear from half the time Joe had no idea. Plucky Jack could sell a cat its own fleas. That's what they said round Pound's Field.

'Makes two of us then, don't it?' said Joe. 'Plucky Joe and Plucky Jack.'

'Sounds like a music-hall act.' Joe could hear the smile in Jack's voice. 'We could try out at Nimms's on Saturday night after the rattin'. How's your singin' voice, Joe?' And Jack launched into a raucous improvised song: '*Oh there's gold in them there shores, if you don't mind the stink . . .*'

'Shut up your racket!' A rough voice came from one of the beds – a tramp in from the country for the winter probably.

'Shut up yourself, you old bone-grubber,' Jack snarled back. Joe had seen Jack fight men twice his size right in this room, but the man in the bed, invisible in the darkness, didn't want a fight. He grumbled some more to himself, and then there was silence. Jack lowered his voice: 'What you say we tip that old muck snipe out and you nail his bed for your eight hours?'

Joe let out a snort of laughter through his nose. When Joe laughed, his mouth stayed tight shut and his eyes disappeared.

You couldn't help laughing around Plucky Jack, even if a dozen Billys had been thumping your bones.

'I'll stick to the floor,' he said finally. 'Not so many bugs down 'ere.'

'Don't know about that.' Jack reached down under the piece of sacking that covered him and scratched.

'Sleep a bit more, Jack. I don't need the shakedown just yet.'

'You woke me up to tell me you don't need the bed? You're as daft as the rest of 'em in this stinkin' den.'

'I'll be back in a bit, Jack. Somethin' I gotta do.'

Joe felt his way quickly back across the room and down the stairs. From behind the kitchen door came the sound of a mouth organ, a sudden shout of laughter and the sweet smell of cooking – cabbage, maybe some bacon. But Joe didn't think about his hunger now. He picked his way soundlessly over the boards, which were already rotten in places, crept down the crumbling wooden steps to the cellar, and stepped thigh-deep into water, feeling his feet sink into a familiar layer of sludge. In Pound's Field all the houses with cellars were like this. Some said there was an underground river somewhere, others that it was just cesspools overflowing. Either way, to a tosher it was nothing.

'Catch Mother shellin' out to the pump-gang,' Joe murmured aloud. He talked to himself down here sometimes, just as he did in the sewers. 'She'd rather we all slept in a cesspool than part with a penny she don't 'ave to.' Joe extracted the tiny leather pouch once more from the pocket of his soaked and tattered breeches. 'Now then, my little joey, Billy don't know about you, does he? Mother don't know about you. Joe's little joey!' He gave that tight little laugh again at his own joke. 'She got her pirates and bullies all full of bluff and bustle, but ain't none of them game to follow where you're goin', my friend. Only Joe Rat got the nerve for that . . .'

Still murmuring softly to himself, he waded across the pitch-black cellar to the far wall, clambered onto a pile of rubble and reached up to the ceiling, feeling for a strip of sacking which was wedged tight into the corner. The bricks were different on this wall, red and smaller than the ones that lined the rest of the cellar, and behind the sacking they were loose. One by one Joe removed the loose bricks, placing each in turn in the water at his feet. He hung the sacking on a nine-inch nail, driven into the loose mortar. A draught of air touched his face. He could see the clouded night sky.

Joe pulled himself up, bare toes feeling for familiar holds in the brickwork. The hole was no wider than his shoulders, and he'd propped it with timber to stop the whole wall collapsing. Beyond was overgrown grass, bushes, tangled bramble and thorn, and further still a clump of tall trees holding the last of their leaves – the only trees standing outside the churchyard in the whole of Pound's Field. From the Whitechapel Road to the docks Mother controlled everything that moved, but this was one place her hand didn't reach, one place even she wouldn't expect her minions to go. He lay still in the damp, tussocky grass. There were night sounds here you couldn't hear anywhere else in Pound's Field – the hoot of an owl, a fox's bark. The smell of the grass and the earth was different from anything else he knew. It made him think of secrets and danger. But that was because of what he did here and what lay beyond the trees.

He made his way along the back wall of 16 Holywell Court to where it formed an angle with the cow sheds. You could see how at one time the old timber buildings had had doors on this side, which were now boarded up. You could also see how number 16 and a couple more houses had been built straight into the old garden wall. But no windows looked out this way from Holywell Court. If you stood way over on River Lane outside the docks, you could see the trees over the high, spiked wall, but from the court there was no hint that this place of grass and earth and secrets existed.

Twenty yards further on, the garden wall was completely hidden by a group of enormous bushes. The glossy green leaves of their lower branches were tangled with thorny scrub, but in the spring Joe had seen great pink and red flowers hanging from the upper branches, like the paper lanterns in the market on Saturday night. He pushed through, holding the brambles back with careful fingers.

In the middle of the dense bushes in a wide oval of ground, a line of old stone tombs stood out, pale in the darkness amongst dying ferns and trailing ivy. There were a dozen of them in all, each with a pair of low double doors set into the base and topped with the statue of a sleeping animal. Joe liked to run his fingers along the writing carved into each block, feeling the sharp edges on some of the stones, the worn roughness of the oldest. He hesitated, eyeing the monuments in turn. Which one had he used last time? Oh, yes . . . Time had weathered some of the statues to the point where you couldn't be sure if they were cats or dogs. But there was no mistaking this one – the heavy-set shape of a bull mastiff, eyes closed, ears drooping, snout resting on folded paws, tail curled around its hindquarters.

'All right, boy?' murmured Joe. He reached up to give the stone dog's head a pat. 'Bin lookin' after Joe's tosh then?'

He squatted down at the base of the statue. Carved into the low wooden doors was a pair of torches, burning upside down. One night Joe had noticed the keyholes were upside down too. The blue paint on the doors was cracked and peeling, gone altogether in many places, and one door had rotted at the bottom, leaving a gaping black hole where the hinge had been. Joe reached in, deep into the burial chamber, up to his shoulder, stretching his fingers . . . Panic gripped him. He grasped wildly at nothing. It was gone . . . No. There it was.

Joe drew a grey cloth bag out of the tomb as tenderly as if it had been a living thing. He loosened the drawstrings and felt inside, fingering the contents an item at a time, recognizing each by its shape – three silver teaspoons and a fork, a glass scent bottle, a pewter tankard and an inkwell, a small leather bag containing copper coins and a few silver ones too, two pearl earrings in a silk handkerchief and his best find ever – a silver signet ring wrapped in oilcloth.

For all the more valuable items and most of the silver coins, he could remember the exact moment he had found each one, sieving the foetid sludge of the sewers or probing deep with the long-handled hoe that was like another limb to him. He'd lost tosh worth maybe twice as much to Billy and his gang; there was no counting how much had gone to Mother. But Joe never thought about that stuff – it was gone, and it wasn't coming back. But this was something Billy didn't know about, something Mother didn't know about, something he hadn't even told Plucky Jack. This was Joe Rat's secret. He had no idea if he would ever be able to dispose of his hoard, but, as he opened the little leather purse and added his silver joey to the coins inside, he was glad. His guts and his knee still hurt him. But he was glad.

Joe closed his bag and scuttled, silent as the shadow of the great bushes, over to another tomb. This might be the safest hiding place in Pound's Field, but he still liked to move his tosh every time. Some kind of terrier lay on the top of this one, like the dogs he'd seen going into Nimms's – stumpy tail, paws stuck straight out in front, eyes closed. But this statue was older or maybe the stone was different, because the rain had got into it, tunnelling out tiny holes. The ears were gone, and the back of the head and nose were worn and stained in patches. But the doors were still solid, locked and immovable. He scrabbled quickly at the foot of the plinth, slipping the bag into a shallow hole, replacing the flat stone which concealed his hiding place. Then, as he pulled the ivy back to cover the stone, a cry came from high in the damp November air.

'*Yes! Yes!*'

A shiver ran down the back of Joe's neck. Didn't matter how often he heard that cry, it always did the same thing to him. This was what kept Mother and Billy and Plucky Jack and everyone else in Pound's Field away from the garden. Joe twisted sharply. The wind was blowing now, tossing the trees, sending the clouds scudding, letting the moon shine out fitfully. Through a gap in the dark surrounding bushes, the pointed wooden gables and broken chimneypots of the big old house stood out, silhouetted like jagged teeth against the night sky, towering over the surrounding buildings. Only the tall stack of the sugar works next door rose higher.

'*Yes!! Yes!!*'

The voice echoed from the walls around the garden where Joe cowered motionless amongst the gravestones. It echoed out into the darkness, through the stinking courts and alleyways of Pound's Field, down to the docks and out across the river. It stopped the talk of the men lounging on the wharf. It turned the Watchman's head, halted the police on their night patrol, stilled the drunken arguments in the sailors' tap houses on River Lane.

'*Yes!!! Yes!!!*'

The people of Pound's Field called him 'the Madman', as if there was only one. They told tales about the Madman to frighten the kids and each other – how he was a gentleman once and lost everything at cards and sold his soul to the Devil for one last stake at the tables and could talk to ghosts and raise the dead from their graves. They said he shouted to the Devil to come to him at night. Some said that years back they'd seen him after dark walking the streets. But nobody ever saw him now. It seemed he never left the huge, crumbling house. Even when the local kids dared each other to throw stones over the high front wall – smash another windowpane – even then no one appeared. The only sure sign that there was still anyone living in the house at all was a smudge of smoke from one broken chimney and the awful cry in the night.

There it was again. As Joe hurriedly finished burying his tosh, it rang out once more from somewhere high in the house, a raw scream of affirmation – '*Yes!!! Yes!!!*' – but in a voice that was hoarse, desperate, lost.

Chapter 3
THE WHITE BIRD

There was frost across the whole countryside. Bess shivered, pulled the blanket around her shoulders and rubbed quickly at the windowpane. The sky was beginning to lighten beyond the wood, and across the lane she could make out the dim shapes of the cows in the field. On the other side of the room her mother still slept in the big bed.

Bess pressed close to the window and thought about her father, Reuben Farleigh, who last year would have been the man taking the cows up to the Manor Farm for milking in the morning. She wondered where he had spent the night. She wondered whether he would be back that day, and if he was, whether it would be good news this time. But Bess wasn't watching for her father, not at this hour. It was something else she was waiting for, something that had meant the difference between a special day and an ordinary day ever since she was a little girl. A dog barked somewhere in the village and the cockerel which had woken her crowed again. Then there was a sudden flurry of white wings, and he was there.

Bess held her breath, not wanting to mist the glass, while the barn owl perched lightly on its usual tree stump in the hedgerow. Her lips moved silently, forming words: 'I wish . . . I wish . . . I wish . . .' The great bird swivelled its head left and right and was still, merging into the frosted landscape. For a moment the huge black eyes seemed to look straight at her; then the broad wings spread again, and the bird flew low and silent up across the field and away towards the steep escarpment of the downs.

Bess followed the flight of the bird northwards in the early dawn, as it disappeared at last beyond the point where she herself had ever travelled. She let out a deep sigh, got up from the cot, which was now so small for her she had to sleep curled up, dressed quickly and bent close to examine her sleeping mother's face.

The habitual furrow between the brows was gone. The lines at the corners of the mouth were smoothed out. Bess thought of the stories her father had told her of their wedding day, when Jane had walked up to the church all in white, the prettiest girl in Hartingham – the prettiest girl in the whole of Kent, that's what Father said. And he would be home that day. Now that she had seen the white bird she was sure of it.

She tiptoed across the dim room and eased up the latch. The single room downstairs was as dark as the bedroom above. She raked out the wood ash from the hearth and laid a new fire, fetching logs from the dry stack in the corner. Near the wood-pile a dozen hand-woven fruit baskets were stacked on the bare, flagstoned floor, along with two more waiting to be finished. A month ago her mother had suddenly announced they were to take up weaving. She had hopes of a big order, she said, and here was an answer at last to their money worries. Bess had twisted the long willow sticks until her hands bled. Then abruptly Jane had abandoned weaving, and they'd gone back to taking in washing.

The fire was starting to burn, warming the dampness from the room. Bess cut a slice from the remains of yesterday's loaf, and set it near the flames to toast. There was water still in one of the two buckets by the front door. She filled the copper kettle, and set it on a hook over the fire.

While she waited for the water to boil and the bread to finish toasting, she fetched the washboard and the wooden wash pans, and set them outside the front door. This year she was tall enough to have to duck under the overhanging thatch. The sky was a heavy grey and the air was chilly, but she and her mother would work in the open air, if the rain kept off. There was more light there, and the floor of the cottage didn't get soaked.

The room was full of the smell of toasting bread now. Bess crumbled the toast into the teapot and added boiling water, setting it down to stew. They had been calling this tea for the last six months, since her father first got sick. She lingered over the basket of mending, fingering the delicate white muslin dress that lay on top. There had been a stain at the waist, but that was gone now, and her mother had been repairing some tiny tears in the delicate silk lace trimming around the neck and sleeves. She'd also added red satin ribbons. Bess held the dress up against her own plain white pinafore.

26

'What you at, you timbersome girl? Put that down now. Do you want to be a-dirtying it up again?'

Bess started violently and dropped the dress into the basket. She hadn't heard her mother come downstairs. The girl fetched tea in small wooden bowls, and they drew close to the fire, her mother in a chair, Bess kneeling by the fender. Jane Farleigh winced at the taste of the 'tea'. 'Filthy muck. That I should ever be a-drinking this kettle-bender, like the pauper-folk. He'll have us all in the workhouse, that father of yourn.'

'It's not Father's fault.' Bess's eyes flashed, as she leaped quickly to her father's defence. 'He didn't get sick a-purpose.'

'Ay, take his part, won't you? Still, 'tis I as has to earn the money now, annit?' Jane pulled the fancy muslin dress out of the basket and held it up herself. 'Why shouldn't I have my own lace to wear?' she demanded. 'I'm not so old and wore out. There's those still reckon Jane Farleigh a handsome woman.'

'The beauty of Hartingham.' Bess smiled and her mother smiled with her. 'That's what all the girls at school used to say.' Bess bit her lip, wishing she could take the words back, not wanting to remind her mother of how she'd had to leave the village school in May to help with the washing and save on the tuppence a week. Sure enough, the sour expression was back on her mother's handsome face at once.

'I'll never have any nice things again now,' she said. 'Not now your father won't never make no money again most like.'

Bess changed the subject quickly. 'Shall we take it back to the big house today then, Mother?'

'Take what back?'

'The dress. It's finished, isn't it? And you've added those beautiful bows. I didn't hear the housekeeper ask for you to do that.'

'You hear what you shouldn't hear and you don't hear what you should,' her mother pronounced. 'The dress is not finished. But we'll call at the manor on our rounds and see if there's more work needs a-doing.'

Mother and daughter sorted swiftly through the dirty laundry in the big canvas bag. Then they set out in the direction of the village green, picking their way down the rutted lane.

Business was poor. Bess could see the villagers didn't really like her mother and, though she knew it was disloyal, when she saw her through their eyes she could understand why. There was something in her manner which suggested that even though it was Jane Farleigh who was taking in washing, she was nevertheless superior to these ordinary village folk. After all, wasn't she 'the beauty of Hartingham'?

As they passed the pump, Bess spotted a man doing the rounds of the village directly after them. With his heavy walking stick and battered stovepipe hat, Harry Trencher had been a regular visitor to Hartingham since Bess was a child. At hop-picking time he was the lollyman who sold sweets and buns to the children. The rest of the year he would arrive one week with a patent medicine promising to cure every human ill, and the next week it would be brushes or some wondrous mechanical invention from across the seas. Mr Trencher was from London, and he could do conjuring tricks and talk like no one Bess had ever met before, but this last year there was something about the man she didn't like – something about the way he looked at her. She didn't know if it was a change in Harry Trencher or a change in her.

Her mother didn't look round, but Bess sensed she had spotted Mr Trencher too. Her walk became slower, and the salesman soon caught up with them. 'Mornin', Mrs Farleigh. Miss Farleigh.' He lifted his hat with exaggerated politeness, and swished his walking stick, cutting at the wet grass at the side of the lane. Bess had always liked it when Harry Trencher called her Miss Farleigh. Somehow she didn't seem to like it so much any more.

'Why, good morning, Mr Trencher. What a surprise! Say good morning to Mr Trencher, Bess.'

As they talked, Bess found herself watching her mother. It was all pleasantries and the weather, but there was a manner in her mother she'd never seen before – the way she looked down and then up suddenly from under her eyelashes at the man, the colour in her cheek. This week Trencher had pictures of a machine he was showing at all the houses. 'Change the lives of women for ever, this will,' he claimed grandly. 'Take a look, Mrs Farleigh.'

Bess looked over her mother's shoulder. Mr Trencher stood rather close. The picture showed a woman washing clothes in a barrel, using a long-handled dolly-mop. 'Looks no different to our own,' she said shortly.

'Hush up, Bess,' said Jane quickly. 'What do you know of it?'

'But see what it says there, Miss Farleigh.' Mr Trencher put his hand on Bess's arm, as he pointed to the bottom line of the advertisement. Bess could smell pipe tobacco and a sharp, stronger smell on his breath.

'Go on, read it out,' said her mother.

For a moment Bess found herself unable to speak. With the man so close, touching her like that, surrounding her with his smell, she felt as if she had been struck dumb. Mr Trencher prompted her, spelling out the words: 'Corrugated galvanized steel.'

'I can read well enough,' interrupted Bess. 'I been to school.'

'I know you have, Bess,' said Mr Trencher, patting her shoulder. Bess shrank from him. 'You're quite the young lady these days, my dear. Your mother's very proud of you, you know.'

Was she? What had her mother said about her to this man? And when? Bess couldn't remember her mother ever saying anything about her schooling at any of their meetings with Mr Trencher around the village.

'I haven't been up to the manor yet,' said Trencher, taking the handbill back from Jane. 'Don't want to take the bread out of your mouth, Mrs Farleigh. If they order one, they might not want your services no more. Still, maybe you won't have to worry about that for too much longer, eh?'

Bess looked quickly from the man to her mother. What was he talking about? Her mother gave an almost imperceptible shake of the head, and Trencher's mouth tightened. He swung his stick again, harder this time, shredding the fronds of a fern

30

that grew in the ditch. Bess took a step back, startled by the sudden violence. Her mother spoke quickly.

'Don't stand there grinny-grogging, Bess. You just cut on up to the big house now, while I finish the rest of the round. And if they asks about the muslin frock, you say it's not finished yet. You mind me?'

'Ay, Mother.'

'And take the gentleman's picture with you. Save you a climb, won't it, Mr Trencher?'

'Very civil of you, Mrs Farleigh.' Trencher raised his hat again.

Bess smoothed the front of her pinafore, and walked up the hill towards the gates of the big house. Her father had worked the manor land for nearly fourteen years, ever since he came to Hartingham to marry Jane. Then in April he had fallen ill and by the time he was well again his job had gone to a local man. Reuben didn't complain – 'Local men first is only right.' But then Bess had never heard him speak a hard word about anyone.

The housekeeper at the manor had nothing for them this week. But instead of going straight home, Bess took the footpath past the church, aiming to meet up with her mother. The men were working along the hedgerow by the church. Hands were raised in greeting as she walked by: everyone knew Bess and she knew them all.

There was no sign of her mother. Down on the green some women were drawing water at the pump, but her mother wasn't among them. Bess turned up the lane, and she was almost opposite the very last cottage when she heard voices. She looked around. There was no one to be seen. The sound came again. Someone was talking in very emphatic tones in the field behind the hedge.

'I'm tellin' you it's money in the bank. And no harm done neither. White Street Market – it's like the hirin' fair in Maidstone. Only more respectable-like.'

As far as Bess was concerned, the London accent meant it could only be one man – Harry Trencher. She leaned close to the hedge, trying to peer through the tangled thorn. She could see the outline of a woman's dress, but the man was still doing all the talking. 'All you've got to do is the persuadin'.'

'Won't be no trouble with that, Harry.'

Bess put her hand to her mouth to stop herself crying out. It was her mother. She crept on up the road to a gap in the hedge, her mind racing. A hiring fair? That meant it was something about a job. Work for her father at last. But why this secret conversation? And first names? Peering round the gate into the field, Bess could see her mother and Harry Trencher standing very close together, though she was too far away now to hear what they said. Then Trencher slipped his arm around her mother's waist, something she had only ever seen her father do before, and her mother did not pull away.

Something closed off inside Bess. She refused to believe what she was seeing. They were discussing a job for her father. That was all. Mr Trencher was more of a friend to the family than she had ever known, and he was helping them out of their trouble. Her mother was right to meet the man like this if he could do something so important for them. She, Bess Farleigh, was the one who was in the wrong, to be spying on her own mother. She turned and stole silently away back to the cottage, ashamed of her suspicions, determined she would say nothing to her mother or her father about what she had seen.

Reuben Farleigh came through the door before dark, but Bess felt none of the joy she had expected. The events of the day had knocked it out of her and her father's face told its own story. He didn't need to say that he had found no work; that he had tramped twenty miles a day for the last fortnight, calling at farms the length and breadth of the county with the same answer at every door: 'Times is hard. We be laying men off, not taking on new hands.' That evening her mother was uncharacteristically quiet, sewing more ribbons onto the muslin dress from the manor. She seemed to be altering the neckline now too. Bess watched her father in profile, as he stared silently into the fire. He had hardly looked her or her mother in the eye since he came home.

She went over to where he was sitting, knelt down and slipped her hand into his. The touch of her father's rough, labourer's hand had always held a special message of comfort for the girl. 'It'll be all right, Father. I just know it will.'

Her father looked up slowly and a half-smile touched his lips. 'Up the wooden hill for you now, Bessie.' It was what he had said at bedtime when she was a little girl. She wasn't a little girl any longer, but she still liked it when he spoke to her like that.

She kissed him and her mother, and climbed the stairs,

hoping sleep would bring a quick end to this miserable day. But it didn't. Almost as soon as she was in bed, she began to hear raised voices downstairs. In the last few months Bess had got used to the sound of her parents arguing. Usually she tried not to listen, feeling guilty and embarrassed to overhear their endless talk of money and work or the lack of it. But tonight she wanted to know exactly what was being said.

Trying not to let the floorboards creak under her, she tiptoed to the door of the bedroom, lifted the latch as silently as she had that morning as her mother lay sleeping, and sat shivering in her petticoat at the top of the stairs. The voices were clearer now. Her mother was talking.

'. . . there's nothing on offer round here, and a friend I was a-talking to suggested London.'

'What friend?'

'Someone as knows a bit more about the world than you does.'

Trencher! Bess knew who her mother was talking about. She felt his hand on her again, smelled his clothes, his breath, saw his arm slipping easily around her mother's waist. But – London? Were they to move to the city? Her mother was talking quickly now, not giving her husband the chance to interrupt.

'It's a chance for her to do something to help the family – more than work the dolly and the mangle. We go to this place called White Street Market, and—'

Reuben interrupted. The anger in his voice was gone. He sounded tired. 'I don't like it, Janey. You know I'd do anything

34

for you, but she's never been over Maidstone way, never mind London. I've never bin there meself!'

She? They were talking about *her*. Bess clasped her knees tight in surprise.

'Ain't no shame in service with a good family, Reuben. And she's a pretty one now. You know how all the gentlemen likes to pat her on the head when they rides through Hartingham. She just might make all our fortunes. You think of that now.'

If her father said anything in reply, Bess didn't hear it. Her ears were deaf now. Maidstone. London. White Street Market. The names whirled in her head. 'She just might make all our fortunes.' That's what her mother had said. She was the one who would save the family. Not her father, not her mother. She was the one! It was exactly what she had wished for that morning as the white bird beat its wings in the light of dawn.

Chapter 4

MOTHERS

A face loomed out of the darkness, a single candle throwing shadows across the features – hollow eyes, snout-like nose, pock-marked skin. It was the face that woke Joe each morning, winter and summer, but it still sent a shock through him every time.

'Shake a leg, boy. Two a.m.'

If they knew the man's name, no one ever used it. They called him the Watchman, because that was his job at St Saviour's Docks. Officially the Watchman worked a shift from noon until midnight, but Joe knew he could be seen at his post any hour of the day or night, eyes on the road – like last week when he was running from Billy and the gang. Some days he'd seen the Watchman stopping characters he didn't like the look of at the dock gates, or throwing out angry wharfmen the company had no work for, or searching porters suspected of thieving on the job. The Watchman wasn't liked in Pound's Field. People respected him all right, feared him even, and not just for his size – it was his silence and the long, still hours of watching on River Lane, as if he was waiting for something to happen or guarding something more precious to him than St Saviour's Docks – but nobody liked him.

Joe had his own ideas about the Watchman. Mother had a deputy in all her houses – someone who looked after the place, kept a check on who came and went and made sure they didn't hop the twig without paying the rent. Greasy Tyler did the job at number 16. But everyone knew she also had spies everywhere. Some people in Holywell Court pointed the finger at Joe, but Joe would have staked his life on the Watchman being Mother's nose, and his greatest fear was that the big man wasn't so far from nosing out his little secret. Because if you followed his gaze outside the dockyard gates, the Watchman's sunken eyes were fixed most often not on the street or the passers-by, but on the old timber-framed house across River Lane, the house with the broken chimneys where the Madman shouted in the night, the house with the overgrown garden where Joe hid his tosh.

The Watchman set his candle down on the floor, sending shadows flickering across the ceiling of the room. 'Going to be another fine November day.' The voice was soft, almost expressionless, but there was something in the accent, not to mention the good wax candle, that made Joe wonder yet again what he was doing sleeping on the floor in Holywell Court. Was he just saving his money? Or had Mother put him there to keep a sharp eye out for anything a young tosher might have hidden away?

When Mother had first sent Joe to number 16, he had spent his nights on the bare boards of the kitchen floor. It was only a penny to sleep there, and the room was warmer than upstairs. But in the kitchen there were always people coming and going, fights breaking out at all hours, and you never got more than five minutes' rest at a time. Then Plucky Jack came up with the idea of sharing a shakedown on the floor upstairs to keep down the price, and the Watchman had come in on it. Joe couldn't remember just how that had happened. Certainly hadn't been his idea. The Watchman had the shakedown after Joe from two until ten in the morning, but according to Jack the man was hardly ever there when he came to take his turn at ten.

Joe scrambled out of the sack he used as bedding, rolled it up quickly and buried it under the shakedown. The Watchman spread out his blanket. He'd offered to share it with Joe once. Joe had said no. Don't put yourself under an obligation. That was one of Mother's lessons: if you owed anyone anything, sooner or later they'd come collecting, and you never knew just what they might want. He watched the man remove his cap, kerchief and coat – all decent quality clothing but showing wear, like the man had come down in the world.

'You all right for the rent, Joe?' Why was he asking that? Joe didn't need reminding it was settlement day with Mother and he was behind on his payments. 'I could let you have five shillings maybe . . .'

'A bull? What you wanna give me a bull for?'

'Not give you, Joe. Lend.'

'Keep it, Watchman. I don't want your money.'

Joe knew about loans. Back when he first went under, Mother had lent him the price of the sieve and the long-handled hoe that were the tools of his trade. Two guineas, she said they cost. Working flat out in the sewers, he had kept up with the rent and the interest on the loan at sixpence a day – more or less – and most often Mother threw him enough back to eat on. But nearly four years on he still owed her the two guineas, and as far as Joe could see he would owe them for the rest of his life.

The boy was up and out of the room without another word, his mind working quickly. All the drains led down to the Thames in the end, where twice a day the tide made the river rise and fall by up to twenty-five feet, so for four or five hours around high tide you couldn't work the sewers at all. First high tide yesterday had been around seven – two hours after midnight now – so the water would be low enough in the sewers right this minute to go under for maybe three hours. If he'd had a lantern like most of the other toshers, he'd have done it. But with no light it was impossible. So, the tide would be low enough again about an hour before noon; November meant it was too dark to work by four, even right under a grating; result: he'd have maybe five hours.

The numbers shuffled easily in his brain, though Joe didn't have words like adding and subtracting for what he was doing and he had never seen a tide-table. The rise and fall of the river was in his bloodstream.

The stairs were still in darkness. He could slip into the kitchen, and catch another couple of hours' rest if he was lucky. If it was ever going to be quiet, this was the time. With the fire going all night it would be warm, and there might even be leftovers in Greasy Tyler's pot. Joe dismissed the idea. It was settlement day. He was all right on his interest payments, but if he had a bad five hours in the sewers he was going to end up short on the rent. He had to go and see Mother right now.

Bess woke suddenly from a heavy sleep. The room was light and silent, and her parents' bed was empty. She went quickly to the window, but it was broad daylight and there was no chance of seeing the white owl at this time. Why had no one woken her? She could smell toasting bread from downstairs, so someone else must have made up the fire, filled and boiled the kettle. Then she caught sight of the white muslin dress laid out at the bottom of her bed where her heavily darned woollen frock usually lay. Today was the day.

It was not the thought of putting the garment on that filled her with a terrifying thrill: her mother had said it was all right to borrow it, so she accepted it must be. It was what putting on the dress meant. From today everything would be better for the family, and it would be because of her, Bess Farleigh.

She could hear the voices from downstairs before she opened the bedroom door. 'I know what I said, woman, but it's you as made me say it. 'Od rabbit it, you gets an idea in your head and you goes on until a man can't think right.'

'And when was the last time you thought right? Or did anything right, for that matter?' Bess was used to arguments, but she had never heard anything quite like this. There was no attempt to keep voices down or hide what was happening. Her mother went on furiously, 'This is my decision, Reuben. The girl's plenty old enough, and for once I'm a-doing what's right for myself and right for the whole—' She broke off at the sight of her daughter standing at the bottom of the staircase. Jane had been working on the dress for weeks, but Bess could see that the sight of her wearing the thing in the kitchen in the light of morning was a shock.

She looked from her mother to her father. Reuben was the first to step forward, but he seemed unable to say anything. Instead he led her to the chair by the fire, and sat her down, while her mother brought a bowl of kettle-broth and a piece of bread and dripping. It was more than any of them had eaten at breakfast for months.

'Dear heart's alive, but she's a picture, now ain't she, Reuben? Ain't you proud of her?'

Her father still said nothing, but there was an expression on his face which Bess knew meant he approved of what he saw. 'I still says it hadn't ought to be so low-like at the front,' was all he managed in the end.

'Oh, you don't know nothing about it.' Her mother was good-humoured now, her tone light-hearted. 'That's the way all the young ladies in London wears them. Just the hair wants a-doing.'

And while her mother busied herself tying a ribbon in her hair, Bess wondered at the expression on her father's face, as he watched her shyly from the door. He looked almost in awe of her. The way they were behaving it was as if she had turned into the young lady from the manor, simply by putting on her dress.

No one said much, as she ate and drank, her parents standing and watching her awkwardly.

'Cart's here,' her father announced finally, looking out of the door. 'Reckon it's time then.'

The yard where Mother lived didn't have a name. The sign had disappeared long ago, and the dingy houses lined up on either side of what was barely more than an alley were known throughout Pound's Field simply as Mother's Court. In the archway at the entrance to the court a figure lay bundled up under the gaslight. Man or woman, boy or girl, Joe couldn't tell which, but it was Mother's lookout. He knew that much. As he passed, the figure let out a low whistle. There was a whistle for strangers, a whistle for someone the lookout knew, and there was a special whistle for the crushers, though Joe had never heard it used. Mother's Court was at the dead centre of an intricate web of alleyways and tiny streets in which strangers often got completely lost even in broad daylight. It was the kind of place the police avoided, which was probably the reason Mother lived there, when she could have had her pick of the houses in Pound's Field.

There was a back way into Mother's house that Joe was allowed to use, but tonight he went straight through the front door, ignoring the silent man on guard. It was still three hours until dawn, but a line of people stood waiting in the darkened hallway, and Joe knew Mother would see him. Voices grumbled as he edged past.

The parlour was shockingly bright after the darkness

outside. A coal fire blazed in the grate, making the place oppressively hot, and a pair of oil lamps burned on each wall. Sure enough, Mother was awake – in fact Joe had never seen her sleep, any more than he'd ever seen her stand upright. At the opposite side of the bare room she lay propped up on an ancient four-poster bed, a massive figure enthroned amidst cushions and cloaks, shawls and rags. The bed sagged under her weight. She was draped, as always, in layer upon layer of clothing, so much that it was impossible to tell where she began and the bedding ended. Winter and summer Mother looked the same – like a ragged and immovable mountain of flesh and fabric.

Apart from the bed there was no other furniture in the room, so Joe stood in a corner and watched as Mother dealt with an old man paying his rent. For casual lodgers just passing through Pound's Field Mother's deputies took rent by the day or week, but for regulars she collected in person once a month – 'Mother likes to keep a personal eye on her little brood' – that was how she put it. A pudgy hand extended slowly from the bed, tips of the fingers trembling slightly as if from the effort of reaching out. The old man dropped coins into the hand, careful to avoid touching – Mother didn't like to be touched – and the money disappeared into a capacious leather satchel strapped to her side.

As Mother collected her tribute, coin by coin, a dozen white mice ran here and there across the bed and over the mountain of rags and clothes, vanishing into the folds of a cloak, re-emerging from a pocket with whiskers twitching and bright little pink eyes blinking at the light. And as each new tenant or debtor edged warily towards the bed, Mother fed the trembling mice with tiny morsels of cheese. Joe stood by the door and tried not to salivate, and another figure shuffled in from the hall.

Joe knew them all. This woman sold tapes and laces behind St George's. She'd been on the same pitch as far back as he could remember, maybe taking sixpence some days, other days nothing at all, and every month she was here in Mother's Court just like him and all the rest, paying the old monster her whack. Could be a tenth part. Could be as much as a quarter. It depended on where you worked and how close to the law your line of work ran. Mother took all of what Joe brought her from the sewers – all that wasn't hidden in the Madman's garden anyway – and paid him maybe a quarter of its value. But whatever he found, somehow it was never enough even to make a dent in that two guineas he owed her.

Without shifting her gaze from the tape-seller, who was struggling nervously to open her drawstring purse, Mother made a movement of her head, acknowledging Joe's arrival. A lift of the right forefinger meant she wanted him to stand by her. One of the two men flanking the bed gave way, disappearing into the kitchen, and Joe took his place. He had never seen the man before: Mother never kept anyone close to her for too long. Joe had been one of the ones who lived here for a time, stood by the bed while Mother received her rents and tithes, slept on a shakedown by the fire alongside Mother's bed, even fed those white mice. Then she had suddenly announced he was to move to the house in Holywell Court. Standing here now at her side made Joe think of those early days, of his first time groping through the maze of sewers under London's streets and the old toshers who had shown him the sinkholes where you could disappear over your head in sludge and the gratings down near the docks that in those days were almost always good for a couple of dozen copper nails.

Joe shook his head to clear his thoughts: the heat in the room was making him sleepy. Another woman came in. She had a room underneath Joe's in Holywell Court, making matchboxes at tuppence ha'penny a gross with every one of her brood of kids working alongside. If they all worked day and night at it, Joe didn't see how she could clear more than two shillings a day, and that was when the work was there, which it wasn't always.

Mother collected one shilling and tenpence from the woman, enquiring in a kindly voice into the health of her children as she dropped the coins into her bulging leather satchel. Joe caught the woman's eye as she left. There was a hard loathing in it she dared not show Mother herself, and he suddenly realized what he must look like standing next to her like one of the bodyguards. He wanted to call the woman back, tell her he was no different from her, that he was only there because he owed money and he couldn't pay. But the woman was gone, and more than likely she wouldn't have believed him anyway.

Abruptly Mother switched her gaze to Joe. The heavy jowls of her face shook and her eyes seemed to disappear further into deep folds of skin.

'Joseph! Joseph!'

Nobody ever called him Joseph except Mother. She held out her arms. A white mouse poked its head out of her sleeve, scenting the air. Joe went closer, near enough to see the dampness on Mother's pallid skin and the mouse's pink eyes. He tried not to look at the cheese, but he knew Mother could tell where his thoughts were. 'Such a long time since Mother saw you, Joe. You don't visit the poor old soul.' Mother's laugh was more like a cough. It brought up phlegm, which she spat into a silk handkerchief and examined with interest.

'I've had a bad week, Mother.' Joe was talking fast. 'The old spots is gettin' worked out. Can't find nothin' decent. And Billy and his mug-hunters—'

Mother interrupted him. 'Mother wasn't talking about money, Joe.'

'No?'

'No. She just likes to see you once in a while. You don't think about Mother any more, now you're a big man out on your own.'

Joe never knew what to say when Mother started talking like this. It was as if she could just forget that he came there every day he had something worth money – every day Billy didn't thieve the lot off him anyhow. He started again about how hard things had been, but Mother turned away, apparently losing interest in him altogether.

She was dealing with a couple of men now. These weren't tenants. They'd come in through the back door and their eyes were quick and furtive. The older man had a sack open on the

bed, and Mother had raised herself up to peer inside. Joe could see her little black eyes gleam as she picked over the contents. There was no mention of theft or stolen property. Joe had never heard those words in Mother's house. It was just a businesslike negotiation over prices.

'A bargain!' Mother shouted aloud, as a deal was struck, and without being summoned, a man in shirtsleeves appeared through the kitchen door, face red and sweating. 'More chicken for the pot,' said Mother, laughing and spitting into her hand-kerchief, as she passed the sack to the man. Joe caught a gleam of silver from the open bag. Baldock – that was the man's name – would take the stuff into the kitchen, where he kept two pots always ready on the fire – one for silver, one for pewter – then he'd melt the whole lot down so it could never be recognized again.

Mother counted out two gold sovereigns and the two men left, looking less than happy; then she lay back on the bed with a sigh of contentment, holding a piece of cheese between her lips for the bravest of the mice to nibble. There was silence in the room. No one else came through the door. Joe decided it was time to take his chance.

'Fact is, I know I ain't up with the rent this month, Mother. Can you see your way to maybe lettin' me have till next week? Things is bound to get better and—'

'Joseph! Joseph!' The voice was reproachful. 'With all Mother's brood coming to see her today, what would they say if she did that for you and not for them? Would they think it was fair, Joseph?' Joe hung his head. He'd known there was no chance. 'You'll have something for Mother before midnight.' There was steel in her voice – no need to spell out what might happen if he didn't have something for Mother before midnight. 'But you're looking so ragged, my boy,' she went on in quite a different tone, and Joe knew there was no point in trying to go back to the subject of money. 'Do get yourself some decent clothes. And are you eating proper? I don't believe you are. You'll get sick, Joseph.'

'I'm all right, Mother.' Of course she knew why he couldn't afford new clothes or more food, but Mother always said the same things. 'Toshers don't get sick' – he repeated the phrase he'd heard all the old sewer-hunters use. 'Must have been forty or more with the fever in our court last summer. Not me.'

'But the filth in which you work, my boy. Can't be good for a growing lad.'

Mother turned to the man standing silently on the other side of the bed and issued quick commands. He pulled back the heavy brocade curtains and drew down the sash window. There was the first hint of light in the sky. She was turning back to Joe, about to speak, when they all heard the sound, quite distinct in the quiet before dawn – '*Yes!! Yes!!*'

The man at the window went rigid. The colour drained out of his face, and he began to mutter to himself.

'What you muttering about, you idiot?' snapped Mother.

The man ducked his head at the rebuke. 'I was just sayin' it's bad luck. Hearin' 'im when it's gettin' light.'

'Hearing who?'

'The Madman.' The man lowered his voice, as if he didn't

even want to say the word aloud.

Mother gave a snort of disgust, but Joe knew she was as superstitious about the Madman as any of her gang. It was what made the garden such a good hiding place. Thinking of his tosh hidden under the tomb, with Mother there in the room, Joe fixed his eyes on the floor. There had been times when he was almost sure she could read his mind.

'What you thinking about, Joe?' she queried sharply, as if confirming his fears. But the man at the window spoke again before Joe had to answer.

'We'll burn 'im out of there one of these days,' he said. 'That old house'd go up like a bale of straw.'

'You and who else?' snarled Mother. 'You wouldn't have the nerve to go near the place. None of you would.' The man shook his head and looked away, abashed. Mother went on quietly, 'That old madman is a part of Pound's Field, same as any of Mother's brood. He was here before Mother, you know that?'

'Never!' The idea seemed impossible to Joe, who couldn't imagine Pound's Field without Mother sitting at its centre like a huge, fleshy spider. Amazing really that Billy could operate on his own . . .

Mother's voice droned on, low and soporific. She could be like this – soft, even soothing: 'They say half the parish belonged to that house once – back before any of the courts was built. They say there were orchards and a river running through all the way down to the mucky old Thames. 'Cept it weren't mucky in them days.' Suddenly Joe remembered lying on the bed as a little boy of maybe seven years old with Mother reading him a fairy story.

'Send the next one in. Come and sit with me, Joe.' She patted the bed next to her.

Joe sat down gingerly, avoiding the mice. It was warm in here and comfortable and it was hours yet until low tide. Joe closed his eyes, but he knew he would still have to be down the sewers before noon. Never mind what kind of mood Mother was in now, he owed her money, and that came before anything.

Chapter 5

FRIENDS

'Dear hearts alive! All dogged up like one of them Maidstone doxeys! Did you ever see the like of it?'

Bess shrank back behind her father in the doorway of the cottage. The voice belonged to Mrs Ackerman from next door. She stood with arms folded next to her husband; she'd kept her voice low, but not so low that it didn't reach Bess's ears in the stillness of the misty November morning. Already up on the driver's seat, her mother heard it too, and shot the old woman a filthy look. They had been enemies since the days when six-year-old Jane had chased the Ackermans' hens.

'Don't you mind her, Bessie. You look just grand.' Her father's hand on her arm was meant to be reassuring, but there was a tremor in his voice that made Bess more uneasy than anything Mrs Ackerman had to say. Suddenly the borrowed clothes felt awkward on her.

She leaned close to her father and whispered. 'I won't go, Father. Not if you says I mustn't.'

Reuben looked around at the people gathered to watch,

then up at his wife on the cart. 'Your mother's got an aching tooth for London, Bessie,' he murmured finally, trying to summon a smile. Then he looked away, and his voice was so soft, Bess could barely hear him. 'I want – what she wants.'

It was like a confession of weakness. She felt frightened and at the same time proud that her father should suddenly be talking to her so differently, as if she was grown up, as if he was looking to her for reassurance. She patted his arm awkwardly, feeling herself blush,

'I'll be all right,' she said. 'Don't you worry.'

The horse and cart in the lane had drawn out all the neighbours. Three boys who were supposed to be bringing in the cattle from the field opposite had left their work too, and were lined up on the other side of the hedge to watch. They gave a ragged cheer, as Bess climbed up next to her mother.

'Cart must have cost you a pretty penny, Reuben.' Old Mr Ackerman limped across to Bess's father.

'Ay,' agreed Reuben. 'Can't make bricks without straw.' Bess knew the hire of the cart had cost her father most of what little cash he had left.

'That old nag'll never make it to London,' called out one of the boys behind the hedge, voicing Bess's own thoughts. The horse stood patient and quiet in the traces. Suddenly Reuben was yelling.

'Go on, clear off out of it, the lot of you!' He was shouting at the boys, who scattered across the field, laughing, but most of the other onlookers began to drift away too. To see Reuben Farleigh lose his temper was a mighty unusual thing. Only Mrs

Ackerman stood her ground, her husband hovering behind her.

'Not a-going yourself then, Reuben?' she said. 'Reckon your wife and daughter ought to be on the gammock in the big city without 'ee?'

Bess looked desperately at her father. He had told her there was no room in the cart for all three of them, but she knew why he wasn't coming. He wasn't going to stand in his wife's way, but he still didn't like the idea of his daughter working in a stranger's house so far away, especially when it wasn't settled who she'd be working for. It was her mother who spoke. Jane had obviously had enough.

'You mind your business and let others mind theirs, Alice Ackerman. You has two healthy boys a-working at the manor and keeping you and your old husband fat and fettled. I has a husband as can't find work and one daughter. So what would you have me do, eh?'

Jane's voice tailed off in something close to a sob, but before Mrs Ackerman could say anything, Bess spoke up herself. Seeing her mother so near to tears had made her find her own courage. 'My mother and father think it right for me to go and earn my way, Mrs Ackerman,' she said in a loud, clear voice. 'I think it's right too. And I'm glad to be able to. Let's be a-starting now, Mother.'

And it seemed as if the horse had understood what Bess said, because with hardly a stirring of the reins in Jane Farleigh's hands it began to pull them up the lane away from Hartingham, past Kirby's farm, north towards the high road and the line of the downs, the way the white bird flew at sunrise. Reuben stood at the front door, his right hand raised, as still as a statue, until they were out of sight.

The morning was cold and damp as Joe cut briskly down Greenfield Passage and out onto Flower Street, but there was no sign of real rain. That was good: the sewers got difficult in a downpour. The clock at St George's struck the half-hour, so levels were just getting low enough for him to go under. Perhaps he should have taken a chance and tried a new patch, somewhere he might stumble on something really valuable. But venturing into sections of the sewers you didn't know was mighty dangerous work. Apart from the sinkholes that could drown you, there were stunt ends – underground blind alleys where you could choke on the bad air in a minute. Then there were gangs of toshers who would defend their patch to the death. Stray into the wrong part and Joe knew he could finish up with a thumping that would make Billy and his boys look like a Sunday stroll. Right outside the church gates, at the corner of Flower Street and River Lane, he ran into Plucky Jack.

'Come on! Best apples! Three for an ha'penny. Finest fruit this side a Covent Garden. Come on, sir. Farthin' a piece or three for an 'a'penny!'

River Lane was a prime spot for selling, but Joe wondered how much profit there was in it. For a pitch like that Mother would be taking at least a quarter of everything Jack earned.

'Joe!' Jack had a booming voice when he was selling. 'Smell you comin', didn't I?'

Two women laughed and bought apples from Jack's basket. When he'd finished doing business, Jack turned back to Joe. 'Have an apple, Joe boy. Looks like you could do with some peck inside yer.' Joe took the apple and bit into it. It tasted sweet. He knew he was eating a part of Plucky Jack's profit, but he was too hungry to refuse. Mother would have called it putting yourself under an obligation, like borrowing from the Watchman, but with Jack it was different.

'Where'd you get the apples?' Joe asked, mouth full.

'Ask me no questions and I'll tell you no lies.' Jack winked to suggest they were stolen, and turned back to a group of men coming up the street: 'Come on! Best apples! Three for an 'a'penny. Just fallen off the tree. Finest fruit this side a Covent Garden.'

'What about Mother? How much you payin', Jack?'

'Mother!' Jack's tone was scornful, dismissive. 'I can't let that old monster stand in my way. I don't pay her nothin'.' Joe's mouth tightened into a smile. He wanted to believe it. He wanted to believe there was someone in Pound's Field apart from Billy who wasn't under Mother's thumb. 'You should get away from her, Joe,' Jack went on, lowering his voice. 'Between Billy and Mother you're gettin' bled drier than last week's loaf.'

'I'm doin' all right.' Joe finished his apple and threw the core in a wide arc over the churchyard wall.

'Sure you are, Joe boy. Billy don't get you every time, does he? And I'd wager Mother don't get it all neither, eh? You get away from both of 'em once in a while, don'tcha? You're a fly boy, I reckon. You got pluck. Like me. Where d'you hide the tosh then, Joe boy? Not in that bug-infested ken, eh?'

Joe listened to Plucky Jack. He liked to hear him talk. He liked the way he could string words together and make them dance. But he wasn't going to tell him about the stone mastiff or the terrier with the ears missing or the little silver joey he had saved from Billy and the gang last week. He wasn't going to tell anyone that.

Her father had said it was twenty miles to London, and Bess reckoned the horse had been plodding close to an hour through the gentle countryside north of Hartingham. It was chilly in the cart, and her mother hadn't let her wear her bonnet – just the ribbon tying up her blonde hair at the back. Bess smoothed the white muslin over her legs and drew the brightly coloured shawl her mother had produced that morning a little more tightly around her. The excitement of first thing had gone, and her mother's mood seemed to have changed too in the last half-hour. She looked anxiously ahead, scanning people they passed on the road, as if hoping or fearing to meet someone along the way.

The horse crested another rise, and a neat, prosperous-looking village of half-timbered houses lay spread out in front of them along the course of a small river. An ancient stone bridge, wide enough for a single cart, was the only way across, and leaning against the parapet on the nearer side stood a man in a battered stovepipe hat. As they drew nearer, Bess could see him swishing the heavy stick he carried, trimming the heads off the weeds which grew in crevices in the stonework. There was no mistaking him. It was Harry Trencher.

She turned quickly to her mother, but Jane was already talking. 'Now, Bessie dear, we're a-going to meet up with a friend of ours here. Mr Trencher has very kindly agreed to come with us the rest of the way and show us where we need to go in London.'

A friend of *ours*? Harry Trencher was no friend of hers. And certainly not of her father's. Or was he? Bess had tried not to think about that day – less than a week ago, it was, though it seemed longer – when she had overheard her mother and Trencher talking near the church, seen the man slip his arm so easily around her mother's waist. They hadn't been talking about a job for her father: that was clear now. It had been *her* they were discussing. So did she have Harry Trencher to thank for giving her the chance to save her family? Was he a friend after all?

'Mornin', Mrs Farleigh. Miss Farleigh.' Trencher raised his hat in his usual style. 'Very nice,' he went on, giving Bess an appraising look up and down. 'Just the ticket, Jane – er – Mrs Farleigh.'

'Thank you, Mr Trencher.' Her mother's smile was at its most artificial, as if in warning. 'Reuben and I wanted our Bess to look as nice as possible for her trip to the big city, didn't we, Bess my dear?'

Bess didn't speak. Before her mother could suggest any other arrangement, she climbed over the back of the seat and set herself down where the miller usually carried his flour sacks. If the famous dress got filthy, she couldn't have cared. Anything was better than sitting near Harry Trencher, having him sway against her as the wheels caught the ruts in the road. But even from where she was she caught a strong smell of tobacco and cheap gin, as he clambered heavily up onto the seat next to her mother.

They jolted across the bridge and on towards London with Trencher holding the reins. Bess watched the backs of the two figures on the seat, saw their shoulders touching and listened to their talk of 'Bethnal Green' and 'White Street'. She thought of her father, of the cottage, of Hartingham, where she knew everyone and everyone knew her, and for the first time the certainty that she was doing the right thing faltered – just a little.

Chapter 6

GOING UNDER

Ten yards from the loose grating on Flower Street Joe slowed to a casual saunter. There was a police reward for snitching on toshers, but he knew there was nothing to fear from any of the inhabitants of Pound's Field. He was one of Mother's brood and no one snitched on Mother's brood – they had seen what happened to those who did. But a stranger might not be so careful. He stopped to let a group of sailors go past. A glance back down the street showed all was quiet around the police station itself. For a moment there was no one on the street looking in his direction.

Joe slipped both hands through the rusted iron and pulled. The grating was heavy, but it came away easily. In a single accustomed movement he slid through the hole in the roadway and down the shaft of the drain through a gap too narrow for an adult man to pass. As he braced his feet against the side of the shaft to slow his fall, Joe dragged the grating back into place. Anyone who had been watching the ragged boy loitering in the street and looked away for an instant would have thought he had vanished into thin air.

Right up at the top of Flower Street the sewer ran more than fifteen feet underground, but here the drop was less than half that. With the tide not yet at its lowest Joe landed in two feet of water, hands reaching out in the near darkness to steady himself against the curving brick walls of the sewer. He let the dark water swirl around his bare feet and legs, waiting for his eyes to adjust to the gloom.

A little light filtered down from overhead. This was one of the newer drains, big enough for Joe to stand upright and with gratings at every junction in the road above, so even without a lantern you could see to work. He waded downstream, oblivious to the stench which rose to his nostrils, counting his steps aloud – 'Five, six, seven.' Joe reached up to a ledge and lifted down his precious long-handled hoe and flat-bottomed sieve. A spade would have been handy too, but from Mother that would be another guinea more than likely, and if he used some of his hidden tosh to buy a spade or a lantern elsewhere, then she'd know he had cash hidden somewhere, and then . . . Joe didn't want to finish the thought. He'd seen what happened to people who were caught holding out on Mother.

As he lifted it down, the iron double-hook at the end of the hoe clattered sharply against the brick wall of the sewer. Sounds were magnified down here, so that where the tunnel ran near the surface, the rumbling of a heavy cart overhead was like thunder. Joe balanced the ten-foot wooden handle of the hoe easily in one hand, gripped the sieve under his arm and started down the echoing tunnel.

Where the new Flower Street sewer joined the old drain that ran under River Lane, almost exactly beneath the place where he had talked with Plucky Jack a few minutes back, Joe came to a drop of about four feet. Over the years the water flowing over the spill had washed out the lining of the old drain below, and mud and sewage had been gathering in the hole so long there was no bottom to it. This was what the toshers called a sinkhole. Joe could remember falling into this very one the first week he went under: over his head in the mud, he was, breathing it in. One of the old toshers had pulled him out that time – with one hand.

He reached over the drop, probing with the hoe down into the old drain. The hooked end sank a foot into sludge. Joe shifted his hoe a couple of feet to the left. There was a softer place there, but he could still reach a hard bottom. Then suddenly there was no resistance at all, and the hoe sank down as far as he could reach. That was where the hole was, and that was the first place to try: all kinds of gear gathered in the sink-holes, but he'd have to get nearer to reach it.

Joe shifted the point of his hoe to a solid spot, and slid easily down its long shaft into the old drain. The roof was lower here, so that even Joe had to stoop. You didn't want to bang it with the wooden end of your hoe, or even with your head, because it didn't take much to bring a fall of bricks, and it might be just a couple or it could be the whole roof. There were tales of toshers buried alive under roof falls, just as there were stories of men losing their way and being pulled out days later, skeletons picked clean by rats. Some said there were wild pigs down here somewhere that thought nothing of attacking a full-grown man.

For an hour Joe worked his hoe methodically through the mud and sewage that filled the sinkhole. He talked softly to himself as he worked, re-telling old toshers' tales of fabulous finds, of great balls of copper and tin and coins all rusted together, weighing two hundredweight and jammed in some drain so tight you couldn't shift it. All you could do was chip bits off, and the deeper you went into the ball the older the coins got, until in the middle there was money from a thousand years ago when the Romans built the first shores in London.

The water was cold around Joe's bare feet, but the air was warmer in the sewers than up above. Clouds of noxious gas bubbled to the surface, but the suffocating stench meant nothing to Joe. He didn't even notice it any more. Gradually the water level fell as the tide continued to ebb, and he could reach deeper into the hole with the iron end of his hoe. That was when he started to find things. He hooked out a rusted horseshoe, a tin kettle and half a dozen fresh animal bones. The metal was all worth something for scrap. The soap works bought bones. But it wasn't even the start of a month's rent.

Joe had just made up his mind to move on, when he caught sight of a light flickering towards him along the sewer. Someone was coming. It could be a rival tosher or a whole gang of them, but whoever it was Joe didn't want to meet them. Silent and slow, he pressed his hoe down flat into the sludge. Then he pushed the sieve carefully up into the narrow entrance of one of the ancient drains which ran into the main sewer and

pulled himself up the slime-encrusted wall after it, taking care not to disturb the brickwork.

The man stopped opposite Joe's hiding place, bent almost double, breathing heavily. He wore a long coat and canvas trousers and in his left hand he carried a wooden cage. Joe held his own breath. The man must have been close to standing on the hoe, which would have been quite a find for a tosher, but with that empty cage in his hand Joe knew the man was looking for different game. He was a rat-hunter, probably picking up vermin for the Sunday night sport at Nimms's. Joe could have told him places not a hundred yards from where he was standing which were alive with rats, but he stayed silent where he was. Look out for yourself and let others look out for themselves. That was another of Mother's lessons.

They had crossed London Bridge some time back. Bess was beginning to get used to the chaos of noise and traffic and choking air that was the great capital city, and she had long ago stopped listening to her mother's exclamations at the sights and sounds of London. Now the cart had come to a dead stop. A drayman had halted his wagon immediately in front, and a crowd of people surged about the vehicles. The heavy drayman's horse was accustomed to the uproar, but the old country nag which had pulled them nearly twenty miles from Hartingham had never seen anything like it and was backing and whinnying anxiously. Trencher climbed down from his seat to hold the animal's head, shouting to find out what was happening.

'Pump's on!' came the answer.

Up ahead Bess could see a gas lantern shining brightly in the gathering gloom of late afternoon, the thin fog making a halo about the light. She stood up in the cart to see what was going on. The lantern was fixed to the top of a tall stone column at the side of the road, where a man in shirtsleeves worked a pump and water gushed from a pipe. Around the base of the column crowded a sea of humanity – men, women and children, shouting and complaining, fighting and cursing. There must have been two hundred people with buckets, copper kettles, tin pots, cups and broken bottles clutched in their hands – all desperate to reach the water.

The drayman was standing up too, shouting to Trencher: 'First water in three days. You'll 'ave to wait.'

'I got to get this lot to their lodgin',' Trencher shouted back. 'Over White Street way.'

'Oh, yes? White Street, is it? Nice little racket.' The drayman looked Jane over slowly before turning his gaze to Bess, who was still standing in the back of the cart. He nodded slowly and a smile twisted the corners of his mouth. 'I reckon you've got the merchandise for it, Captain.'

Bess caught the leering expression on the man's face and sat down quickly. The drayman turned to another man holding the head of his horse and said something. The man laughed uproariously, and several on-lookers who didn't want water, but were there simply to watch the crowd, began to gather to see what the joke was.

'Mother, I don't like it here.' Bess's heart was thumping

and she could feel the blood making her cheeks glow.

'No more than any of us,' said her mother, who had paid no attention to the drayman's remarks. 'We just has to wait.'

'Tell you what,' observed Harry Trencher in his most jovial voice, 'since we're stuck here, now might be the time to try out a drop of this 'ere potion I was able to obtain at considerable cost.' As if he was performing a conjuring trick for the children of Hartingham, he produced from the pocket of his coat a tin pot with a screw-top lid. 'Don't really need it until tomorra mornin', but we might as well see if it works. They calls it the sympathetic blush, Bessie my dear.'

Perhaps it was the way he called her by the pet name her father used or something about his expression, but Bess made a violent movement away from him that almost tipped the cart over. She would have leaped from it that moment if Trencher had come an inch nearer with his pot of cream. But Trencher stopped, seeing her movement, and turned to her mother, still with a genial smile on his face. 'P'raps you'd better do the honours, Mrs Farleigh.'

'Right. Hold still then, Bess.'

Jane twisted in the seat, and scooped a dollop of the cream out of the pot. It was a pure white.

'What's it for, Mother? I don't want it.'

'Don't start acting about, girl,' snapped her mother, taking Bess's chin firmly in one hand. 'Hold still where you are.' And she rubbed the cream first into one cheek then the other.

'Just takes a little minute to turn colour,' said Trencher, watching the girl's face. 'There now,' he purred. 'Just like magic, that is! Don't she look a picture, Mrs Farleigh?'

Bess looked from Trencher's leering face to her mother's. There was a strange expression there too – half smile, half disgust.

'Why don't we let Miss Farleigh see the total effect herself?' announced Trencher, adopting the voice he used for selling patent medicines around the village. 'Now, I just happens to have with me a small lady's lookin' glass.' And with a flourish he drew a hand mirror from another pocket, holding it up so that Bess could see her reflection.

There was a crack across the mirror, splitting Bess's face into two jagged halves. Her cheeks glowed red on either side of the crack, as though someone had painted her with a brush. Her shawl had slipped from her shoulders, and the mirror caught the bright red ribbons her mother had sewn onto the dress and the whiteness of her skin where the neckline had been lowered.

Alice Ackerman's voice was in her head: 'All dressed up like one of them Maidstone doxeys . . .' With an abrupt movement she swept the mirror out of Trencher's hand, sending it crashing onto the roadway. There was a roar of laughter, and Bess looked round to see that a dozen people were now gathered by the cart, staring up at her, pointing and laughing. She looked to her mother. She was trying to suppress a laugh too, and Trencher's arm had slipped around her waist. One woman's voice was raised above the laughter, and she pointed straight into Bess's face – 'White Street! She looks about ready, don't she?' And suddenly Bess wanted to be anywhere but where she was.

She sprang from the cart, heard Trencher and her mother shout out, felt the jostle of the crowd pressing in on her, as she thrust out her elbows and hurled herself at the wall of people. Even in their desperation for the water, the crowd fell back, and before she knew it Bess was in the clear and running, one hand holding the hem of the muslin dress so that it didn't trip her, scanning desperately this way and that – any road, any alley would do. She could hear shouting not far behind, knew it was Trencher and her mother, but there was not a way in the world that she was going back to them, back to that cart or the crowd of people pointing and laughing. She ducked down a narrow passage between two buildings, where the way was darkest, past a flickering gas lamp, into a maze of alleys and lanes and court-yards where the walls pressed close on every side, turning left and right at random, breathless and panting in mingled fear and relief.

Chapter 7
TOSH

The light was failing, and the water around his legs had stopped flowing towards the river. The tide was on the turn. Joe knew he had maybe another hour before work in the sewers became impossible. Once the tide started coming in, you got sudden surges and the shores could fill up quick as a flash. He'd had to swim for it more than once. One time the water had been just an arm's length from the ceiling when he got out of a little side drain not thirty yards from where he was now, and he didn't want that happening today.

Joe liked to work slowly and carefully. There were toshers who went racing from one grating to another hoping for a big find, but to earn a steady living you had to search every inch, sieve through every scrap of mud. On the other hand Joe also knew that sometimes you had to do the opposite, and that time was now. There was no need to check the contents of his bag. He knew exactly what was in there and how Mother would value it to within a couple of farthings. He had an hour, and in that hour he had to find something that was worth real money or he couldn't pay Mother what he owed her. That had never happened to Joe, but he'd seen it happen to others, and not all of them were still around to tell the tale.

Joe hurried down the old River Lane sewer faster than he knew was safe, feeling ahead of him with the hoe. He was at the end of his usual pitch. After the next grating he'd be beyond the entrance to the docks and into an area he'd worked maybe once or twice but never on his own. Today there was no choice: the light was going and the water was rising too fast.

The sewer ran close under the roadway here and the roof was lower, but Joe could stand upright where a man would be bent almost double. 'Come on now,' he murmured softly, groping with his arms in the soft sludge under the grating, and lifting armfuls into the sieve. 'Joe wants to see yer, don't 'e? He wants to see somethin' shiny. Somethin' with an 'ard edge to it. Somethin' *nice*.' He hissed the last word through his teeth, as if he was trying to conjure something valuable out of the sieve. He swirled water through the steel mesh, peering for what was left. Nothing. Stones. Scraps of bone too small to sell.

He plunged his arms in deeper, more desperate now. A spade would have made the work easy but he didn't have a spade. No sense in thinking about that. Thinking didn't make a spade, did it? Thinking got you nothing.

A swirl of the sieve and the black water washed the mud through again. Nothing. This time he stirred deep with the hoe right under the grating, then plunged the sieve itself down into the mud. That could easily damage his precious implement, but he was in a hurry now. As soon as he lifted it from the water, he knew by the weight that there was something there.

Joe's hand moved across the surface of the mud in his sieve quick as a spider, probing, feeling – too dark to see now even right up under the grating. His fingers stopped. He didn't feel tired or cold or hungry any more. He couldn't smell the stench of the sewer or feel the cold of the water around his legs. All he could feel was the tingling in the tips of his fingers as his right hand closed around a handle.

Joe's heart thumped as he felt around the object with both hands. It was a tankard and it was undamaged. It could be silver or pewter or tin. If it was silver, then that was enough and he could quit. But by the time he got it into the light to check, the tide would be too high to go under again. Better to assume it was tin and keep going. There was more than one way a decent tankard could end up in the sewers, but the most likely was that it had been thieved and then ditched when the crushers got too close. And if it had been thieved, there was a chance it hadn't been thieved on its own. If only there was another half an hour, even a quarter of an hour, but the water was at his waist now.

He didn't use the hoe again. If it had moved one piece of decent tosh near the surface, maybe it had shifted more. He probed with fingers and toes; then he dug deep with the sieve. He had to hold the sieve above chest height now to keep it clear of the water's surface. The black water washed through the mesh, as he felt with accustomed fingers. Nothing.

He took a breath, plunged his head under the filthy water and groped desperately at his feet. Nothing. Up for air and then under again. Nothing. The third time he felt them – one, two. There were four. Four spoons. He surfaced, gasping, sucked in a breath as the spoons disappeared into his bag, and he was under again. There was another. And the next time one more. And now, even if it was all tin, he definitely had enough. Maybe not enough for food as well. But enough to pay Mother.

There could have been more gear right there, but Joe knew he couldn't wait another instant. Half wading, half swimming, half vaulting with the pole as his support, he struggled back up the old sewer to the junction with Flower Street. At the sink-hole where the big drop had been, the water was deep enough now for him to swim straight up over the ledge. He gripped the hoe and sieve with one arm and kicked out strongly with his legs. Even up in the new drain the water was deep, flowing strongly in with the rising tide, but the flow was helping him, and he knew he was safe.

Joe stowed his tools back in their hiding places, and stopped under the loose grating, feeling in the dark for holds in the brickwork. Now he felt the cold in his fingers and toes as he worked them into crevices in the bricks, levering himself painfully up the wall towards the narrow slits of grey light in the roadway above. He braced his back against the shaft of the drain, holding himself just under the metal grating. It hurt to hold still there, but you couldn't just pop up out of the road-way like a jack-in-the-box. Anyone could be passing, and if they didn't give him to the crushers, they might just want a look inside his bag for themselves. Billy and his boys could be out there right this minute. But the only sound from the street was the piano in Nimms's gin shop.

Joe pushed up with his head and one arm. In a single

movement he was through the opening, the grating was back in its place and he was pressed against the blackened wall of the warehouse. Easing the tankard out of his canvas bag and scratching at it with a broken thumbnail, he peered at his find. The metal gleamed dully. Pewter. He rubbed one of the spoons quickly on his sodden breeches, but his clothes were too wet and filthy to make any impression. He spat on each spoon in turn, wiping it with his finger, and they gleamed faintly in the gaslight. Silver. All six of them.

Joe grunted with satisfaction. It was probably the best single find he'd ever made, apart from the silver signet ring which he could never quite believe was real except when he was holding it in his hand in the Madman's garden. But finding the gear was only the start. Now he had to avoid Billy and strike a bargain with Mother that would leave him enough to eat on. He would never make the mistake of straying near the cookshop again with tosh in his bag.

With no coins to hide he had no use for the leather pouch – you couldn't swallow spoons. So Joe gripped the bag tightly under one arm and set off at a brisk walk straight down Flower Street. *Don't run now*, he told himself, *that only draws attention*. He was scarcely past the light at the entrance to Greenfield Passage when he heard a shout. Another voice answered. He'd been spotted.

Mother's Court was no more than a hundred yards on down the passage, past the piggery and through the arch, but it was no good going that way. They'd have the direct route blocked. Joe spun on his heel and sprinted down Flower Street directly above the sewer he'd just been searching, his brain working fast.

Glancing back, he could see four of them coming down Flower Street after him. For a moment he thought of cutting up the alley to the police station. Maybe he could hide the bag somewhere outside and duck in with the crushers. None of Billy's mob would follow him there. It was a trick he'd considered before but never tried. No. Better to take his chances with Billy than finish up with three months in quod.

He rounded the corner into River Lane, slipped between three men walking past the church, and hunched his shoulders, trying to disappear in the crowd. He walked almost straight into Jack.

'Hey, smell you comin', Joe.' Jack pulled at his wet sleeve. 'In fact' – he grinned – 'I reckon they can smell you across the river tonight, boy. Come on!'

Joe froze. He saw the other boy's eyes run quickly over his dripping bag. It obviously wasn't empty. Jack was trying to thieve his tosh. Was that it? Jack smiled, as if he could read his mind. 'I ain't after your tosh, Joey boy. But I know who is.'

Joe glanced over his shoulder. The four boys were at the corner, jumping, trying to spot him amongst the carts and pedestrians. Billy couldn't be far away.

'Come on!'

This time Joe let himself be pulled out of the surge of traffic down Church Lane. 'Get off of me,' he spat at Jack. 'This way ain't no good.'

'You're not gonna make it to Mother's on your own, Joe.' The older boy held him in a grip from which Joe couldn't escape. 'Now, I happens to know a way out of 'ere that Billy doesn't. So d'you want it or not?'

'What's in it for you?'

'Ain't nothin' in it for me.' Jack's voice was a soothing murmur. 'You got to have a little faith in people once in a while, Joe Rat. Too much time in that sewer's got you lookin' for rats everywhere.'

Joe relaxed in his grip and Jack let go, smoothing Joe's sodden jacket, grinning. 'Come on,' he said. 'You got too used to looking at Pound's Field from underneath.'

Right next to where they were standing, an iron ring had been bolted into the churchyard wall at knee-height – an old hitching post maybe. Jack put his foot on it, reached high and hooked himself up onto the top of the wall. Joe copied the bigger boy, using the ring as a foothold, reaching up for the top of the wall. Without Jack's help he wouldn't have made it.

'I don't like it, Jack.' Joe's voice was a whisper. 'There ain't no way out of there with the gates closed.' He looked down into the darkened churchyard. Somewhere amongst the tombs and broken gravestones was the pit where his mother was buried. He'd never fancied hiding in the churchyard.

'Not down there,' said Jack with a quiet laugh, following his gaze. 'Up there.'

Balancing easily on the old stone wall, Jack led the way. The railway viaduct cut straight across the corner of the churchyard and then on over the junction of Flower Street and River Lane. At the corner of the churchyard wall an ancient yew tree towered into the dark sky. The navvies who had built the viaduct had simply sliced off the branches on one side, splitting the blackened trunk and leaving the rest behind. But somehow the old tree had survived and fresh green foliage had already sprung out to cover its wounds.

Jack pointed to where a thick branch reached out towards the viaduct. 'I've done it. You'll make it.'

Joe looked up. The trunk and branches of the tree were so gnarled and pitted he could see hand- and footholds all the way up even in the semi-darkness. But whether you could really drop from the branch down onto the viaduct, which was what Jack was suggesting, Joe doubted. 'You go first,' he managed at last.

'I ain't goin', am I? Someone's got to lead Billy and his lot off. If we both go, they're bound to come back this way.'

Still Joe didn't move.

'Go on,' hissed Jack. 'Trust me, Joe Rat.'

Joe hesitated. He didn't like the word. He shared a shake-down with Plucky Jack and he liked being with him, but that didn't mean he trusted him more than he trusted anyone else. Jack looked after himself and no one else – same as everyone in Pound's Field – same as Joe. Again Jack seemed to know what he was thinking.

'All right' – he laughed – 'don't trust me. But you still ain't got a choice, have yer?'

That was true.

Joe scurried along the top of the wall to the tree, found a handhold on its rough bark and scrambled up into the branches. It was easy climbing. Looking down, he could see Jack watching for a moment. Then he was gone.

Climbing more slowly, Joe made his way cautiously up through the tree and onto the branch that reached out towards the viaduct. There was a drop of maybe ten feet to the railway tracks. But it wasn't a straight drop. He would have to jump out from the tree, clear the parapet and then land between the tracks. If he missed altogether he would break his neck. If he landed wrong on the tracks he would probably break his ankle. He could go back and hide in the churchyard until Billy gave up or found him. He could take his chances in the alleys of Pound's Field, where he had a chance of making it to Mother.

Maybe any other day Joe would have taken the safe option and climbed back down the tree. But that afternoon he had taken a chance in the sewers and finished up with a bag full of tosh. Maybe today was a day for taking chances.

Chapter 8

A Meeting

Joe slid quickly along the tree branch, which ended abruptly at the workmen's saw cut. From here the jump looked worse. He looked out beyond the viaduct. He could see over the buildings as far as Flower Street. He could see part of the police station. The other way he was looking through the branches straight at the spire of St George's. Jack was right: Pound's Field did look different from up here. If he was going to do it, it was better not to hang around too long thinking.

Joe slung the precious bag over his shoulder and jumped – hands and feet extended like a cat. He landed feet first, pitching forwards onto his hands. The rough cinders between the railway sleepers scuffed his palms. He had made it.

Scrambling quickly to his feet, he ran bent double along the viaduct. Below was the open ground of the piggery – no way down there. Joe hurried on. Where the viaduct crossed Sweetwater Lane, a row of houses stretched away at right angles. There was a chimney stack almost within touching distance. He looked quickly down into the road. It seemed quiet enough. He climbed up onto the parapet. If he made it to the ground, from here he could come up on Mother's Court from the other direction, and Billy couldn't cover every way.

Then he heard footsteps below him – running. Joe's first thought was 'Billy'. The running figure stopped under the gaslight. It wasn't Billy. It was a girl.

Frozen under the light, she glanced sharply behind her. She didn't look right for Pound's Field. To Joe she looked like she could be 'quality'. For those clothes Billy would hit her over the head as soon as look at her.

So intent had Joe been on the figure under the gaslight that he hadn't noticed the trembling of the viaduct. Now it had become a shaking on the lines and a roar of steam and screeching metal as a train rattled towards him. He leaped up onto the parapet as the engine came level, catching a glimpse of two sweating faces in the red glow of the cab fire. But no one saw him, balanced on the wall in the darkness thirty feet above Sweetwater Lane. As the great iron monster steamed past, he glanced down at the drop. The girl was still there, backed up against the brickwork, cowering almost to the ground, staring straight at him, wide-eyed, terrified. He made a gesture as if to tell her he meant no harm. Then he realized it wasn't him she was staring at; it was the train thundering over her head.

The last of the trucks groaned past and Joe darted across to the other side of the viaduct. From there he could see up the darkened lane. A man and a woman were walking swiftly down from the main road, and they weren't the usual strollers or a sailor out with his girl. The man carried a heavy stick and they stopped at every doorway and alleyway. Joe knew a hunt when he saw one. Without pausing to think, he stepped lightly off the parapet and onto the chimney stack, then swiftly across the roof and down a drainpipe. He was on the ground within fifteen seconds.

At his touch the cowering girl jerked upright. She was taller and probably stronger than him, and it was only because he caught her off balance that he was able to pull her back into the shadow of the viaduct. But he wasn't quick enough to get his hand over her mouth, and she cried out sharply.

'Go on then,' he hissed, 'shout, if you wants them to get yer.'

'What d'you care?' she demanded, struggling with him. 'What do you want of me?'

Joe hesitated at the strangeness of her accent. 'I don't care and I don't want nothin',' he managed finally. 'They'll 'ave you anyway, shoutin' like that.'

'Who?'

Joe couldn't see her face in the darkness, but he could feel the softness of the woollen shawl and the lace under his fingers. 'There's a man and a woman.'

'Leave go of me, will you?'

Joe let go his grip. She didn't want his help and he didn't know why he'd even come down from the viaduct where he was safe. He was turning to leave, when he heard more hurried steps coming up the lane from the other direction: this time it was Billy with three of the gang. He had nearly broken his neck escaping over the viaduct and now he had walked right into them – all on account of this girl. What had possessed him to get involved in the first place?

In the shadow of the viaduct Joe flattened himself against the arch, the girl close beside him. As Billy passed almost within touching distance, the man and woman rounded the corner. Joe knew exactly what Billy would do. The man looked pretty rough in his battered hat, but the woman was well dressed enough and between them they had to have something worth stealing.

Billy clicked his fingers once and made a quick circling gesture with one hand, and in an instant his followers were in a ring around the couple. Joe didn't wait to see what happened. Sliding his back across the rough brickwork of the railway arch, scarcely breathing, he edged sideways into another pool of darkness. The gas lamps on Sweetwater Lane were spaced pretty far apart and Billy was busy. Now was his chance.

'Well, now, what have we got 'ere, boys?' Billy's sneering voice rang sharp and familiar in Joe's ears, but for once it was someone else on the receiving end. He glanced back in time to see one of the gang come up behind the man and get a stinging blow with the stick for his trouble. Two more closed in. The man struck out again. Joe turned away. At the corner he looked back one last time. The girl was following him.

Joe walked on more briskly, cut down an alley and waited in a doorway. From inside the house came the sound of raised voices – 'I told yer, didn't I?!' – then a slap, a short scream and a child crying. The girl stopped at the entrance to the alley, took a look behind her and a look ahead, clearly with no idea which way to turn. Joe watched her for a moment, then he

stepped out of the doorway and she saw him. He didn't say anything, but when he turned to head on up the alley, he stayed in
the middle where he could be seen, and he could hear her footsteps behind.

Fifty yards before the entrance to Mother's Court he
stopped by the piggery. If the lookout saw the girl, Mother
would know about her in a minute – that is if she didn't know
already. He waited for her to catch up.

'So what's it about?' he demanded in a rough whisper. 'Why
they after yer?'

The girl was silent. Joe could see the cheeks now, flaring red
from Harry Trencher's cream, and the fancy ribbons and the
white skin where her dress was cut low. He'd taken her for
quality, but close to, he saw that she was done up more like one
of the local bobtails that hung around the docks when the
sailors came ashore. Only there was still something about her
that didn't fit – the way she looked him in the eye all fierce one
minute and then suddenly looked down and away like she was
just plain scared. And the voice . . .

'Right.' Joe made up his mind. 'Don't tell me nothin' if you
don't want to. Better not if somebody wants you that bad. I'd
blow the gab if it came to it. Wouldn't take a beatin' for yer.
Why should I? You wouldn't take a beatin' for me.'

The girl stared at him as if he was speaking a foreign
language, and Joe realized he was talking too much. That wasn't
like him. Keep your gas shut and there ain't no danger of
nothing flying out nor nothing flying in – that was another of
Mother's sayings.

'I got some business 'ere with Mother,' he spat out finally, 'and if you know what's good for yer, you'll stay out of the old monster's reach. Slip in there and keep out of sight.' Joe nodded towards the piggery. The girl hesitated. 'Might get your fancy togs mucky, mind,' he scoffed. 'I'll help yer over the wall.'

'Don't need your help,' snapped the girl.

'Suit yourself,' said Joe, and he was gone.

Bess eased herself over the low wall and squatted in the mud. After Harry Trencher and the endless, echoing, brick-walled alleys of Pound's Field and the roaring engine belching fire and smoke, the smell of pig made her think of Hartingham and her father and the home she had left just that morning. She gave a sharp sniff and dashed the back of her hand across her face, as if to wipe tears away before they could form. 'Stop your snivelling, you cruppish girl!' she murmured, borrowing a phrase of her mother's.

There was a low whistle from the direction the boy had gone. Then there was silence – no sign of Trencher or her mother, and with the number of turns they'd made in this maze of tiny streets, Bess didn't see how they could follow her. On the other hand she had no idea where she was or how to get back to a proper road or what to do if she got there. There was no choice: she would have to wait for the sharp-faced, filthy little boy to come back – if he did come back. She would have to trust him. After all he hadn't given her up to Trencher back there in the lane, had he? Even if he did talk like he hated her. But the smell! She could hear pigs grunting in the darkness.

They smelled. But the stink that came off that boy was like nothing she'd ever smelled before. Was there some kind of sickness in him that he stank like that?

Footsteps were coming down the alley now, and Bess crouched lower in the mud. She risked a peek over the wall as whoever it was passed close in front of her. It wasn't Trencher or her mother. In the spill of light from the lamp where the boy had disappeared, Bess recognized the big lad who had fought Trencher back in the lane. He was holding a bloody handkerchief to his nose. Bess heard the same whistle she'd heard when the boy left her. She settled down in the darkness and the familiar pig smell to wait.

It couldn't have been more than five minutes before a light, pattering step she already recognized came hurrying straight past. Bess climbed quickly over the wall and caught the boy at the corner. He was muttering to himself like the crazy man that came tramping through Hartingham sometimes – '. . . quality tosh and I end up with a deuce – two miserable pennies . . .' He turned back in the lane and raised a fist. 'I'll get out one day, Mother. You'll see. Get out on my own hook. Won't 'ave to pay you a miserable farthin'.'

'That lad . . .' Bess tried to interrupt.

The boy stared at her as if he didn't know who she was. 'What? What lad?'

'The one as was a-laying into Harry – into the man back there.'

'Billy. What about him?'

'He went down the same twitten you went in. You didn't see him?'

'The same what?'

'Down the alley. There was a whistle like and he—'

Joe interrupted sharply, 'What kind of whistle?'

'How d'you mean?'

'There's a whistle for strangers and there's a whistle for someone 'e knows.'

'Well, it was like—'

'Don't do it!' This time he did manage to clamp his hand across Bess's mouth, but she fought out of his grasp at once.

'I wasn't a-going to do it,' she hissed angrily. 'I bain't stupid, you know. It was the same whistle as when you went down the – down the alley.'

'Was it now?' The boy stood nodding his head, his mouth set hard. 'Was it? You sure it was Billy?'

'It was the same lad as back there.'

As Bess watched, horrified, the boy seemed to go mad. He beat his head and his chest with clenched fists; he kicked out at the brick walls around them with his bare feet; he cursed himself in a low, intense, hissing whisper: 'Just a fool! A damned fool! How come Billy's not under Mother's thumb? He is, isn't 'e? Workin' for her the whole time! The old devil!' Then his voice changed, as if he was imitating someone – '"You owe me rent, Joseph. You owe me my whack, Joseph. You owe me two guineas, Joseph." And all the time she's runnin' Billy and his boys and thievin' the whole lot off of me every chance she can.' He hammered on the wall at the corner with his fists. Then suddenly the passion went out of his voice and he shrugged.

'Yeah. Makes sense. Billy and Mother. Should've known it. Billy and Mother.'

'Your mother?'

The boy whirled round at her. 'What are you – Irish?'

'No, I bain't Irish.'

'How come you talk like that then?'

'Like what?'

'Like tha-a-a-a-t.' The boy put on an odd, drawling voice.

'Well, how come you talk like you do?' Bess shot back.

The boy let out a peculiar snort that Bess didn't recognize as a laugh. His shifting eyes disappeared into his face. 'Come on,' he said quickly. 'She knows about you now. That's for sure. And after the game she's played me, I ain't givin' you to her. You want to stay away from that bloke with the stick?'

'Yes.'

'There's a lodgin' house down past the docks. It's mostly sailors down there. I'll take yer. You can stay the night and go wherever you're goin' in the mornin'.'

'Thank you.' Bess wasn't sure what the expression on the foul-smelling little boy's face meant. His eyes narrowed and he seemed to wince at being thanked. Perhaps he hadn't understood. She repeated the words slowly as if to a very young child. 'Thank you.'

'Don't thank me,' he spat out. 'I don't like it.' And he was off again, turning this way and that through the dark streets and alleys with Bess hurrying alongside.

Chapter 9

HOLYWELL COURT

They passed under another railway arch and alongside the high stone wall of a churchyard and, to Bess's surprise, emerged onto a busy thoroughfare. They'd seen hardly anyone in the last few minutes, and when they had seen a figure approaching, the boy had always drawn her back into a dark doorway. Now there were carts and wagons, men in working clothes and light flooding out from shops and taverns. Bess scanned the faces anxiously, expecting to walk straight into Harry Trencher and her mother. Instead it was a heavy-set man she didn't know who stepped out unexpectedly into their path.

'Where you off to then, Joe?' The voice was level and surprisingly soft for such a big man. Bess noted the name he called the boy and the way Joe seemed to shrink instinctively away.

'Ain't goin' nowhere, Watchman,' Joe said quickly.

The man turned a penetrating gaze towards Bess, and all at once she was intensely conscious of the white muslin dress, now heavily stained at the hem, and her flaming red cheeks. She drew the shawl around her and took a step backwards. A group of sailors staggered past, pushing between them, shouting and singing at the tops of their voices. At the same moment a heavy wagon laden with two enormous barrels emerged from the archway behind the Watchman, horses straining to draw the load. Out of the corner of her eye she saw Joe take a couple of steps sideways, slipping away amongst the passers-by. But the Watchman was too quick.

'Who's your friend, Joe?' The voice wasn't raised, but one hand snaked out to hold the boy firmly by the shoulder.

'She ain't nobody. Let go, will yer!'

'Mother know about her, does she?'

'She will now you've seen her, won't she, Watchman?' Joe snarled, twisting in the man's grasp.

The Watchman's expression didn't change. He let go of Joe. 'You could try Palmer's, if she needs a place.'

Bess looked quickly at Joe. The boy was staring suspiciously up into the pock-marked face of the Watchman. 'Never said she needed a place, did I?'

The Watchman shrugged, and stepped back under the arch of the dock entrance, as if to say he was finished with them. Joe hurried on down the busy road with Bess at his side, but when she looked back she could see the heavy-set man still watching them.

Joe cut off the main road and led the way down a narrow court with lines of washing strung between the houses above their heads. He stopped in front of a pair of green gates that looked to Bess more like the entrance to a stable yard than a house of any kind.

'Now why's he want us here at Palmer's?' It was a question, but the boy wasn't addressing her. He was talking to himself.

Bess sat down heavily on the dirty cobblestones, leaning her head against a gatepost. Suddenly she was exhausted and hungry. She could lodge here, or she could lodge with the pigs. She didn't care which. The one place she wasn't going was back to Harry Trencher and her mother.

Somewhere inside she had always known Trencher was no friend to her. She'd tried to make herself believe he was helping her mother and father, but she'd had to blot out the smell of the man and his ugly, wheedling ways, and above all the memory of that hand slipping so easily around her mother's waist. What set her heart racing again, as she slumped on the wet ground, was the fear and humiliation she had felt as the cart stuck fast in the crowd and her mother had rubbed that muck on her face and then tried not to laugh with the rest. She'd told her father that she, Bess Farleigh, could make all their fortunes. She'd said that. Then she'd made her feel like a calf fattened up for market.

Bess shook her head quickly, dismissing the image of her mother smiling as Trencher's filthy cream took effect. She held onto the thought of her father, trying to fill every corner of her mind with the last sight she'd had of him, standing with his right hand raised outside the front door of their home. She forgot the strange weakness she had heard in his voice that morning, the way she had felt the need to reassure him. In her mind Reuben was once again the solid figure that would make everything all right. Somehow she must get back to him. If she could just rest tonight, perhaps tomorrow there would be a way . . .

Joe's urgent voice cut in on her thoughts. 'You can't stop here!' He pulled awkwardly at her sleeve, and Bess struggled back to her feet. 'There's a place up past the church.' Bess looked blank. 'You go up by the docks again, and then . . . Oh, come on, I'll have to take yer.'

They tried up past the church. Then they tried the place Joe had thought of going to first. Then they tried Palmer's lodging house after all. But everywhere was the same. 'Mother know about her, does she, Joe Rat?' 'Who's after her then, Joe Rat?' 'Why don't you take her back to your own crib, Joe Rat?'

Finally Bess had had enough. She turned away quickly as the last door was shut in their faces and headed off at random down a narrow passage. She walked straight into a blank wall, striking her head sharply on the bricks. She hadn't heard him come up behind her, but Joe's hand was on her arm.

'Come on,' he said.

'You just let me be. I'll be fine.'

'No you won't.'

'Well show me where those pigs are then and I'll stop the night with them.'

'Right on Mother's doorstep?' The boy let out a derisive snort. Then he pulled at her arm. 'Come on.'

'Where we going? You know another lodging?'

'No use. They all know me, and they don't know you. No one'll take the chance.' He sighed heavily. 'Have to be my crib.'

Bess followed him back past the church once more and on

amongst houses crowded so close together it seemed as if the inhabitants of the upper storeys could have shaken hands across the alley. She made no attempt to follow where they were going. She was too tired. Finally they ducked through a particularly dark and foul-smelling archway and emerged into one of the larger yards. Bess looked up to see a soot-encrusted sign high on one wall. It read HOLYWELL COURT.

Joe led her through the open front door of one of the houses. 'Mind out,' he called out without looking round. 'Boards is goin'.' At the end of the passageway he threw open a door, and a cloud of smoke and cooking smells and noise burst out.

Bess followed him into the low-ceilinged kitchen, and the noise stopped abruptly. Every face in the room turned to stare at her – a man still holding a mouth organ, a clutch of wide-eyed, ragged children, several more figures who could have been male or female slumped across the trestle table that ran the length of the room. There was a single low window above the sink, crusted with dirt so you couldn't see through. A small fire smoked in one corner. Over by the stove a rocking chair was still in motion, but the man, who had obviously been sitting in it when the door opened, was standing, a wooden ladle raised in his hand as if it was a weapon. Like all the others in the room he had his eyes fixed on Bess.

Joe was the first to speak. 'What you got there then, Greasy Tyler? Nice bit of bow-wow mutton, is it? I got the chink.' He produced one of the two pennies Mother had given him and held it aloft.

'That's Mister Tyler to you, Joe Rat,' the man with the ladle growled. 'And it ain't no dog meat; it's a nice bit of soup and some sawney what Charlie's boy found in Leadenhall Market last night.'

Charlie, the man with the mouth organ, blew a mock fanfare at this. Then he cocked an eye at Bess. 'Looks like young Joe got hisself a nice slice of meat of his own, don't it? Who's yer bit of muslin, Joe Rat?'

'Ain't nothing to do with me,' said Joe. 'Don't even know her name.'

'Oh, dear!' Tyler and Charlie chorused together, and there was laughter from around the room. Even the children joined in. 'He don't even know her name.'

Greasy Tyler crossed the room to where Bess was still standing by the door, and inspected her at close quarters. His breath reminded her of Harry Trencher. 'Fancy little chickster and he doesn't know your name, my dear.' There was another shout of laughter. Bess felt her face burning. She dashed a hand across her eyes.

'Might have to wash yerself every now and then, Joe Rat,' another voice called out.

'Ain't you a bit young, dear, for all that painting?' asked Tyler, his nose almost touching hers now, fingering the material of the shawl that hung loose about her bare shoulders.

Unable to speak, Bess threw the brightly coloured shawl from her and began to rub fiercely at her cheeks, spitting on her hands. The laughter in the room grew louder. It was the same as the crowd that had surrounded her in the cart, except here in this cramped and dingy room she felt even more trapped. She turned desperately for the door with nothing but escape in her mind. She saw Joe. He had a rag in his hand, which he was holding out to her. She stared at him, not understanding. Joe spat on the filthy rag and offered it again. Bess hesitated; then she took the rag and began to work at her face, shrinking down onto one of the wooden benches.

The people in the room seemed to lose interest in her at once. Tyler was ladling out the contents of his enormous pot and taking coins from those that had them. Joe sat near her, spooning the thin soup quickly into his mouth with one hand while the other circled the bowl as if guarding it from the rest of the room. She looked round to see the four young children eating in exactly the same way.

'Hungry, my dear?' Bess looked up with a start to find Tyler bending over her. 'Ain't he given you no money then?' He tut-tutted in mock disapproval over Joe, who didn't look up from his bowl. 'He don't know how to treat a real angelic like your-self. Now a man such as me—' Bess turned away, unable to suppress a shudder. Tyler's tone changed sharply. She noticed he was holding her shawl. 'Reckon this shawl you didn't want might be worth a ladleful.' He handed her a steaming bowl and a spoon and went away, fingering his payment.

'That weren't nothin' but workhouse skilley,' grumbled Joe, pushing his bowl away empty. Noises of agreement came from around the room. 'Feel like you swallowed a bowl of dirty water.'

'You should know, you filthy tosher,' Tyler hurled back

at him, and the rest of the room laughed, back on Tyler's side.

Joe got up from the table and gestured to Bess to follow. There were cat-calls and shouts of laughter as the two left the room and headed in complete darkness up the rickety stairs.

'Watch your step.' Bess heard Joe's voice in the darkness. 'Ain't no banisters. Got broke up for firewood last winter.'

Bess was on hands and knees, feeling her way. Some of the stairs were broken so badly you had to climb over two or three at a time. Eventually she came to a dead stop. 'Wait!' she demanded.

'Whasamarra?'

Bess reached out and felt for Joe's tattered jacket. It was wet. He grunted in surprise but he didn't shake her off, and they started up another flight of stairs with Bess holding onto him.

'Don't make no noise,' he told her. 'Some of 'em don't take kindly to bein' woke up.'

With one hand still holding Joe's jacket and the other groping in the dark, Bess followed the boy into the black room. She choked on the air. It smelled as if you'd taken every piece of dirty washing in Hartingham and thrown it on the smoking fire they'd just left downstairs. There was a heavy snoring somewhere in the darkness and the sound of a woman muttering in her sleep. There might have been others sleeping in the room, but she could see absolutely nothing. The fingers of her right hand touched the glass of a window. Not a glimmer of light came from the outside, but she could feel the night breeze seeping through the rags and paper that had been stuffed into the broken panes. The chill November air didn't thin the all-enveloping fug but it calmed the girl just a little, reassuring her that she hadn't been buried alive.

Joe's sharp little fingers dug into her arm, pulling her down towards the floor. She heard the hiss of his voice, but he wasn't talking to her.

'Got a girl, Jack.'

'You what?' The second voice was groggy with sleep.

'A girl. An angelic. She ain't mine,' Joe added quickly, and in a whisper he outlined the events that had brought the pair together. 'Old cow up at Tinker's Alley wouldn't take her, so I brung her here,' he finished, as if admitting some guilty secret. 'Don't reckon she's got much of a chance though. Watchman's seen her.'

Suddenly Bess felt hands on her, feeling her face, her hair, her bare shoulders.

'Here! What you think you're a-doing?' She recoiled from the touch. It wasn't Joe's voice that answered in the darkness.

'Stow it, girl. Just trying to work out what we're dealing with. Sounds like a Jenny Raw up from the country, Joe boy. What you doin' round Pound's Field, Jenny Raw?'

Bess didn't answer. It was Joe who spoke. 'You won't say nothin', will yer, Jack? I'm gonna keep her here for the night.'

'Don't sound too clever, Joe.' The other boy's voice was deeper than Joe's. Bess guessed he might be a year or two older. 'Any money involved?'

'No,' Bess lied quickly. She had no intention of telling anyone of the plans to hire her out as a servant. 'Ain't no money involved.'

'If there's chinks anywhere, Mother'll know before light. You know that, Joe.'

'Yeah, I know.' Joe sounded miserable about the whole affair. 'You won't say nothin' though?'

'What you think I am? A dirty snitch?' The other boy sounded indignant. Bess had been long enough in the dark now to discern his outline as he squeezed past her, but she couldn't see his face. Joe had stretched out on the floor, but it was hard to tell if he was lying on a mattress or on the bare boards. Without another word, she curled up by his feet, making herself as small as she could. It wasn't a mattress, but there was something between her and the boards. She shifted, trying to find a way to lie comfortably.

Joe sat up, not certain whether he should be making more room for the girl on his shakedown. 'You can stretch out a bit if you want,' he offered. There was no answer. The white dress stood out faintly in the dark room. Joe reached out a hand and shook her gently. No response. She was fast asleep. All those fancy clothes and yet there she was kipping on the floor just like – well, just like him.

Chapter 10

THE MADMAN

Joe was struggling to wake up. In his dream the high walls that surrounded the Madman's garden had grown up to the sky and were dotted with barred windows through which eyes peered. Then suddenly they collapsed like rotten timber, and a crowd of people – Mother, Billy, the Watchman: too many to count – were all lined up outside, watching him check his tosh. Then the walls of the buildings behind them collapsed the same way, and he was in the middle of a wide open space that stretched away as far as the eye could see and he didn't have a notion which way he was supposed to go . . .

A hand was shaking him. 'There's someone on the stairs.'

Now he was awake. The room was still pitch black and the snoring and muttering was the same. But somewhere in the house – maybe the landing below – Joe could hear boards creaking under a heavy tread. That wasn't the way Greasy Tyler moved day or night. Of all the occupants of 16 Holywell Court only the Watchman had that kind of firm step, but it was too early yet for him, unless he'd come looking for the girl.

Joe grabbed his canvas bag and slipped out of the sack. He

saw the outline of the girl's dress, pale in the darkness, gripped her arm and pulled her towards the door. He damned himself as a fool for bringing her here in the first place, but he was relieved to find she moved as soundlessly as he did in the darkness.

Out on the landing the light of a candle flickered up from below, casting the huge shadow of a man across the stairwell. A noise of sleepy grumbling and complaints mixed with a few drunken oaths came from the rooms on the first floor. Then a voice rang out, loud: 'They ain't in none of these rooms!'

It wasn't the Watchman or any voice Joe knew, but he could feel the girl go rigid at his side. She had recognized it all right.

'You're on the wrong floor, you idiot! He's upstairs. They're both upstairs.' That was Tyler.

Joe risked a peek over the edge where the banisters should have been. On the landing directly below him was the man in the stovepipe hat who had laid out two or three of Billy's gang on Sweetwater Lane. Then he heard Billy's voice. They were working together! The man was after Bess. No doubt about that. But if Billy was there, then this was going to end badly for Joe too. It was no good just handing her over now. That wouldn't get him off the hook.

'I'll get him, Mister Tyler. I know that little rat boy's hole.'

There was a stamping on the stairs, which Joe knew was too heavy for the rickety structure. A sharp oath showed that Billy's foot had gone through one of the rotting boards. It gave Joe the time he needed.

He drew Bess away from the stairs and through another

door. More oaths, more grumbling in here. The whole house was being woken up. That might just give them half a chance. They could wait it out here, while Billy and the man went into his room, and then hope to get past Tyler on the stairs. But there was a better way if the girl was up to it. All the upstairs rooms looked straight out onto Holywell Court, with most of the windows too warped to shift. But in this room one window actually opened, and right next to it was a drainpipe Joe had been up and down more than once when occasion demanded.

He turned to the girl. She was already at the window, silhouetted against the night sky.

'Oi, what you at?' A rough voice came from the darkness. It would be only a matter of moments before the whole room was awake and Billy and the man with the stick were in the room and they had had it. Joe wrenched up the sash, swung himself out onto the window ledge and slid quickly and easily down the drainpipe, landing in a crouch in the dark courtyard. He looked up to see if there was any chance of the girl making it. She was standing next to him.

'Come on!' he hissed, making a move for the passage that led out of Holywell Court. The girl stopped him before he could stand upright. Two of Billy's boys were stationed that way, and where the blind alley led down to the back wall of the warehouse two more figures waited. They could have tried fighting their way out, but that wasn't Joe's way. Suddenly there didn't seem to be a choice. He was going to have to do what he had always sworn he wouldn't – he was going to have to take this girl to the Madman's garden where he hid his tosh.

Joe took the girl's arm, heading back for the front door of the house. 'It's all right,' he whispered, as he felt her pull away. To his surprise she didn't argue or speak; she came with him.

They crept down the hall with the upper part of the house in uproar. Tyler was on the first landing, shouting; a woman was screaming at the top of her voice; a couple of the kids were bawling; doors were banging, and everyone from downstairs seemed to have gone either to join in the hunt or to watch. The door to the kitchen was open, but the room was empty. Swift and soundless, Joe led Bess down the wooden steps to the cellar. He turned quickly to warn her they were rotten in places, but she was placing her feet at either end of each tread just as he did. Only at the bottom of the steps, as he slid thigh-deep into the water, did the girl hesitate. Then she followed him there too.

They waded across the floor of the cellar. Joe climbed onto the familiar pile of rubble in the far corner, and ripped back the sacking. One by one he passed the bricks back to Bess. It was easier than having to climb down and lower each one into the water himself. Then came the familiar draught of air, and he wriggled through and into the long, damp grass of the garden. Behind him he could hear Bess struggling at the opening in the wall. It was wide enough for his narrow shoulders, but she was bigger than him. As she finally emerged from the hole, Joe could see that her clothes were torn where they weren't soaked from the cellar water. If she'd ever looked like quality or even one of the fancy tarts at Nimms's gin shop, she certainly didn't look that way any more.

Gradually the noise from Holywell Court died down as the searchers gave up. They would find the upstairs window open and assume that somehow Joe and Bess had got past the guards at the entrance to the court. No doubt Billy would give his boys a good thumping for their carelessness. That was some satisfaction, Joe thought grimly.

He had never been in the garden this late before. A thin mist hung low over trees, grass and brambles, and high overhead a semi-circle of moon shone faintly in the milky sky. There was silence from the old house, which rose dim and ghostly in the damp air. Perhaps even the Madman was asleep at this time. But it wasn't the lateness of the hour that made the garden feel eerie and different and less like a place of safety, it was the other person crouching in the darkness next to him. His secret was a secret no more. It was done now and there was no use in wishing it undone, and they could hide here until morning. But there was one part of his secret Joe certainly wasn't going to share with this girl: they wouldn't be going anywhere near the stone tombs that concealed his grey cloth bag.

He led the way at random, away from his usual route into a part of the grounds he had never visited before. There were tall plants around them here, and the grass still stood thick and high from the summer, holding onto the last of its seeds. Every now and then Joe could feel bricks set into the earth under his bare feet, the remains of pathways that wound through the undergrowth.

In the middle of a clump of bushes they came upon an old stone seat, but the brambles grew over it so thickly they couldn't sit there. In the end Joe squatted down amongst the fallen leaves as far from the animal graves as he could get and turned to Bess, who hadn't spoken since they entered the garden.

'You want to know where we are, don'tcha?' She didn't answer. 'Well, I ain't gonna tell yer.' His aggressive tone prompted no response. Bess slumped down amongst the leaves. He could see she was shivering. Joe realized he was shivering too. 'So what's it all about then? You gonna tell me now? I got you away, didn't I?'

The girl looked at him, narrowing her eyes, as if she was trying to make up her mind about something.

'Well, what's your name at least?' Joe pursued. 'You ain't even told me your name.'

'You didn't ask.'

'I did.'

'No, you didn't.'

'All right, well I'm asking now.'

And slowly, unwillingly at first, she began to tell her story – or *a* story. 'My name's Bess – Bess Farleigh. Do you know Kent?'

'What's that?' asked Joe, instantly suspicious.

'It's a place. The place I'm from.' There was a tone in her voice Joe didn't like – like he was stupid for not knowing what Kent was. He scowled. Bess went on: 'I come from a town in Kent called Hartingham. Big place, it is, and we're quite an important family there – fields and cows to the Farleigh name, there are. And you want to know for why a girl from a good family ends up in a place like this on her own, don't you?'

Bess hesitated. Then, with growing confidence, she began to unfold a tale that came so easily she almost believed it herself.

'See, what happened is this. My mother died. Near on two year ago it was. She got sick and she died. And my father, he was on his own for a while and then he met this woman – this very beautiful woman with black hair and he married again . . .'

Joe forgot about Greasy Tyler and Billy, and he even stopped thinking about his tosh for a while. This girl named Bess had a mother who'd died too. Perhaps that was what made her story sound vaguely familiar.

'Anyway,' she went on, 'she seemed nice enough to start with. But then it seemed like my father gradually loved her more and more and me less and less. Till in the end they said I had to go and live with Uncle and Aunt here in London. So I come up on a big coach this morning. Only we was crossing this big bridge over the river – the Thames, right?'

'River Thames. That's it.'

'We was on this big bridge – well, just coming off the other side – and we had an accident, see? And I made a run for it. Didn't want to go and live with Uncle and Aunt.'

'So it was them as was after yer? Your uncle and aunt?'

'That's right. Only I didn't want to go with them, see?'

There were things about the story that didn't make sense to Joe. The girl looked prosperous enough – or she had before she'd started hiding with the pigs and wading through a cesspool. But the man with the stick and the stovepipe hat – he didn't look like part of any 'good family'. But then again, Joe didn't know much about 'good families', and what was the difference anyway? A lot of folk around Pound's Field had tall tales to tell about themselves. He let it go.

'Shouldn't have sold that fancy shawl for a bowl of Greasy Tyler's skilley,' he said finally. 'Worth a sight more'n that.'

'My father won't mind,' Bess returned brightly. 'I got lots of shawls like that at home.'

''Cept he don't want yer no more,' said Joe.

That seemed to set the girl thinking, because she didn't have anything else to say. It occurred to Joe that she had told him her story and perhaps he'd better tell her some of his. Why not, seeing as how they had hours yet until morning?

'My ma died too,' he said abruptly. The girl looked up, surprised, as if she had forgotten he was there. 'Only I ain't got no pa neither. He was a soldier, Ma said, though I didn't never meet him. Army sent him off across the ocean when I was a nipper.'

'But you said you were going to see your mother.'

Joe let out his tight little laugh. 'She ain't my mother. Everyone round here just calls her that. No. See, my ma got sick when she was on her own and we ended up in the pike.'

'In the—?'

'The pike. Whitechapel Workhouse.' Joe's face took on a grim, set expression. 'You keep yourself out of them places no matter what.'

'Yes. That's what my mother says – said, I mean.'

'My ma washed clothes there.'

'Really?'

Joe looked at her sharply, misinterpreting her interest. 'Yeah. Ain't nothin' wrong with that. Anyway, I had two big brothers, and they both went workin' in this tailor's shop, only I couldn't stand it. Too shut in like. Shut in the pike and then shut in the shop. So I run off. Like you. Only I was younger. And after a bit I met up with Mother – her they call Mother, I mean. And she set me to – outdoor work. Suited me better.'

'Outdoor work? What's that?'

'Well, it's stuff as goes on in London,' said Joe evasively. 'You wouldn't know about it.' There was something about this girl that made him unwilling to tell her he earned his living searching for scraps in the London sewers. He went on hurriedly, 'Anyways my ma got sick with the tramp fever last time there was a big go of it.' The girl looked blank. 'Tramp fever. Cholera, they call it.' Joe pronounced the word carefully. 'Done for her and Matt and Jimmy. Never touched me though. Healthy, I am. It's the way of life.'

'What way of life?'

'I told yer – outdoor work.' Like as not she'd make fun of him if he told her what he did – girl from a 'good family' with a load of shawls at home. She'd call him Ratboy or something.

'Is that why you – why you're so—?'

'Dirty?' finished Joe with something that was meant to sound like a laugh. 'Yeah. Course, I sometimes cleans up on a Saturday. Clean clothes and all. I got some,' he lied weakly.

The boy stood up abruptly, stretched his stiff limbs and headed off into the darkness without another word. He was cold and his stomach felt like it had been hollowed out and scraped clean, but he was familiar with those sensations. Less familiar was the sense that he didn't want to sit near Bess Farleigh with her good family and her fancy clothes another minute. The moon had disappeared, and it was hard to be sure of the pathway, but more than likely there was an outhouse or a shed where he could sit out the rest of the night – maybe even catch a little sleep. Of course, she'd probably follow him, but what could he do about that?

The night was very silent. The owl hunting in the darkness had stopped its hooting and the distant sounds from River Lane had ceased. Joe picked his way between some tall trees, his feet rustling in the fallen leaves. These must be the trees you could see over the wall from down by the docks. Their thick trunks were regularly spaced, as if they had been planted carefully a long time ago. High above his head he could make out their bare branches laced together against the dark sky. Then his sharp ears caught another sound – like the rustle of the leaves at his feet, but different. Joe stood quite still. In the darkness almost straight ahead he could hear the faint trickle of water.

He moved forward carefully, peering into the gloom under the trees. Further on, the line of the garden wall was just visible, but here all was darkness. Then, quite suddenly, the mist lifted, the moon sailed out into an open sky and a clear blue light bathed the whole garden, reflecting in the dewdrops on the grass, silvering the cobwebs on the bramble bushes, casting a deep shade beneath the thickest undergrowth. The trees stood in a patient circle, throwing long shadows across the uneven ground, and right in their very centre amongst the thick, tussocky grass was a low stone structure, half buried in the earth. Joe moved closer, expecting another tomb, though this stonework looked even rougher and older.

Twenty paces and he was looking down at a brick dome, overgrown with weeds and moss, which rose no more than a foot above ground level. Joe worked his way around the side, and a black hole opened up suddenly at his feet. He reached out on both sides to steady himself, and edged carefully down ten narrow stone steps into a deep hollow in the ground. The sound of water was clearer now. Then, deep in the ferns and weeds at the bottom of the hollow, a gleam of light caught his eye: it was a thin stream, shining, twisting and sparkling in the moonlight.

Joe reached down. There was an edging of ice to the narrow stone rill where the water ran. He cupped both hands and scooped the liquid up into his mouth. He drank deep and scooped again. He had never tasted anything so good in his whole life: it was like drinking the moonlight itself. Then, as he put his lips to another deep draught, a high, piercing scream rang out through the garden.

His first instinct was to duck deeper into the earth – to a tosher the dampness and the running water meant places to hide. He told himself it could have been anyone screaming in the darkness. Maybe the sound hadn't even come from inside the garden. But somewhere inside Joe knew that it was the girl, Bess Farleigh, and that he had to go and see what had happened to her.

He scrambled up the stone steps on all fours, scuttling back along the leaf-strewn path, expecting to find Bess where he had left her. Then he heard something to his left. The moon had disappeared again into a thickening mist, but he could see the girl struggling amongst the long grass, tugging at her leg.

'What happened?'

Bess didn't reply; only a low moan of pain emerged from her mouth.

'I'll get you out of it.'

She was caught in some kind of metal contraption – animal trap, he guessed. Together they heaved at the heavy iron clamps that gripped her ankle, but they couldn't shift it. If it was a trap, then there had to be a release mechanism somewhere, but Joe couldn't work out where it was and Bess was in too much pain to think straight. The whole thing was held by a chain to a metal spike, driven deep into the ground. Joe strained at the spike. It was immovable.

Then Bess stiffened abruptly and stopped struggling with the trap. She was staring over his head, eyes wide and unblinking. Joe turned quickly to follow her eye-line. Amongst a tangle of brambles three stunted trees held their branches up straight and leafless in the damp air. Then one of the trees moved. Joe blinked. Couldn't have. Must be the night playing tricks. He was good in the dark; ought to be after all the long hours under. Wasn't nothing there. Just a dead branch falling, or—

The tree moved again. Except that it wasn't a tree. Stiff and slow, as if each step was a terrible effort, a hugely tall, stick-thin figure loomed out of the mist, arms held straight out in front.

At every other step it bent slowly almost double at the waist, was still for a moment, then came on again with the same halting stride. Joe had never seen him. He had never heard of anyone who had seen him. But there could be no doubt who it was. It was the Madman himself.

The boy didn't pause to think. His feet silent even amongst the fallen leaves, he melted into the darkness. Keeping low, never looking back, he moved quickly through the overgrown garden, dodging between bushes, keeping to the darkest places, always heading back in what he thought was the general direction of 16 Holywell Court. There was the line now where the houses had been built straight into the garden wall, and there was the entrance back into the world he knew. His hand was already reaching through, feeling for the strip of canvas that concealed the hole in the wall, when Joe stopped.

He told himself it was the thought of Billy and Greasy Tyler and the man with the stick who might still be waiting. He told himself it was because Mother would be after his blood when she found out he had helped the runaway escape her. He turned and made his way back as swiftly as he had fled – to where he had left Bess Farleigh with her leg caught in the Madman's iron trap.

Without the circle of trees he would never have found it, but they made a clear landmark to aim for. Where the grass was trampled, Joe came to a halt, breathing heavily. The sound of water was faintly audible. Peering amongst the grass and feeling on all fours with his hands, he found the edges of the trap. It had been reset. There was no sign of Bess or the Madman, but

THE MADMAN

Joe knew where they must have gone. He took the widest of the paths that had been trampled through the overgrown garden, and headed straight for where the towering wooden gables and broken chimneys of the old house rose dark and solid in the shifting mist.

Chapter 11

The House

Weeds and brambles reached right up to the back wall of the house, but in one place there was still a clear brick path which led directly to a doorway. The upper storeys were wider than the lower ones, so that when Joe looked up, the building jutted out over his head, hanging in space as if about to come crashing down on anyone foolhardy enough to try that back door.

Not a sound or a glimmer of light came from inside as Joe rubbed the grimy glass of the door with his sleeve, trying to make out what lay within. He pressed too hard. The brittle glass shattered, sending broken shards cascading onto the hard floor inside with a noise that seemed deafening in the silence. Joe froze where he was, one hand on the doorknob. He waited a minute, then another, his heart thumping. But no one came. The house stood absolutely silent in front of him, but through the hole where the glass had broken he could now see light.

The boy took a deep breath to try to calm the beating of his heart. This was the Madman's house. The Madman! In all the tales he'd heard told around Pound's Field, no one had ever claimed they'd been inside the place, and yet here he was with his hand on the doorknob. It was partly curiosity that drove him on. He'd been in the garden so often now, looked up at the towering building where the Madman shouted: there had always been a part of him that wanted to see what lay inside. But there was something else – he called it stubbornness. He'd helped keep Bess Farleigh from Mother and Billy and the man with the stick, and now the Madman had got her, which was probably a thousand times worse. And he wasn't going to just let it happen. If anyone had told him he was doing something for someone else which was against his own interest, he would have laughed in their face. Mother had taught him better than that, hadn't she? It was just plain stubbornness – the same thing that kept him adding tosh, piece by piece, to his hoard in the garden when he knew he might never be able to spend it. Anyway, the door was probably locked . . .

He turned the doorknob gently. The door wasn't locked. It swung open, hinges protesting, and Joe stepped into the Madman's house.

He was standing at the end of a long passageway. Doors opened to left and right, and an oil lamp flickered dimly on one wall. Joe edged forward, making no sound, picking his way over shattered glass and broken floor tiles. The fingers of his right hand scraped a thick coating of dust as he felt his way along the wall. There was a smell of dead things in the air.

He tried one of the doors. It creaked open, but behind, all was darkness. Each door he passed was the same – opening to his touch, but inside, nothing and no one to be seen. At the end of the passage a stairway led upward. Joe mounted gingerly: every creak set his heart thumping again and seemed to echo away down the passageway and through the empty rooms, but no one came. At the top of the stairs a door stood half open, and Joe emerged into a room such as he had never entered in his life.

The first thing he saw was a huge crystal chandelier – maybe twice the size of the one he'd glimpsed one night at Barton's Music Hall. Only this one wasn't hanging from the wood-panelled ceiling, because there was a great jagged hole where it had been ripped out of the timber. One half lay more or less intact in the middle of the long table beneath and the other half lay shattered on the floor. In the part that survived, four or five good wax candles burned brightly. There were smashed plates and glasses on the table where the chandelier had crashed down, but spread across the rest of a massive tablecloth were plates, glasses, bowls, silver knives, forks, spoons – enough for every inmate of 16 Holywell Court to sit down to dinner. Joe's eyes widened at the sight of all the silver, and he found himself making quick calculations of its worth – one for solid silver; one for silver plate.

Gilt-backed chairs stood ready for the diners, except that every one had had the stuffing ripped from its seat, as if a wild animal had been let loose on them. The silverware looked wrong too, not glinting brightly in the candlelight, but stained and tarnished like something Joe might have picked up in the sewers. And over the remains of the chandelier and the plates and the glasses and the chairs and the white tablecloth lay a thick, grey coat of dust and dead insects and the webs of a thousand spiders.

On the opposite wall hung three sets of tall curtains. Once deep red, their colour was faded and hidden, as if the autumn mist had come stealing through the windows and shrouded them in grey. Just by Joe's right hand stood a small table with an unlit lamp. A book lay upside down open on the table and next to it in a bowl – more silver! – the remains of a cigar, a long ash still attached. Table, book and silver bowl were all covered in what Joe recognized at once as old rat droppings. Looking more closely, he could see the same ash-grey muck scattered over the white tablecloth.

Detail by detail Joe took in the entire room – the carpet worn and faded, wallpaper hanging from the walls in long festoons, a huge mirror with half its glass in pieces on the floor. There were pictures on the walls too – dark landscapes, a massive black horse rearing up, portraits of men and women in old-fashioned clothes, and in each of the portraits the face had been clawed out, leaving a tattered hole in the canvas. On the far side, so far that Joe thought you could have fitted his entire lodging house inside the room, a small coal fire burned in an enormous marble fireplace. Chunks of stone had been split off the mantelpiece and stacked where the iron grate had been to create a rough base for the fire. Over the burning coals a makeshift stand supported a blackened cooking pot, and next to the fireplace, bending over a long, low couch with his back turned, was the gaunt figure Joe had seen in the garden.

The Madman's feet were bare and nearly as filthy as Joe's

own. The ends of his heavily stained trousers were frayed and the tails of his coat looked as if they had been hacked off with a pair of shears. As he inched closer, Joe could hear the man murmuring softly to himself, but he couldn't distinguish any words. Half hidden by a tall wing-backed chair with its stuffing torn out like all the other chairs in the room, Joe stopped to watch.

The man straightened up for a moment, and Joe saw Bess stretched out perfectly still on the couch, eyes closed, face a deathly white. The man bent over her again. Joe couldn't see what he was doing, but the muttering continued, becoming more agitated as the skeletal figure stooped lower over the motionless girl.

When the sound finally came, Joe was shocked to find it was his own voice: 'Stop!'

The Madman turned quite slowly and looked straight at him. Joe's stomach turned over. Long, grey hair hung round a face so lined and seamed and blackened, it looked as if dirty water had scoured the skin year after year until it had just worn it away. The eyes were pale, almost colourless, and sunk deep in folds and shadows, but they were focused on nothing. They looked at Joe, but they didn't flicker. Joe stood rooted to the spot, unable to stir or to make another sound. If the man saw him, he gave no sign, as he turned away to the fire, moving with the same stiff-legged walk Joe had first seen in the garden.

The man picked up a battered copper kettle, poured steaming water into a bowl and carried it carefully back to the couch. Then he bent again, and Joe could finally see what he was

doing. With a slow, caressing hand he was washing blood from Bess's left ankle. Joe watched open-mouthed, more surprised than he had been by anything else in the house. There was a tenderness in the man's movements that was completely at odds with his horrifying appearance. But the muttering was louder now, and Joe began to distinguish some of the words: '... terrible ... evil ... a corruption of the air ... comes up from the ground, comes down from the air ... death ... it's bringing death ... like they bring the blood ... that's the smell ... it's the smell of blood ... innocent blood ... a miasma, that's what he said ... keep the stink back, he said ... keep it back ... yes ... keep it back ... yes!'

The voice rose to a shout, something like the terrible voice that rang out across Pound's Field in the night. Still Bess gave no sign of life. Joe would have fled if he could have moved his legs. Instead he opened his mouth and spoke again almost without meaning to.

'It's me.'

The man's eyes shifted around the room, as if searching for the source of the sound. Joe saw Bess's eyes flick open. So she wasn't dead, he thought blankly. Finally those pale eyes fastened on Joe. This time he saw him.

'What's you?' demanded the man, his whole frame shaking with the intensity of the question, as if his life depended on Joe's answer.

'It's me as smells,' Joe said simply. 'I'm the one.'

'You're the one?' For the first time the man's eyes seemed really to focus, except they didn't look at Joe, they looked through and through, as if they could see past or inside him. 'You're the one?' he repeated.

'Yeah,' said Joe. 'Sorry,' he added awkwardly.

For a moment the Madman's face seemed to soften. 'No, boy, you're not the one.' The rasping voice was different – steadier, almost normal. 'You don't live any deeper in filth than the rest. It's the world around you.'

The man made a wide, sweeping gesture that seemed to take in the room and the city that lay beyond it, and the bowl he was holding clattered against the wall. The water made another mark on the stained and peeling wallpaper. Then he turned away to the fireplace, the muttering too low again for any words to be heard.

Bess stretched out her injured leg, feeling the ankle carefully with both hands. The blood had stopped and it was clean now, but when she flexed her foot, a stab of pain shot right up the leg. Still, the ankle moved, and if it moved, there were no bones broken, and that meant it would get better. It might take days, but it would mend. Joe was perched next to her on the tattered couch now, shoulders hunched up tight to his ears as they always seemed to be. His pinched face looked even thinner than usual and his eyes were wide and staring. Bess realized that for some reason this boy hadn't run away: he had followed her into the house, and she felt she should say something to him. But she didn't know what effect it might have on the man if she spoke.

As she reached out a hand towards Joe, the man turned from the fireplace, holding the blackened pot. He looked quickly from Joe to Bess and back again, then he placed the pot on the floor in front of the couch and held out a tin spoon, jabbing it towards Bess. She shook her head, shrinking back. The man held the spoon out to Joe. Joe stared at him for a moment, not understanding. The man said nothing, but he made a gesture with his head towards the food in the pot and a kind of animal grunt. Joe took the spoon and began to eat hungrily, tasting meat in the mixture. He couldn't tell what kind, but whatever it was, it tasted good. He reached out to move the pot nearer, but the metal handle seared his hand. Apparently it had had no effect on the man.

After a while Joe passed the spoon back to the man and he ate with it too. There were unbroken china bowls and plates and silver forks and spoons on the table but the man made no move to fetch any of them. He and Joe ate in turn from the pot, and Bess watched them spoon the food into their mouths, and tested her ankle with careful fingers.

'It's good. Have some – Bess – is that what you said your name was?'

It was the first time Joe or Bess had spoken since entering the house. It was also the first time he had used her name and Joe spoke it hesitantly, as if reluctant to let it pass his lips. Bess only shook her head, but the Madman swung round, eyes glittering as he peered close into the girl's face.

'Bess?'

His voice was gentle, wondering. He reached out a hand and took a lock of her fair hair between his fingers. Bess let out a sharp exclamation, tried to get up from the couch and sank down on the floor in pain. Joe was on his feet at once, placing himself in front of the fallen girl, knees flexed, ready to spring back or forward or out of the way – he wasn't sure which.

'You,' he stammered. 'You dirty old tramp. You lay off of 'er, right?!'

In spite of herself Bess almost laughed at the fierceness in his voice. The man didn't seem to notice. He was spooning the remains of the food into his mouth, but his voice was a quick mutter now with a note of panic just below the surface: 'There was a house, you see. And this man. And he owned everything, he did.' The voice droned on and on. Sometimes it sounded like a story. Sometimes it just sounded like words. Sometimes he seemed to be arguing with invisible people he could see around him in the room. Bess and Joe sat motionless on the couch, while the heat from the fire began to dry their sodden clothes. 'Profit,' the man was saying. 'There was profit. That's business, man. That's just business. But there was sacrifice. Too much innocent blood. Animals. Children. Too much blood. Casks of it. Wagonloads. Blood comes in and sweetness out. Blood in and sweetness out. Blood in and innocence out. Do you see what I mean? Do you understand?'

His voice was suddenly very clear, as if what he was asking them made the most perfect sense. Joe could make nothing of it. 'They bring the blood in,' insisted the man, gripping Joe's arm now with fingers that felt as if they might cut straight through to the bone. 'That's the business. But is it right? Blood in and sweetness out!'

'Sugar – is that what you mean? Blood in and sweetness out?' It was Bess who spoke.

'Yes.' The man let go of Joe's arm and seized her by the hand. There were tears in his eyes. 'Sweetness,' he crooned, almost singing the word.

'Schoolteacher told us about it.' Bess's voice was low, soothing. She knew she couldn't have escaped the man's grip if she tried. At times he seemed gentle, like when he'd washed her ankle or offered them food, but at other times the shining in his eye looked like danger. He went from one extreme to the other in an instant. She put her other hand on top of the man's where he held her. He flinched and drew away, releasing her. 'They use animal blood, don't they, mister?' she said gently. 'Cattle blood. Part of making sugar, it is.'

'Blood in and sweetness out,' repeated the man dully.

'Bowman's,' said Joe suddenly. 'It's right next door here. Sugar works.'

'Refinery,' corrected Bess. 'Sugar refinery.'

'Oh, right. Sugar refinery. You know all about it, don'tcha?' Joe's voice was raised. Quite suddenly he was close to hysteria. He had taken an almighty chance following this girl into the Madman's house, something no one else in Pound's Field would have done, and now she was trying to make him feel stupid again – like in the garden when he couldn't bring himself to tell her he was a tosher.

Joe stood up. He had had enough. He was leaving. But his anger seemed to have awakened something in the Madman, because he was on his feet too, shouting: 'Lost it, you see . . .

lost it . . . all that money but it wasn't any good . . .' He was stumbling around the room, throwing aside tattered cushions, wrenching back the curtains, sending clouds of dust flying into the air. He tore back one corner of the tablecloth, peering underneath, sending more plates and glasses crashing to the ground. 'Lost it. My treasure. My treasure!'

'What treasure's that then?'

Joe forgot about being angry with Bess and he forgot about leaving. Treasure was a word that could make a tosher forget anything. He struggled to make sense of the man's random cries and ramblings as he rampaged through the room. To begin with he seemed to be talking about money. Then it was a person he was looking for. At times it sounded more as if he was talking about himself and his own lost wits.

Suddenly the man seized a burning candle from the broken chandelier. Wax ran down his hand, but he didn't seem to notice. He threw open the double doors at the end of the room and stormed out, Joe in pursuit, that word still beating in his head – *treasure!* People around Pound's Field had talked about it for years – a madman shut up in a big old house: he must have something hidden away in there. When it wasn't how they were going to burn him out, it was plans to break in and rob the place; only no one had the nerve for it. They were all too scared of the Madman himself. But now he was searching for something and he didn't seem to know Joe was there, so, if he stuck close maybe he'd be around when the old man found it. There was gear lying around that room worth a pretty penny – Joe knew that – but maybe there was something a lot better hidden away in this crumbling old dump. His fear disappeared in the excitement of the hunt, as he followed the man through the house, struggling to keep up with the light from his guttering candle.

They went into rooms with wood panelling and heavy furniture where everything was smashed and covered with years of dirt like the big room downstairs. They searched below stairs, where Joe had got into the house, and everywhere they went, hanging from hooks, lying on the floor and furniture, were dead animals – big birds, small birds, foxes, mice, squirrels. Some had been stuffed and mounted so skilfully they looked as if they were still alive, standing on stiff legs, glass eyes glittering in the candlelight. Some were freshly killed, blood still sticky in wounds around the neck or legs. Some were rotting where they lay, crawling with maggots, savaged by rats, filling the house with the putrid smell Joe had noticed as soon as he stepped inside – the smell of death.

They were in a stone-floored room in the basement when Joe caught the familiar sound of running water. The man was rummaging in cupboards, sending pots and pans clattering, while Joe bent to peer through the heavy metal grating in the floor. He couldn't see it, but it was down there all right: water. Only there was something odd. Instinctively his mind sifted times and numbers. The tide wasn't right for the sewers to be running that fast, was it? Or had he lost track of what day it was? Then it struck him what else was wrong – no smell. The smell of the London sewers was so familiar to him it was a jolt when water in Pound's Field didn't stink. There was a smell that sifted up through the grating, but it wasn't the smell of drains: it was the same smell that had come from the bright and sparkling water he had drunk in the garden. He tried the grating, gently at first, then straining with all his strength, but it was set firmly into the stones of the floor.

Joe followed the man upstairs, watched him overturning beds, digging into mattresses that were already hacked open, sending clouds of feathers flying into the air. More dead animals were everywhere and the rats were thicker. Rats meant nothing to Joe – he'd worked amongst them in the sewers long enough – but it would be impossible to sleep up here. All that meat got the rats excited, and they'd be biting as soon as you were still.

The man moved on, throwing open doors to more rooms and cupboards. From the junk strewn across all the floors it was clear this wasn't the first time he had made a hunt like this through the house. Joe's hopes began to fade. Just what were they looking for anyway? He couldn't have lived here all these years and not been able to find his own money, however crazy he was.

They climbed another flight of stairs, Joe following the flickering light of the man's candle. As the boy's hand reached out for the banister at the top of the stairs, a great winged shadow seemed to leap out of the dark, swooping down towards him. He ducked, throwing up his arms instinctively to protect himself. Then he took a glance up and snorted derisively at his own stupidity. On the broken banister was the stuffed carcass of an enormous white bird. It was mounted on a piece of wood, wings outstretched, talons reaching out as if to grab its prey. The candle had made a shadow: that was all!

They were high up under the eaves now. As the man stumbled on down another long corridor, Joe began to throw open doors himself at random. He had his hand on yet another doorknob when the man fixed him with those pale eyes again. It was the first time during the crazed hunt through the house that Joe had felt the man knew he was there.

'Not in there!'

The voice was low and clear and carried an absolute command. Joe heard what the Madman said quite distinctly; it was the strangeness of his tone that made him respond as if he hadn't.

'What?'

'Don't – search – in – there.'

In spite of himself Joe tried the handle. It turned but the door didn't give. It was the only locked door in the whole place.

'Not in there!'

The man was shouting now and he moved towards Joe, hands outstretched. Quick as a flash the boy ducked under the tall man's grasp and was gone down the dark staircase. It might be a strange house and bigger than any he had entered in his life, but Joe didn't get lost that easily. On the ground floor there were oil lights burning in the hallway and the double doors to the big room still stood open. Bess hadn't moved from the couch, but she'd pulled a tattered old rug around her shoulders.

'No treasure then?'

Her voice was heavy with sarcasm, but Joe didn't seem to

notice. He talked on about a locked room upstairs and water running under the floor, but Bess hardly listened. There was a throbbing in her ankle and the numbness of total exhaustion in her whole body. Joe's voice grew softer, and she slipped into an uneasy sleep.

The boy watched her for a moment. The fine clothes were stained and filthy now, but there were still traces of an unnatural redness on her cheeks. This girl had a father and a mother – well, a stepmother; she had an uncle and an aunt; yet here she was hiding in the Madman's house with him. He had the same feeling he'd had in the garden when she told him her story: that there was something that didn't make sense. Then he shrugged quickly, lay down on a scrap of rug in front of the fire and fell asleep too.

Later he woke in the darkness. From high in the house he could hear shouting – '*Yes!! Yes!!*' The fire had died down. Joe crept across the floor a little closer to the couch, and drifted into sleep again. The locked room upstairs – that was his last thought – and all that silverware spread out across the table amongst the rat droppings.

Chapter 12

CHOICES

For two days neither Bess nor Joe stepped outside the house and garden. At night they slept in the big room. There were no dead animals there and whatever food might have been on the table had disappeared long ago, so the rats left them alone.

If the man slept at all, they didn't know where or when. Sometimes in the night they heard shouting from high in the house, but through the day he was mostly silent, working on the dead creatures that littered the rooms. It was easy to see how every chair and mattress in the place had lost its stuffing. The man used it to fill the animals, and he fashioned eyes by chipping pieces of broken glass. The rest of the time he wandered through the house, apparently aimlessly, or checked his traps in the garden. Each night he cooked in the same blackened pot. It was the only food they ate.

Without anything being said, Joe took over the job of fetching water from the garden. He could sit for hours, fascinated by the way the clear liquid bubbled up from a hidden spring deep in the undergrowth. The water ran along a narrow stone rill,

128

through an open wooden pipe and then down, down, down, spiralling and cascading into the darkness. Joe could hear a faint plashing as the thin stream hit the bottom of the well far below. The stone structure overhead prevented leaves from falling into the well and cast a deep shadow that made it hard to see down. But set into the stone maybe five or six feet below, Joe glimpsed an iron rung. A man might have been able to lower himself down onto it, but it was too far for Joe to reach, and whether there were more rungs further down it was impossible to see.

As the days passed, slowly the throbbing in Bess's foot began to grow less. She forced herself to walk on it, hobbling up and down the worn carpet of the big downstairs room, then, as the ankle began to feel stronger, venturing out into the damp garden. She stuck to the beaten tracks close to the house, avoiding the thick undergrowth where the Madman set his traps. And as she limped painfully along, her thoughts ran on to her father and her home. She searched her memory, working backwards, trying to visualize the route she had run through the alleys of Pound's Field, and before that the way the cart had travelled along the streets of London. But the truth was that even if she was fit to travel, she had no idea of the way back to Hartingham, and though Joe might know every back alley in the wretched part of the city he called Pound's Field, he'd obviously never been outside the area in his life. He couldn't help her either.

Joe spent less and less of his day searching the house for treasure and more and more peering into the sweet-smelling well, wondering what to do next. He knew Mother wouldn't give up looking for him – or Bess for that matter. The best hope was that she'd think they'd got clean away and be casting her net out beyond Pound's Field. In that case the safest thing was to stay right where they were.

Exploring the first floor of the house, picking his way through the animal corpses, he found a broken window where he could see over the front wall and out onto River Lane. The sight of the Watchman, impassive as ever at the dock gates, sent a shock through the boy and he edged back out of sight behind the half-closed shutter. The next time he looked the Watchman was still there, but this time he was talking to Plucky Jack – pumping him for information more than likely.

From then on Joe spent at least an hour of every day watching River Lane from his upstairs window. Always the Watchman was there – eyes on the old house: sometimes it seemed as if he was staring straight at him. A couple of times Billy came loitering down the street amongst the sailors and the dock-workers, as casual as you like, but every now and then Joe could see his head turn up towards the big house.

For a week Joe twisted the problem this way and that. He could see three choices and he didn't like any of them. They could stay where they were and hope for the best. That was the simplest way. But Billy strolling by and the Watchman staring up at the house could mean Mother had already guessed where they were and it was just a matter of time before she persuaded or forced someone to come and get them.

Second choice: he could make a run for it now and leave

Bess to take her chances – she couldn't travel yet with her leg like that. Joe told himself he was still holding this as the best option, but inside he knew he was never going to do it.

The only other way was to try somehow to square himself with Mother, and after what had happened that would take a sackful of chink: nothing else would do. And where was he going to get that kind of money? He could hand over every brass farthing of his hidden tosh. But that wouldn't work: she'd know he'd been holding out on her all these years and she'd have him killed. There, he'd said what he'd never admitted before. Mother would have him killed. She'd have to – couldn't be seen to let a tosher get ahead of her.

Joe turned the alternatives over and over in his mind, staring deep into the dark well, but there was no answer to be found there. 'What's the old monster planning then?' he murmured aloud, patting the stone mastiff, as he checked on his grey cloth bag once again. The dog had nothing to offer either.

One afternoon, as she walked outside, Bess spotted Joe heading quickly across the garden, making for a distant part of the grounds she'd never been to. There was only one way she was ever going to get home and that was if she kept pushing her ankle harder until it was strong enough to carry her there. So she set off after the boy, past the well and on to where a group of tall bushes blocked off a corner of the garden.

She hadn't meant to hide, but with her ankle slowing her down, Bess couldn't keep up with the boy, and she didn't like to call out in case her voice carried beyond the garden walls. She felt her way carefully through the bushes, avoiding the brambles, watching every step for hidden traps.

In the open ground beyond the bushes was a line of grey stones, overgrown with ivy. She didn't see Joe at first. Then she spotted him crouched in the tall grass at the base of one of the stones. She was just about to call out, ask him what he was doing, go over and take a closer look at the weathered stones which made the place look like a miniature version of the graveyard outside Hartingham church. Then he turned slightly, and she saw what he was doing.

The boy was poring over the contents of a small grey bag which lay open in front of him. There was something about the way he hunched low over the bag, as if he was trying to disappear into the tall grass, which told her at once he wouldn't welcome finding her there. She turned away, letting the branches of the bush fall silently back into place, and limped back towards the house.

She didn't go back to the big downstairs room. As she walked along the passage in the basement she heard muttering coming from one of the stone-floored rooms. This was where the man worked on his animals and mended his traps, and in the last couple of days Bess had got into the habit of sitting with him as he worked. Sometimes when he wasn't there she fiddled with the traps herself. It wasn't hard to see how the mechanism had made such a mess of her ankle.

The man was sitting on a tall stool, as usual, an oil lamp burning on the tabletop next to him. She sat down alongside him without a word. He didn't look up, but she knew he was aware of her presence. He often muttered as he worked.

Sometimes, after ignoring her presence for hours, he would turn suddenly and stare at her, murmuring her name – 'Bess . . . Bess . . .' – until she grew uncomfortable. But he never spoke directly to her and he never tried to touch her.

She had no idea why he produced these endless stuffed animals, but she had soon understood the process well enough. This afternoon, as he reached out for his knife, she passed it to him. He looked up – surprised, questioning, searching her face – then he took the knife without a word and went back to the beautiful, red fox skin he was working on. Within an hour he seemed to have accepted her help, reaching out without pausing in his work for Bess to hand him knife or needle or stuffing material as he needed it.

The way his fingers moved, gutting the creatures with quick, delicate hands, peeling off their skins, reminded Bess of her mother mending lace, and that set her brooding yet again on her home and the problem of how she was to get back to Hartingham.

'Don't know how you can do that.' Joe was standing in the doorway. The Madman had gone, and Bess was alone, setting a piece of amber glass into the empty eye socket of the fox.

'You eat them all right,' she said irritably. The memory of the boy hunched over his secret in the garden that afternoon somehow still rankled.

''S diff'rent.'

'I mended this here trap and all.' She held up the metal contraption proudly. 'Only needed a bit of wire.'

'You never!'

'Why not? You reckon yourself such a mannish little lad, don't you? And you don't think Jenny Raw from the country can do a thing. That's it, annit?'

'No, it ain't.'

'I been to school, I have. You been to school?' When Joe didn't answer, Bess went on, 'What you want anyway? No treasure in here.' Joe made a movement to protest, but Bess hadn't finished. 'I seen you looking at the silver on that table too. Not above a little thieving, I bet, you pikey little gutter-grub.'

'You ain't got no call to be usin' names like that,' grumbled Joe, slinking away. 'I ain't no thief.'

But the truth was he had been looking at the silver, because here just might be the sackful of chink that would set him right with Mother. Closer examination had revealed the cutlery on the Madman's table wasn't solid precious metal, only plate, but it was still worth a deal of money even at Mother's rates – far more than the two guineas he still owed for the hoe and sieve.

Joe rolled the word around in his mouth: '*Guineas . . .*' In his mind it had come to mean something you could never have, however much you wanted it and however hard you worked; and now here it was literally spread out on a table in front of him. With this stuff he could pay off what he owed, and there'd be enough over to square both him and Bess with Mother.

He stood in the wide, double doorway, gazing along the length of the table with its smashed chandelier and its rats' muck and its silver. He was a tosher, he told himself, and toshers weren't thieves. Thieves were different and they ended up in quod with bars on the windows a sight thicker than the ones at the Whitechapel Workhouse. But this wouldn't be like thieving. There it lay, day in, day out: no one touched it and no one used it, and the Madman would never notice it was gone. Swag like that was the only way he'd ever get near Mother again – that was certain.

'Toshers ain't thieves,' he muttered through clenched teeth, smacking a hand hard against his forehead. Then he sighed, and added softly to himself, 'But toshers got to live . . .'

Chapter 13
THE CRUCIBLE

The clock in St George's was striking two as Joe hooked his old canvas bag over one shoulder and slipped out of the back door of the Madman's house. He had checked the big front door in the hallway, but it was locked on the inside and no sign of the key: this was the only way out. He rounded the side of the building onto what had once been a broad sweep of gravel, but was now soft underfoot with moss and choked with weeds. Ahead were the main gates onto River Lane, but Joe wasn't planning to try them.

Set into each of the solid, timber gates was a small door. The one on the right needed a key to open it. But in the left-hand gate was a door with a bolt top and bottom and a latch – but no keyhole. That was what Joe had spotted, prowling the grounds of the house that afternoon after Bess had finished calling him names. He couldn't go back through Holywell Court. Too risky. He could climb the wall, but he knew the other side was bare and too high to scale, which meant he could never climb back. This way, if he undid the bolts in the left-hand door and left it on the latch, he could sneak out and get back in later. Of course, anyone else could get in too, but why should they guess that suddenly, after so many years, all they had to do was poke a finger through that little hole and lift a latch? And anyway, who would have the nerve for it?

A wagon rumbled down River Lane. This was the danger moment, because even this late there could be people around, and if anyone spotted him coming out of the Madman's gate, that would be an end to the whole game. Joe waited until all was quiet. Then he eased back the rusted bolts, lifted the latch and glided like a shadow through the small door, shutting it instantly behind him.

It was dark on the street, and he could see no one who might have spotted him. Just for a moment he thought he caught a movement over by the dock gates. The Watchman should be curled up all cosy in Holywell Court at this time, but you never knew with him. Joe peered anxiously into the shadows, but there was no one to be seen. He shifted the canvas bag on his shoulder: it was heavy and clanked softly as he moved it. Then he headed quickly down the road past St Saviour's, past Bowman's and right into Sweetwater Lane. There wasn't much chance of running into Billy at this hour, but he'd stay off the main roads and come up on Mother's Court the long way just in case.

There was a guard at the entrance to Mother's Court as always, but Joe made no attempt at concealment. He was banking on Mother not having told more of her crew than she had to that Joe Rat had bolted. She wouldn't want that kind of news getting around too widely – might give others ideas. Sure enough, as Joe walked briskly under the archway, the guard gave the low whistle that meant friend. Now it was just a matter of who he ran into in the house.

He stopped by the front door, which stood partly open. As ever, there were people waiting to see Mother. Joe might not have recognized the narrow-eyed man in the stovepipe hat who was the only one to look up as he peered into the gloom of the hallway, but he did recognize the heavy stick he carried. The woman was with him too. Now, what were these members of Bess's 'good family' doing in Mother's Court amongst the villains and the matchbox-sellers?

The man looked away – there was no reason why he should know Joe – and the boy walked past, heading for the narrow passage that led round the side of the house. The back door was locked. Joe ran his eye over the ground-floor window, but that was too risky. Baldock, Mother's precious-metal man, would probably be in the kitchen even at this hour with his nose hooked over the two big crucibles where he melted down silver and pewter. If he caught Joe breaking in, he'd have the whole house on him. Billy might even be there. Better to try and bluff his way in.

He rapped sharply on the glass of the back door. He didn't have long to wait. A key turned in the lock, a couple of bolts were shot, and a shirtsleeved man with a red face opened the door about six inches, peering suspiciously out. It was Baldock.

'White wood,' said Joe quickly. 'Special delivery.' He'd heard it often enough – they were the words for stolen silver. But Baldock didn't open the door any further.

'That ain't your line, Joe Rat,' he rasped. His voice was always hoarse, as if he'd breathed in too many metal fumes.

'Tosher's got to branch out, ain't he?' said Joe boldly. 'Open up, Baldock. Mother won't want to miss this little lot.'

The man opened the door unwillingly and let Joe past him, checking quickly outside to see if there was anyone else there. 'Heard tell you'd hopped the twig with a bag of swag, Joe Rat,' he said, following Joe into the kitchen. 'There's folk right here in this house that'd like to get their hands on you.'

'Mother knows I'm comin',' lied Joe, banging the heavy bag down on the table. His eyes scanned the room quickly: over a low fire stood the silver-pot, half full of white, molten metal; the door to Mother's room was ajar.

The man looked at the bag, then he looked at Joe. The boy could see the uncertainty in his eye. Baldock had been here long enough to know that Joe had once slept on the floor by Mother's bed and fed her white mice: he'd been a favourite – still was maybe in spite of the stories that were going around. Finally he said, 'You sure you got somethin' more than stinkin' old rope in there, tosher?'

In reply Joe pulled the bag open, and Baldock's eyes widened greedily at the gleam of silver. Joe knew the man would have taken the bag off him if he dared, or called someone to help him do it, but he was too scared of Mother. In the end he shrugged his shoulders. 'Should be in my bed,' he grumbled, and walked heavily out of the room.

Joe closed the bag and tiptoed quickly to the open door to Mother's room. Baldock had talked about bed, but that didn't mean he was going there. Mother might want him at any time or someone else could come into the room. But before they did and before he did anything else, Joe wanted to know what business Bess's uncle and aunt had with Mother.

Squinting through the narrow gap in the door, he couldn't see her properly, but he could make out the corner of the bed and part of the mountain of fabric that covered the woman. A sharp smell reached his nostrils, blotting out the smoke from the fire and the fumes of the silver-pot. It was a stale, acrid, human smell, and Joe realized with a shock that it was the smell of the woman they all called Mother. He had lived with it half his life, but he couldn't remember ever noticing it before. A few days away from her rule, even hiding in the house of a mad-man, and it was suddenly as clear as the scent of rotten meat. Joe felt his gorge rise in revulsion.

There was the low murmur of a man's voice and Mother's familiar cough – Joe could see her spit into the handkerchief as clearly as if she was in front of him – then a stooping figure crossed his eye line, heading for the hallway. Joe looked around quickly, but he was still alone. When he looked back, two more people were coming into Mother's room. He couldn't see their faces, but he could hear the echo of a heavy stick striking the bare floorboards. It was the man Bess called her uncle.

The voices were too low at first for him to hear what was being said. Then suddenly Mother's voice rose, sharp and steely. 'You leave the details to me, my dear sir and madam. I'll find her. Just make sure Mother gets her whack at the end of it!' They were plotting something: something with money involved – almost certainly something to do with Bess and probably him too.

With his hand on the door, Joe stood frozen in indecision. He could walk in right now and put his bag full of the Madman's silver down and he'd be one of Mother's little brood again, standing by that bedside, watching the white mice nibbling on their cheese and no two guineas owing. The door was half open: all he had to do was push on it. It was partly the smell that stopped him – odd that, he thought, for a tosher: it was as if his nose was telling him Mother's room was no longer a place where he belonged. But it was also the thought that he'd have to tell her where Bess was. '*I'll find her.*' That's what Mother had said. It could only mean Bess.

Joe's hand was still on the door, and he still hadn't decided what he was going to do, when there was a footstep in the passage, and he moved instinctively, without time to think whether what he was doing was right or wrong or in his own best interest or just plain stupid. By the time Baldock came back into the room, the boy was sitting with his feet on the kitchen table, the bag gripped tightly in his lap.

'Still waiting, Joe Rat?' grated the man.

'I don't have to wait, Baldock,' said Joe quick as a flash. 'Mother already seen me. I'm just warmin' myself before I go.'

The man's eyes narrowed suspiciously. 'What you up to, you dirty little tosher? I think I might just fetch Billy down to sort you out.'

'Billy kippin' here these days, is he, Baldock?' The man looked quickly away, obviously realizing he had said more than he should. 'You take a look in your chicken pot if you don't believe me,' Joe went on. 'Mother took the lot and I'm all square again.'

Baldock went over to the fire and peered into his crucible. The last inch of a silver spoon was just disappearing into the pool of molten metal. He grabbed Joe's bag quickly away from him and turned it upside down. It was empty.

'Satisfied?' demanded Joe, snatching the bag back. 'See yer, you old sack of bones.' And with that he was out of the back door before the man could say another word.

He cut quickly through the back alleys of Pound's Field, but there was no pursuit. Baldock had obviously believed he was now safely back in the fold. Under the railway arch on Sweetwater Lane, where he'd first seen Bess, he stopped, and one by one from the big pockets inside his ragged jacket Joe drew the Madman's pieces of silver cutlery, replacing them carefully in his canvas bag.

A little smile of satisfaction twisted the corners of the boy's mouth as he thought of the one silver spoon melting in Baldock's crucible. The man had thought the whole lot was in there. He'd walked into Mother's Court with a bagful of silver that wasn't his, and he'd come away with only one spoon missing and the knowledge that the old devil was planning something, and planning it with the couple Bess called her aunt and uncle. A silver spoon was a good price for that kind of information.

And he'd come away with something else too, because as he knocked on the back door of Mother's house Joe hadn't been sure himself whether he was using the Madman's silver as a way of getting into Mother's house or if he'd really stolen it and was planning to give her the lot. But when Baldock's footstep sounded in the passage and Joe breathed in the acrid smell that was both familiar and unfamiliar, he had known suddenly, once and for all, that he was never going back to the old monster.

The boy took a deep, clear breath as he turned up River Lane. He felt as if his whole past life had been dropped into Baldock's silver-pot along with the Madman's tarnished spoon and he had been recast as something new – something that he scarcely recognized himself.

Chapter 14

WELL-WATER

'You thought I wouldn't notice then? Is that it?'

Joe stood looking up at her from under his eyebrows. Bess couldn't read the expression on his face.

'Just because the man doesn't know what's going on around him doesn't mean I don't,' she persisted. 'He's treated us decent, hasn't he? Taken the both of us in. And you pay him back by stealing.'

'Weren't stealin'.'

'So every scrap of silver on this table just got up and walked away on its own, did it?'

'Weren't stealin',' Joe repeated sullenly.

Bess was standing at one end of the long table, Joe at the other. She'd caught him as he came back into the room. It was only just getting light and most likely the Madman would be out checking his traps, but Bess realized she was speaking too loudly. Perhaps Joe had only hidden the silver and she could put it back before the man noticed it was gone. 'Have you still got it somewhere?' she asked, thinking of him crouched over his hoard by the old tombstones. 'We could put it back, and nobody need know.'

Joe didn't reply. Instead he slumped down by the fireplace, poking at the coals with a piece of kindling wood.

'Well, how much did you get for it then?' Bess demanded.

'Didn't get nothink. It was a stall, weren't it?'

'A what?'

'A stall – something to get me in, so as I could find out what Mother was up to.'

Joe threw the stick angrily onto the fire, and glared up at Bess, daring her not to believe him. The only problem was, with the girl standing there accusing him, he still wasn't sure if he believed it himself. It had turned out that way certainly: he'd chucked one spoon into the pot to make Baldock think he'd already seen Mother, and he'd come away with the rest. And he could pull the rest out of his bag right now and Bess would have to believe him. But if the man with the stick hadn't been there, what would he have done then? Wouldn't he have walked straight in and handed Mother the lot? And then more than likely given her Bess Farleigh too?

Joe stared furiously into the fire, brow furrowed, his mouth a tight, angry line. There was a long pause. Then Bess sat down on the floor next to him. Maybe he'd stolen the silver and maybe he hadn't, but he'd helped her get away from Harry Trencher – twice – and suddenly she didn't like the picture of herself standing over him in judgement.

'All right, I believe you,' she said simply.

'You what?'

'I believe you.'

Joe turned to look at her. Face scrubbed clean, hair tied hard back like a washerwoman, she barely looked like the same person he'd found hiding on Sweetwater Lane a week ago. She'd even picked the ribbons out of her dress and sewn a patch on the front so it didn't show her skin any more. If this girl said she believed what he said, then she did. So maybe he should believe it too.

'Only needed one spoon, anyway,' he said. 'Got the rest here.'

Bess's jaw dropped as he emptied the silverware onto the filthy tablecloth. 'Why didn't you say so?' she demanded.

But Joe didn't answer. He knew the question that was coming next, and he was trying to work out what he was going to say.

'So what is she up to?'

Joe made a big show of rearranging the knives and forks on the table. He was playing for time. He'd planned to tell her. In fact, he'd planned to rub her nose in it if she started on about the silver: 'So much for your "good family"!' – that kind of stuff. But now that it came to it, he couldn't bring himself to tell Bess that members of her family had been hatching some scheme with Mother. Wouldn't help for her to know anyway, he told himself.

'Don't know,' he said finally, not looking at her. 'Couldn't hear enough to tell.' The last part was true anyway.

Bess let out a long sigh. The boy was holding something back – that was obvious – but she'd decided to trust him and the fact that he really hadn't stolen the silver proved she was right, didn't it? She found herself examining Joe's pinched and grimy face as he fiddled clumsily with the silverware. The last few months at home had been bad ones – kettle-bender for breakfast and not a lot for dinner sometimes – but however poor folk were around Hartingham, nobody looked the way this little short shunnel of a boy did, with his bony fingers and hungry eyes. And nobody smelled the way he did either . . .

'Well,' she said finally, leaving him to his knives and forks, 'I'm a-going to have a wash. You could try it some time if you haven't got anything more useful to do.'

Joe watched Bess leave the room. The way she walked, it could be another week before she was really ready to make a run for it, and with the Watchman and Billy outside and Mother hatching schemes, that could be too long. But there was no choice now: he couldn't leave the girl and he couldn't straighten things out with Mother, so they would just have to stay where they were.

He shrugged and gave up thinking about it: there was no sense in worrying about things you couldn't do anything about. What was it she'd said? *I'm a-going to have a wash. You could try it some time if you haven't got anything more useful to do.* Joe's mouth screwed up in annoyance, and he headed for the back door. He was tired from the night visit to Mother's but he didn't feel like sleeping. Maybe the quiet of the dark well was what he needed.

But the drip of clean water just brought back Bess's words. She was always washing – washing herself, washing that dress.

Where was the sense in it? You could clean up on a Saturday, but if you were going down the shores to get just as filthy again on Sunday, then why bother?

At the familiar thought of the sewers Joe looked up from the well . . . *if you haven't got anything more useful to do*. There was only one thing Joe called useful, and suddenly he knew what he was going to do. Two days back he'd found an old lean-to at the side of the house with a shovel standing in the corner. He headed briskly down the path, feeling more purposeful than he had since he first stepped into the Madman's house.

The shovel was still standing in the same place. As he tested its weight in one hand, Joe took a more careful look around the shed. Stacked neatly in a corner were six wooden crates stuffed with wax candles; next to them stood several bags of quality coal and a supply of oil in big cans. So that was how the Madman managed to light the house and cook his animal stew. Then he spotted something else; something he'd been wanting for as long as he could remember. On a hook behind the door, tarnished but undamaged, hung a lantern just like the ones the crushers carried – bull's eyes, they called them. It had a thick glass lens at the front that shone a bright beam, and a shutter that could close off the light if you didn't want it seen. Joe ran his hand caressingly over the smooth surface of the lamp. It meant he could work late when there weren't so many about to spot him and he wasn't so likely to run into competition.

It was after midnight as Joe picked up his tools again from the shed. He listened by the front gate. All was quiet on River

Lane. Just like the previous night there seemed to be a quick movement near the dock gates as he stepped silently out onto the street, but just like last night there was nothing to be seen, and Joe decided it was his own nerves playing him tricks. He passed St Saviour's, then Bowman's, and headed on down the road towards the river.

Past Sweetwater Lane and you were outside Pound's Field proper. There was a row of houses down here where the big local merchants lived – men who had trade coming and going from all over the world. Joe had never worked this pitch before, and he knew there was a toshing gang who operated under these houses, but he was gambling that they liked their beds and preferred the midday tide. Going back to his old patch under Flower Street was too risky: Mother would be bound to have someone watching there. It meant losing the hoe and sieve, but however proud he'd felt when he held his first tosh-ing tools in his hand, they'd never really been his. He knew that now. Though he'd only found them lying around in the Madman's shed, the borrowed lamp and shovel felt better in his hands than the old tools ever had.

Testing the gutter gratings as he went, knowing there must be one loose somewhere, Joe worked his way quickly along the edge of the street, fading into the shadows whenever anyone passed. Right in front of the first of the big houses he found it – loose and easy and wide enough to ride a cart down. Joe disappeared out of sight with his bull's eye and his shovel, and all was silent on River Lane once more.

The next four nights he worked the same section. The sewer

was old under the big houses and liable to cave-ins and there were narrow openings heading off towards the river that he didn't dare try. The place was full of rats too, but rats were only dangerous in the sewers if you got between them and their escape route when the tide was coming in. That was how the old toshers said men had ended up with their bones picked clean: they'd stayed under too long when the water was rising and been in the wrong place when the rats panicked and ate their way through to safety.

But Joe didn't have to stay that long. He had his lantern and he could work the hours he wanted, and every scrap he found was his. He couldn't sell rags and bones and scrap – getting out in the daytime was too dangerous – but any money or valuables went straight into the grey cloth bag hidden under the tombs in the Madman's garden. 'And you ain't gettin' a single solitary copper coin, Mother,' he muttered, pushing through the bushes with a silver sixpence clutched tight in one hand. The thought made him feel good.

As he stepped out onto the open ground, heading for the tombs, he stopped dead in his tracks. There was still no more than a faint light in the sky and sunrise was a half-hour away, but crouched in the shadows by one of the tombs Joe could clearly make out a figure. His first thought was the Madman, though he seemed to avoid this part of the garden. Then he realized the figure was too small anyway.

Bess bent low, searching for the inscription she knew must be on the monument. She wished she had waited until it was lighter, but the last few nights Joe had been out at this time, doing whatever filthy work it was that made the downstairs room stink like the dover-house at home, so now was the safest time. She rubbed hard at the lichen that covered the stone. There had to be writing somewhere. Whoever heard of a gravestone with no name on it? A sharp voice from directly behind made her start violently.

'Oi! What you at?'

Joe sprang at the girl, shoving her away from the tomb as hard as he could. Bess fell back, striking her head on the ground, but the turf was soft and she was more shocked than hurt.

'You gone cranky, or what?' she demanded, clambering to her feet, and brushing dirt from her clothes.

'What you at?' demanded Joe again, standing in front of the tomb Bess had been examining, as if to prevent her getting near it again.

'I bain't a-robbing you, if that's what you're thinking.'

'Robbing me of what?' Joe's tone changed suddenly to one of mock innocence, as he realized he was giving too much away.

'I mean' – she was spelling the words out now, as if to a stupid child – 'I mean, you think I be robbing your filthy little bag, annit? That's all you think of me,' she went on angrily. 'A thief up from the country.'

'I never said that.' Joe found himself on the defensive yet again. Then he realized what her words meant. 'How d'you know about my bag? You bin spyin' on me, ain'tcha?'

'I seen you like a squirrel at its hoard. But I bain't at your hoard, am I, my little squirrel, because it bain't in this one. Is it?'

Joe was so flabbergasted, he could barely speak. 'You – you watched me. You bin sneakin' around, spyin' on me—'

'You go and check if you wants to,' Bess interrupted him. 'But I bain't no robber, whatever you reckons.'

'Oh, *bain't* you,' Joe spat back at her, imitating her accent.

Bess ignored the jibe. 'You don't even use this one.'

Joe hesitated. It was true. This tomb was different. Instead of a statue on the top, there was just a seat with a stone shawl draped over the side. It had low doors like the rest, but they were iron and immovable, and the ground around was solid. He'd never tried hiding his tosh here.

'All the same,' he managed finally, 'you didn't oughta be spyin' on people.'

But Bess didn't seem to be listening any more. She was bent to the stonework again, rubbing hard with a corner of the old rug she wore draped around her.

'There!' she announced, standing back to show him. 'What do you think of that?'

Joe peered at the stone. 'There's nothing there.'

'Exactly,' said Bess impatiently. 'No name. And what about the other tombs? What does it say on them?'

'I don't know.'

'What do you mean, you don't know? Look at them.' Then she stopped. 'You can't read, can you?'

'Course I can.'

'Look!' She hurried around the other tombs, pointing to each in turn. 'Rex: 1711 to 1725. Hector: 1803 to 1813. Fidelis – can't read that one. And on this one – nothing.'

'So what?'

'So what?!' Bess couldn't believe her ears. Here she was trying to work out what was going on in this house that seemed to be stuck in time with its tombs in the garden, its crazed inhabitant and its dead animals, and all this idiot boy could manage was 'So what?' She turned away without another word and marched back towards the house. Before she disappeared Joe had time to notice that she had almost stopped limping.

The next day was Saturday. As it began to get dark Joe took a wooden bucket out to the well in the garden, hung it under the falling stream of clear water until it was half full, and carried it back to the house. Then he took an oil lamp from the passage at the back of the house, and carried it into one of the echoing basement rooms. Suspended from the ceiling on a pair of metal hooks was a large black bird and an animal about the size of a small dog with stripes on its back and sides. Joe had never seen the like of it, but Bess had said it was a badger. 'Must be a sett somewheres in the garden,' she'd said, but Joe hadn't wanted to ask what a 'sett' was. Likely as not she'd start going on again about all the schooling she'd had and he hadn't.

In one corner of the room stood a big enamelled sink with a plug and brass taps, though the taps wouldn't turn any more and everything was covered with the same thick layer of dust that smothered the entire house. Joe poured his well-water into the sink, and began gingerly to peel off his clothes. He'd shrugged off the incident at the tombs. If she was willing to believe he hadn't stolen the Madman's silver, then he'd better drop the idea that she was after his tosh. As for the writing on the stones – or lack of it – he couldn't see what that had to do with anything.

But Bess's remark about washing had been working in his head all week – irritating, rankling. *Course I sometimes cleans up on a Saturday.* He could still hear himself telling the stupid lie. Well, maybe this Saturday it was time he actually did it. And he'd told her he had a clean set of clothes. That wasn't true either. He'd *found* decent clothes in the sewers sometimes, but they'd always gone to Mother for cash.

Joe managed to get out of his ragged tosher's jacket with the special pockets, but the vest underneath came apart in his hands as he tried to work it over his head. In the end he had to pick scraps of cloth off his upper body and arms, and even standing right up next to the oil lamp it was hard to tell what was skin and what was filthy clothing. He shivered violently, wishing he'd never started on this stupid washing, but it was too late now.

Hanging next to the sink was a row of cloths, as if someone had just finished washing dishes and gone out of the room – except that the cloths were stiff and dry and the first two dissolved into dust when he picked them up. Finally he found one that didn't fall apart, dipped it in the clear well-water and looked down at his grimy body, wondering where to start.

'Well,' he murmured, 'here goes nothin'.'

Working gently, almost fearfully, as if he thought he might wipe the skin away altogether, Joe began to wash the back of his left hand.

'What you going to wear at the end of it?'

Joe spun round, trying to hide himself as he did so. Bess was standing in the doorway, her face turned away. 'I bain't looking. Only I thought, seeing as how you haven't got those clean clothes you were talking about, you might want these.' She dropped a pile of garments onto the floor of the room. 'Found them upstairs. Nothing for a girl, but there's two cupboards full of boy's stuff. Most of 'em too big for you though.' Joe still hadn't moved. 'Well, don't stand there starve naked,' Bess scolded. 'Finish your washing and put 'em on.'

She was gone, but Joe didn't hear footsteps down the passage. She must be waiting outside the door. Quickly he finished washing his hands and face, decided the rest could stay the way it was, and pulled on a shirt and a pair of breeches that hung loosely on his slight frame. There was a belt, which he tied tightly around his middle, and a pair of sturdy brown boots. Joe picked the boots up and examined them doubtfully; then he stowed them under the sink. He had never worn shoes in his life.

'All dogged up from your head to your hucks!' Bess was back in the doorway, looking at him with her head on one side.

'Don't look like that,' Joe complained.

'Like what? I'm smiling. Anyways,' she went on playfully, suddenly heading towards him, 'your ears is still dirty. Mother wash your weekers for you.'

'What?' Joe shrank into the corner of the room.

'It's all right. I was joking with you. It's what my mother used to say when I was a little 'un.'

'Before she died?'

'Yes.' Bess's smile was suddenly gone. 'Afore she died.'

'Didn't mean nothin',' said Joe, angry at himself. He was stupid – just like she said. She'd looked happy and now she looked sad, and it was him that had done it and he hadn't meant to. He groped for something else to say – something to distract her. 'I work down the shores, see,' he blurted out finally. 'That's why I'm so – why I stink.'

'The shores?'

'Down the sewers. I'm a tosher.' And to his own surprise Joe found himself explaining to this girl with the odd accent and the strange words what the life of a tosher was.

'And that's where you've been going these last nights?' she asked finally.

Joe looked surprised. 'Yeah. I bin workin' a new stretch. And I ain't givin' a rusty nail to Mother neither.'

'Wouldn't you rather do something less— well, something else?'

'Like what?'

'I don't know. Anything.'

'It's what I know,' said Joe simply. 'I did have a notion once for Parson's dust heaps.'

'For what?'

'Pound's Field Mount. It's where they dumps all the rubbish. You can clear a shilling a day for carrying cinders. 'Cept Parson's own brats got it all sewn up. Wouldn't let me near.'

'But there must be something you could do better than—'

'Better than what? It's outdoor work, toshing is. Better than

being shut inside all day. Couldn't stand that, I couldn't.'
Suddenly he felt on the defensive again. 'You and your "good
family" and your "uncle and aunt" and all. What d'you know
about bein' poor anyway?'

Bess was silent. She thought about her home in Hartingham
with the doorway you had to stoop to get through and the one
room downstairs and one room up and the damp in the air
from the washing that hung in front of the fire day and night.
But at least she had wanted to do something better. She had
been going to save her family. *She just might make all our
fortunes* – Bess could hear her mother saying it as clearly as if
she were standing right there in the Madman's basement room.
And at that moment all the reasons she had had for running
from Harry Trencher and her mother seemed to evaporate into
nothing, and all she was left with was the certainty that she had
let her father down. He had wanted her to go to London and
hire out as a servant at White Street Market and help the family
– and if he had wanted it then it must have been the right thing
to do – and she had run away.

'I must get home,' she said simply, looking Joe straight in
the eye.

'What's stoppin' yer? Ankle still hurt?'

'No. The ankle's fine. I don't know the way!'

Bess sat down heavily on the stone floor, and for the first time
since Joe had met her she looked hopeless. It had been *don't need
your help* and *what's it to you?* from the start, but now she looked
so down in the mouth, sitting there moping: he preferred her
with the fight in her, even if it was him she was fighting.

'Come on! I got a fiddler.'

Bess looked blank.

'A fiddler!' repeated Joe. 'A tanner! Sixpence! That's toshing for yer. Not so bad, eh? No rat stew tonight. We'll nip out down the market and see what's good. No one gonna recognize me in these duds and a clean face and all.'

'If you want.' She still sounded miserable, but at least he'd got her up off the floor.

Chapter 15

THE ORGAN-GRINDER

Past the church on the Whitechapel Road there was a glow in the evening air as if the street was on fire. Flaring, hissing, white naphtha lights and smoky, red grease lamps lit up the faces of a great crowd of men, women and children milling up and down the stalls and shop fronts. From tin pots and teacups to turnips and tripe, everything was for sale.

'Eight a penny, stunning pears!' 'Tuppence a pound grapes!' 'Chestnuts all 'ot, a penny a score!' 'Sold again!'

Three big lads stood in front of a donkey-cart piled high with potatoes, bellowing at the top of their lungs: 'Hi-i-i! What d'ya think of this 'ere? A jack a pound! 'Ere's your taties! Five pound for a penny!' The donkey waited patiently amidst the racket, swaying its head slowly from side to side.

The butcher's gaslights streamed and fluttered, lighting up row upon row of animal carcasses, crimson with blood. Dressed in a blue coat and brandishing a shining steel-bladed knife, the butcher bargained in a loud voice with a dozen women at a time, kicking out every now and then as a stray dog got too close.

On the other side of the road a crowd of men and women spilled out from a gin-palace that dwarfed Nimms's drinking shop on Flower Street. As still as a statue amidst the throng stood a shabbily dressed man, head down, holding out a single box of matches in his left hand. Two little boys in clean shirts but no shoes hovered just behind him; to one side a woman held a baby to her breast; a river of people swirled around the begging family as if they weren't there.

Joe tried to stay hidden amongst the bustling crowd, uneasy in spite of what he'd said to Bess that someone might recognize him. Bess stared around her, wide-eyed, bumping into the casual strollers, shouldered aside by busy housewives. She stopped at a barrow covered with toys and artificial flowers and glittering glass jewellery, fingering the goods until the stall-holder spoke up sharply. 'Pull out your chink or 'op it, missy!'

On the next corner she watched open-mouthed as a dark-skinned man tilted back his head and plunged a long sword into his own throat. On a small tasselled carpet at his feet a tiny monkey dressed in a red jacket and trousers held out a tin cup for coins, but no one seemed to be giving the little creature anything. Bess turned away awkwardly with no money of her own.

'Murders! 'Orrible murders! Come and see just how they was done.' Bess peered at the bloody pictures outside a wax-works show, while a man in a dusty top hat and tails shouted close to her ear, ''Orrible murders!'

Instinctively Joe slipped further back into the crowd as a policeman in clean white gloves came down the middle of the road pushing a handcart with a man strapped tight to the top. A crowd of children, mostly younger than Joe, danced around the cart hooting and laughing at the drunk, who lifted his head feebly every now and then to shout back.

They stopped in front of a stove that filled the street with a delicious smell of baked chestnuts. Fire shone through the holes in the stove, reflecting in the eyes of customers and passers-by. A girl lifted brown-stained fingers to her mouth, screaming at the top of her lungs, 'Get 'em 'ot! Get 'em 'ot! Ha'penny a bag! All 'ot.'

A few yards further on a woman was selling baked potatoes, and beyond her a great cloud of white steam spewed out into the night from a brightly lit cookshop, its window packed with pies and puddings and an array of cakes and pastries at two a penny. Joe fingered the silver sixpence in his hand. 'I only got this,' he said finally, holding the coin out towards Bess but not quite able to make himself let go. 'You'll have to do it. They might spot me, see? Then word gets back to Mother. Even up this far – you don't know.'

'I bain't going to rob you,' said Bess, an eyebrow raised in mockery of his distrust. 'I tell you what,' she went on, as Joe still held tight to his food money, 'you stand here and watch and if it looks like I'm a-making a run for it, you can whip off them bits of string and throttle me with 'em.'

Joe followed her gaze down to where he had tied up the legs of his new breeches with string to help keep the cold out. Then he looked back at Bess. In spite of the funny voice, she had Plucky Jack's way with words sometimes. Suddenly he saw his tied up trouser-legs through her eyes, and his shoulders hunched and his eyes closed into a stifled laugh. Then he put the coin in Bess's hand. 'Not sayin' I trusts you, mind,' he said. 'Only some of them stallholders know me. Or they might do,' he finished lamely. But Bess was already gone.

Joe faded back into a crowd that had gathered around a man perched on a box. He was flourishing a black book at his audience and shouting, but Joe wasn't listening. All he could think about was the silver tanner he'd just put into the hand of a virtual stranger. What would Mother have said about that? '. . . the creature next to you is your fellow man . . .' Mother didn't have a saying for that. 'Look at him. Look into his eyes. He's your brother . . .' She'd never imagine anyone being stupid enough to give their food money to someone else . . . 'You. Yes, you, boy!'

Joe had settled himself on the pavement amongst the forest of legs. Now he looked up, bewildered, as the voice of the preacher broke in on his thoughts. Faces were turned towards him, staring. The man on the box was staring at him too. 'That boy!' It was exactly what Joe had feared: the man seemed to know him. But what was he talking about? 'That unfortunate barefoot boy you see there,' he went on: 'He's your son, madam. He's your brother, sir.'

Joe looked around him, bewildered by the sea of unfamiliar faces. What did they want? Something about his brothers?

'My brothers is dead,' he blurted out finally. 'They got the tramp fever. They's dead three years and more – both of 'em.'

For a moment there was utter silence. Then the crowd

erupted in laughter and turned back to the preacher jeering and booing.

'Hungry?'

Bess was standing over him.

'Yeah, I am.' It was a relief to see her face and not just because it meant he hadn't thrown away sixpence.

Squatting in a doorway away from the crowds, they ate the food Bess had bought and drank the quart of sweet lemonade. After two weeks of the Madman's stew the greasy pies and heavy dough puddings tasted so good they could both have gone back and eaten the same again. 'Better not,' said Bess, handing two pennies' change to Joe.

The boy looked at the two brown coins. He looked at Bess. He wanted to say something about the money, about how he'd never trusted even Plucky Jack that way, but he couldn't frame the words. He slipped the two pennies into his pocket. It was time they moved on. But Bess was already on her feet.

'Come on!' she cried.

Beyond the lights of another drinking shop, a crowd of young children had gathered on the corner. An old man with a grey beard was turning the handle of a barrel organ, leaning heavily on the instrument, which was supported by a single wooden post. There was so much racket from the gin shop you couldn't hear the music until you got quite close, but the children dancing in the gutter showed it must be playing. Bess drew nearer. A man with a cart had pushed one of these through Hartingham at hop-picking time a few years back, but he'd only come the once and the music wasn't half as good.

Jangling, trumpeting and tooting, this one filled the air with an irresistible sound.

Bess stepped out into the street with the other, younger children, who stopped capering for a moment to look at the new arrival. The white muslin frock her mother had laboured over so long had lost its lace and its scarlet ribbons, and with the hem all tatty no one could have mistaken her any more for the young lady of the manor. She'd wrapped the old rug from the Madman's couch around her like a cloak to go out into the streets, but she threw this off now and held out a hand to Joe.

'Come on, Joe. Dance with me!'

Joe stared at her, dumbfounded. The tinkling music of the organ had brought a smile to her face he hadn't seen before. He took a step backwards.

'Kids' stuff,' he mumbled, gesturing vaguely at the street urchins, who had started dancing again once they realized there was nothing to be had from the two older children.

'So?'

Bess looked straight at him, her hand still held out, and somehow Joe didn't feel able to turn away. He felt in his pocket for the coins she had handed back to him. The barrel-organist had an empty hat turned upside down on the top of the instrument. That wasn't right. If the man was going to turn his handle, then he needed paying. He had a living to earn same as anyone.

Joe pulled out one of the pennies with a sick feeling in his stomach that was only half to do with the money. He dropped the coin in the old man's black hat, swallowed hard and stepped awkwardly out onto the roadway. With stiff, unaccustomed movements and an expression of grim determination on his face that made his partner smile a little more broadly, he danced on the street corner with Bess while the barrel organ played 'Sing a Song of Sixpence' over and over again.

Chapter 16
The Locked Room

It was three hours until dawn and the fire had died down when Joe felt his way across the darkened room to where Bess lay fast asleep on the couch. Huddling close to the glowing coals to catch what heat there was, he drew the little leather pouch slowly out of his throat with a practised hand. The last three nights there'd been nothing worth hiding, but tonight the pouch contained thirty links of delicate silver chain. The chain was broken and the locket that it had probably once held was gone, but it was still worth money.

He fingered the silver again, counting the links. Then he tucked it away in the pocket of his new breeches and eased the brown leather boots off his feet, standing them in front of the fire to dry. After last Saturday night at the market he'd finally decided to put them on, and in many ways they made working in the sewers harder. He didn't have the same feel for the state of the floor and he slipped and fell more often. Even walking in the dry felt odd, as if you were always wading through something instead of just treading on the ground. But stepping down River Lane in the darkness with a proper lantern in his hand and a pair of real leather boots on his feet, not to mention the new clothes Bess had found him upstairs, Joe walked with a new swagger in his stride – except if there was anyone around, of course, when he could still melt into the shadows as always.

He put a couple more pieces of coal on the fire and settled down to wait for light. He wouldn't sleep now. He'd just enjoy letting the warmth of the fire dry his clothes and banish the chill of the sewer water from his bones, then as soon as it was light enough outside, he'd hide the silver chain with the rest of his tosh.

He was slipping into sleep in spite of himself, when a familiar noise jolted him fully awake. Some nights it was louder than others, and tonight he was really giving it everything – '*Yes!!! Yes!!!*'

It was almost as if there were two men living in the house with him and Bess – one who shuffled around the place in the daylight, fiddling with his dead animals and his traps, never speaking, shooting the odd furtive glance at Bess as she worked alongside him, but more or less ignoring Joe; and then there was another man who shouted in the night and whom he never saw. Well, maybe it was time he *did* see him. Only a couple of weeks ago, in the days when he lived outside the house amongst the rest of the inhabitants of Pound's Field, the sane ones, it would never have occurred to Joe to want to see the man at all, let alone to see him at his maddest, as he screamed from the top of his house. Now it was different, and there was still that word 'treasure' niggling somewhere at the back of Joe's mind.

However much Bess might sneer, the man had used the word. He must have meant something by it.

Joe pulled his boots on carefully. He reached over to check that Bess was still asleep. The girl was gone! He put his hand quickly on the couch where she had been lying: it was still warm and the double doors that led out into the hallway were open.

Bess moved slowly up the wide staircase, pausing on the first landing. She'd never explored high up in the house where the shouting came from. If she was honest with herself, she didn't like the rats that scurried and squeaked around you up there. They were big and black and quite different from the creatures that lived in the barns around Hartingham. Also the upper storeys of the house weren't lit with oil lamps the way the ground floor was, and the feeble glow of a single candle made the rats seem that much worse. But tonight the wall sconces on the first landing were all filled with burning candles.

Joe caught up with her at the next set of stairs. 'What you up to?' he demanded. 'I didn't know where you'd gone.'

'I'm after the treasure afore you get to it,' mocked Bess.

'I never said that,' Joe responded defensively.

'Yes, but you thought it, didn't you?' Bess extinguished the candle she was carrying. 'Have you ever thought where all these candles come from?' she went on. 'Good wax candles and gallons of oil burning at all hours in this old house, but nobody ever goes out a-buying 'em.'

Joe had an answer for that one. He told her about the

lean-to in the garden where he'd found boxes of supplies. 'Three or four sacks of quality coal too.'

'Yes, but where does it come from?' Joe looked blank. 'How many sacks the first time you seen 'em?' she asked with forced patience.

'Four, I reckon. Why?'

'And now?'

'I don't know. Three or four.'

'Three or four? So two weeks ago there's four sacks of coal; now there's still four sacks of coal and there's a fire a-burning the whole time. How's that work then?'

Joe had nothing to say to that.

'Does he slip out once in while, or what?' asked Bess.

'Ain't nobody never seen him. Not for years, they say.'

'You ever heard tell what drove him mad in the first place?'

'I heard stories,' Joe said. 'They used to say he sold his soul to the Devil.'

'You believe that?'

'Prob'ly not.'

'Me neither,' said Bess.

At that moment the shouting started up again, louder now because they were closer. Joe made an instinctive movement back towards the stairs. So many years around Pound's Field listening to that cry, hearing stories about the Madman, and now he was heading up the stairs to see for himself? But Bess didn't flinch.

'Go on down, if you wants,' she threw at him casually over

her shoulder. 'I think it's time to find out what all the shouting's about.'

'You can't go up there on your own,' Joe began. But she was already gone.

From the bottom of yet another flight of stairs Bess could see a yellow glow filtering down from above. There had been light all the way up through the house, but here it was brighter, and to her relief she found the brightness seemed to have banished the rats from the upper storey because there were no scurryings around her feet here.

She was almost at the top of the last flight of stairs, when she stopped, spellbound by the sight that met her eyes. A row of long white candles had been stuck to the banister all the way along the landing, and in the midst of the candles, throwing shadows up onto the ceiling as the flames flickered and swayed this way and that, was the shape of a great white bird. It was the same stuffed bird that had stopped Joe in his tracks as he followed the Madman through the house the first night they arrived. But it sent a shiver through Bess more profound than any she had felt in this house. The white bird, with its glittering black eyes and outstretched wings, was the very image of the white barn owl that had perched on the tree stump in the hedgerow in the dawn light outside the window of her bedroom in far-off Hartingham. It was her wishing bird. It was as if it had taken off that morning, that last time she saw it, that fateful morning when she first heard her mother and Harry Trencher behind the hedge talking about hiring fairs and White Street – it was as if it had taken off, flown north across the Kentish

downs, over the smoke and filth of London, and landed here in this crazy man's house. Only now it was stuffed and dead.

She was still standing quite still, as if she had been stuffed and mounted like the bird, when Joe darted past and across the landing. He knew exactly where he was heading. Steadying his quick breathing, he inched closer to the door at the end of the passage – the only locked door in the house. There was no noise now, except for a faint sound – what was it? – a shuffling, brushing noise . . . What could it be? It sounded for all the world as if someone behind the door was sweeping the floor with a broom! Then a muffled thud. Then more sweeping. The scraping of a chair across the floor. More sweeping. And now there was another sound, a continuous low whimpering of terrible pain. Inside the room someone was weeping – weeping as Joe had never heard anyone weep, weeping as if every care and sorrow in the whole stinking city had come to haunt one single, suffering soul.

Then, abruptly and without warning, the shouting began. Even with the door between them it was as if the Madman was crying his fearful cry right in Joe's face. His hands flew up to his ears to shut out the din, and his mouth opened in a scream of pure terror. At once a hand was across his mouth, stifling the sound. He struggled against the grip.

'Go on then,' came a voice, 'shout, if you wants him to get yer.' It was Bess, and even with his heart pounding furiously in his ears, Joe recognized the exact words he'd used as he pulled her back into the shadows on Sweetwater Lane two weeks ago. She was mocking him – even now.

Anger overcame Joe's fear as he struggled out of Bess's grasp and scurried back down the stairs, away from the fearful shouting. He didn't even look to see if Bess was coming too. He had got so used to the Madman wandering about the place that he'd started to think of him as almost ordinary. Those strange sounds coming from behind the locked door and the sudden shouting had taken him straight back to the way he'd always thought of the man, the way everyone in Pound's Field thought of him: he was bad luck and he was crazy and he was dangerous, and the only clever thing was to stay as far away as you could.

He sat huddled in front of the fire with his boots on, waiting for light, clutching his little leather pouch, not sure what he would do when dawn came, whether he should make a run for it, or if *they* should make a run for it. There was no sign of Bess but nothing would have persuaded him to go looking for her now through that house. One thing he was sure of: he mustn't go to sleep again. But as light began to show under the heavy curtains, he fell into an uneasy slumber.

Chapter 17

TERESA

Joe woke with Bess's hand on his shoulder. A dim grey light filtered around the edges of the curtains. 'Come on,' she hissed. 'I've been watching. He's gone outside.'

Bess made straight for the main staircase, taking the stairs two at a time. Joe followed. He didn't have to ask where she was going. After last night he would happily never have gone near that locked room again – treasure or no treasure – but if Bess did manage to get in, he had to be there too.

On the top landing she edged carefully around the snow-white owl. In the daylight it didn't frighten her the way it had the first time, but the stuffed bird still struck her as an ill omen. At the door to the locked room she stopped with one hand on the brass knob, listening. She had seen the Madman leave the house with her own eyes, but somehow she still couldn't feel certain he wasn't waiting behind that heavy door. Joe caught up with her, breathing heavily from the stairs. There was no other sound. Bess turned the handle slowly, easing her weight against the door, expecting solid resistance.

It swung open on silent hinges.

They were looking into a child's bedroom. A half-size bed with a highly polished brass bedstead stood near the window, one corner of the sheet turned down as if someone might climb in at any moment. Three identical porcelain dolls, immaculately dressed in lilac frocks, lay stiffly side by side in a careful row on a perfect white pillowcase. There was a small painted chest of drawers, a hanging cupboard with oval mirrors set in both doors and a pink, child's-size armchair. The floor was covered with a fine, deep-piled carpet that felt soft under their feet as they entered the room on tiptoe, as if fearing to disturb a sleeping infant. There was a faint smell of lavender in the air.

Bess moved towards the bed, reaching out a tentative hand to touch the dolls. Their dresses were starched and ironed. Their long, blonde curls were silky to the touch, softer than her own fair hair and quite clearly human. Three pairs of vividly blue eyes stared up at her blankly. She turned from the bed to where a small fire burned in the grate. Over the mantelpiece a sampler hung in a silver frame. She stood on tiptoe to examine the brightly coloured stitching. Someone had worked with incredible care and delicacy, sewing an elaborate, flowered border into the cloth, then the alphabet across the top in green, and below that, picked out in delicate blue letters, some words. She leaned closer, trying to puzzle out what they said.

Joe went automatically to the painted chest, though one glance into the room and he had ceased once and for all to believe there were valuables hidden here. The Madman had meant something else when he talked about his lost treasure. Sure enough, the drawers were full of carefully folded clothes – little girl's clothes. So was the cupboard. He turned to the single window. Framed in neat, flowered curtains, its diamond-shaped panes held the only clean glass in the entire house. The room must have been above the one where he'd stood and looked out over the wall into River Lane, because from up here you could see into the street and then clear across St Saviour's Docks to the river, where the dawn mist hung around a forest of ship's masts. The dock gates weren't open yet, but a fair crowd was already gathering outside. The Watchman was there. He should have been flat out on the shakedown in Holywell Court, but it didn't surprise Joe to see him. What did surprise him was that none of the faces were turned towards the docks, waiting for work: they were all looking at the house, and the Watchman's eyes were turned to the topmost storeys. In fact, just at that moment he seemed to be looking straight at Joe.

Joe ducked away from the window as Bess spoke. She was reading softly the words from the sampler: ' "Though I am now in younger days, nor can tell what shall befall me, I'll prepare for—"' Bess broke off abruptly. 'Prepare for what? This part's not finished. We did these in school. You have to put the date and your name. Yes, here it is. Hard to read though.' The stitches here were different from the rest of the sampler – loose and misshapen, as if they had been done by a different hand or a hand that now found it hard to hold a needle. Bess spelled out the letters one by one: 'T–E–R–E–S–'

'*Tess!*'

A great cry prevented her finishing. Bess and Joe whirled round simultaneously. The Madman was in the doorway, his pale eyes wide and staring, his arms reaching out towards Bess.

'*Tess!!*'

Again came the cry, but not the hoarse anguish of the shouting in the night. There was mingled awe and disbelief in the way the man called out the name, as he stretched stiff, awkward arms towards the girl. And suddenly Joe understood. It wasn't 'Yes' the Madman shouted in the night, sending a shiver down the spine of every inhabitant of Pound's Field.

'Tess.' Joe spoke aloud without meaning to. 'That's what you shout, isn't it? Tess! From this window here.' He half-gestured towards the attic window, and as he turned he thought he could hear a sound coming from outside the house, and not quite the usual sound of the morning business on River Lane.

The Madman's eyes flicked sideways to Joe, narrowing as if he was trying to focus on something in the far distance. His mouth opened and closed, forming soundless words. But it was Bess who spoke, her voice low and coaxing. 'Short for Teresa. Like the name in the picture. That's why you like my name, annit? Sounds like Tess.'

The man made a sudden lunge towards Bess, hands groping at the air, fingers extended as if to grip her by the neck. But Bess was too quick for him. She jumped sideways, getting the carefully made bed between her and the advancing man.

'She's your "treasure", ain't she? The one you lost? How'd you lose her then?'

177

At her words the man threw up his hands as if to protect himself from a blow and staggered back against the fireplace, knocking several coals out onto the hearth rug.

'*No!!*'

He let out a terrible scream that had Bess and Joe clasping their hands to their ears and seemed to be echoed by a shout from the crowd outside. Then he collapsed on the floor, clasping his knees with his arms, rocking rapidly backward and forward, uttering a long moaning sound that seemed to go on and on as if he didn't need to draw breath.

A thunderous noise from the street turned Joe's head to the window again. Half a dozen men were attacking the front gates, beating furiously with iron bars and sledgehammers, and the smoke of burning torches rose into the morning air. They'd talked about it often enough, but Joe had never believed it would happen: had they finally come to burn the Madman out?

He began to spot faces in the crowd. Plucky Jack was there at the back. The Watchman was at the very front with several of Billy's gang, waving his arms as if he was organizing the whole thing. And over to one side at the fringes of the mob – what were they doing here? – that was the man in the stovepipe hat and the woman Bess called her aunt.

Bess was at his side now. The Madman was still on the floor, moaning and hitting ineffectually with his hands at the hot coals on the hearthrug. Joe caught the girl's eye as she scanned the crowd anxiously. 'It's your uncle and aunt.' He pointed. 'I seen 'em at Mother's. Didn't want to tell you.'

She didn't even look surprised. 'Like you said' – she smiled grimly – 'makes sense.'

'We gotta go,' said Joe. 'But I got somethin' to do first.'

'Me too,' snapped Bess. 'I know what's in that tomb with no name now.'

Chapter 18

The Coffin

Joe ran full tilt down the long flights of stairs with Bess close behind him. Along the back passage, hurling open the back door, he sprinted for the corner of the garden where the tombs lay. The stone mastiff lay impassive and silent as ever as he scrabbled at the door of its tomb. He reached desperate hands through the gap. 'It's not here!' He was talking aloud now in his panic. 'It's not here! Must have used another one. Come on, think! Bess, it's not here!'

Bess came through the bushes carrying a heavy brass poker she had picked up downstairs.

'You got to help me, Bess. I can't remember which one I put the bag in!'

But Bess wasn't listening. Back braced against the stonework, she was using the poker to lever at the iron doors of the tomb with no name.

'What you doin'?' Joe threw up an arm in protest.

'Got to know!' Bess's voice was strained with the effort. The metal doors buckled under the pressure and she redoubled her efforts. 'I bain't leaving without—' The doors gave way suddenly, catapulting her over backwards. In spite of himself Joe moved closer, peering into the darkness of the stone tomb. He was accustomed to the stench of the sewers, but the strange smell of dust and decay stopped him in his tracks.

'Help me!' demanded Bess, scrambling to her feet.

Together they reached into the tomb, grasping the scrolled brass handles of a coffin. It was heavy – lead-lined probably, thought Joe – but it slid surprisingly easily out onto the grass. They stared at the polished hardwood box in horrified fascination. Still solid and virtually undamaged, it was much less than adult size. Joe could have squeezed inside; Bess was too tall.

A huge cheer came suddenly from the house, as if in comment at what they had done, but, looking quickly up, Joe could see it had nothing to do with them. A pall of black smoke billowed from under the gables, and flames could be seen flickering at the upper windows of the ancient timber building. The house was on fire.

Bess scraped quickly at the lid of the small coffin, brushing loose dirt from a neat, rectangular brass plaque. She blew the last of the dust away, and the letters stood out as clear as if they had been etched in the metal that same day. She turned in triumph to Joe. 'There! What do you think of that?' Then she remembered. 'Sorry, I forgot.' And she read the inscription aloud: ' "Teresa Poundfield. 1836 to 1846." '

'Poundfield?' Joe stared fascinated at the small coffin.

'And you call the whole area—'

'Pound's Field,' Joe completed her sentence. 'Mother said

that was the old name of the sugar works— refinery,' he corrected himself, glancing at Bess. 'It used to be called Bowman and Poundfield's.'

Bess nodded vigorously. 'Must have been the family business. Blood in and sweetness out. That's what he said, wasn't it?'

'Who?'

'The Madman. Blood in and sweetness out.'

'He was talking about making sugar.'

'Yes,' said Bess, 'but what else was he talking about? Teresa Poundfield. Ten years old. That's her room upstairs with the dolls and the sampler with her name on it and the fire still burning. She's his treasure. How old do you reckon he is? Sixty?'

'The Madman? Hard to say.'

'"1836 to 1846".' Bess pointed at the inscription again. 'She's been dead twenty years. Now do you see who's in the coffin?'

Suddenly Joe knew what she was driving at. 'It's his daughter!' he gasped.

'Exactly.'

'Ten years old, and he buried her out here with the family dogs! Why does a man who owns a factory do that?'

'And why does he end up as mad as maybutter?'

Instinctively Joe looked up at the tall chimney of the factory that had once been named Bowman and Poundfield. It was shrouded in thick, black smoke. The upper storeys of the house were fully ablaze now: he could feel the heat on his face, and it seemed to shock the boy back to his senses. Here they were wasting time on something that had happened twenty years ago and his money was lying out here somewhere. 'Forget that, Bess,' he cried. 'You've got to help me. I don't know which one I put the bag in!'

He turned to search amongst the tombs again, but Bess called him back. 'There's no time for your tosh,' she shouted above the rising roar of the flames and the shouts of the mob at the front of the house. She slid the coffin back into its tomb and pushed the doors shut as best she could. 'We've got to go!'

Joe looked at her helplessly. He looked at the tombs and back at the house. And suddenly his mind was very clear. She was right: they did have to go, and now. The house was burning from the top. That meant it was the Madman, or Poundfield if that was his name, who'd fired his own house by accident – probably those coals spilling out of the upstairs fire.

This wasn't some superstitious mob come to burn him out: no, this was what had been hatching in Mother's overheated parlour that night as he peered through the crack in the door. This mob had come for Bess Farleigh and Joe Rat.

With a gesture of despair Joe followed Bess through the bushes and along the back wall of Holywell Court. He could keep searching for his tosh, but it wouldn't do him any good if the Watchman or Billy got him. Better leave the bag where it was and come back when he got the chance. What he wasn't so sure of was how they were going to get out of the Madman's garden. There was no way past the mob to the road. The other walls were too high and his old back entrance to Holywell

Court wasn't safe. He had panicked for a moment at the tombs when he couldn't find his grey bag, but Joe's mind was working now, quick and smooth, the way it always did in a chase. He was used to this. He was good at it. There was another way out of here – just like there'd been another way out of Church Lane up and over the viaduct. Plucky Jack had shown him that one. This time he had to work it out for himself.

'Look!' Bess was pointing up towards the blazing house.

In a long window on the first floor the gaunt figure of the Madman could be clearly seen, smoke billowing thick and dark around him. With a sudden, stiff thrust of his hands he smashed both arms through the glass and they could hear him above the mob and the roaring of the fire. He was shouting, and they knew what he shouted now. '*Tess!! Tess!!*'

Before Joe could stop her, Bess was running for the house. 'We can't go back!' he screamed after her. 'Bess, I'm going!' But she didn't turn, and Joe didn't leave.

By the time he caught up with her she was standing almost under the window where the Madman still shouted. The heat from the fire was intense here, and Bess held her arms in front of her face to shield herself. Joe flinched from the flames and the choking smoke. The mob would be round this side in a moment and they would be caught. The Madman drew another breath to shout, but before the sound came, Bess cupped her hands to her mouth and shouted first: 'Poundfield!'

For a moment the man stood perfectly still. She called again: 'Mr Poundfield!' His eyes searched the smoke and the air for where the name was coming from. Bess felt a little thrill of triumph. They had guessed right. Poundfield was the name on the coffin and Poundfield was his name too.

'We can't do anything,' yelled Joe, making himself heard above the sound of the fire.

'He helped me. I'm helping him.' Bess turned to call the man's name again.

Joe pulled at her sleeve, bellowing in her ear, 'Are you crazy? If that's his daughter, he must have killed her. What else is she doin' in a dogs' graveyard? You want to help a man what murdered his own kid?'

'You've been in his house two weeks. You think he's a murderer?' Bess cupped her hands and cried out again. 'Mr Poundfield! Down here!'

This time he saw them, and even at that distance and through the smoke they could see that his gaze was different, as if at the sound of his name something had cleared in his mind. Kicking out the remaining glass, he leaped from the window, legs working for a moment in mid air, then crashing awkwardly into the brambles and bushes of the garden below. Bess was at his side, hauling the man to his feet. The bushes had broken his fall: he was winded and scratched about the face, but basically unhurt. She turned to shout for Joe, and was surprised to find him already there, cursing, but helping just the same.

Chapter 19

RATS

As soon as they had their backs to the burning house, Joe knew where they were going. Stumbling sometimes on the path, he urged Bess and the ungainly Poundfield through the line of trees to where ten stone steps led down to the clear, icy water of the spring.

'We can't hide here. They'll find us,' Bess protested.

Joe didn't answer. Leaving Bess and Poundfield crouched amidst the ferns, he crawled to where water trickled over the edge of the well and down into the darkness below.

'I'm goin' to need a hand,' he called out softly. Bess joined him at the edge of the well, and suddenly she could see what he was planning.

'I'm not a-going down there,' she declared.

Joe ignored her. 'Him. I need – him.' He didn't know what to call the man now. Somehow he couldn't bring himself to use his name.

Slowly and obviously reluctantly Poundfield moved down to join them. Joe slithered backwards, letting his legs hang over the edge of the brickwork. He held out a hand. For a moment

Poundfield looked at the hand and then at Joe, as if unsure what he was supposed to do; then he grasped the boy's wrist and braced himself as Joe let himself down into the blackness, groping with his feet, feeling for the iron rung. He caught Bess's anxious eye, looking down at him.

'If there's one rung, there has to be more. And if there's a way down, there has to be a way out. Makes sense, don't it?'

'Does it?'

The first part of Joe's calculation was right. A series of cold metal rungs led down into the dark shaft of the well. He counted as he went. Four – five – six. He looked up at the dim circle of light and the two heads silhouetted above him. Spring water splashed in his eyes, as he called to them, 'Come on. It's all right.'

They followed – Bess first, forcing herself not to look down, trying not to think about what might lie ahead; then Poundfield, squeezing with difficulty into the narrow shaft of the well.

Eight – nine – ten. There were twenty rungs in all. The well was deep and almost completely dark this far down. Joe couldn't see the water below him, but he knew he was nearing the bottom by the sound of splashing at his feet. Then he felt solid brick. There was a ledge running at least part of the way around the bottom of the shaft. He murmured softly and continuously to himself, 'If there's a way down, there's a way out . . .'

With Bess and Poundfield next to him there was scarcely room to turn round on the narrow ledge. In the darkness they felt carefully all round the shaft of the well, but there was no way out, no tunnel – only the water below.

'Has to be this way,' hissed Joe, and without another word he let himself slide down into the water. It was icy cold, but once it was all around him he was surprised again by its scent – not the familiar sewer smell he had lived in for so long, but a whisper of earth and growing things – or perhaps it was just that the water had no smell at all.

He could feel no bottom to the well. He hadn't expected one. He was looking for something else. Feeling around the brickwork under the water his hands suddenly groped into nothingness. There was an opening here that led away under-water in what looked like the direction of the house.

'Overflow,' he explained, his voice echoing from the damp brickwork. 'Probably opens out further along.

'And what if it doesn't?' queried Bess. 'What happens then?'

'Yeah,' said Joe simply. 'But it probably does.'

He took a deep breath and let it out slowly. He took another and let it out. Then he drew a shallower breath and ducked down into the dark water, feeling his way into the underwater opening. It was a square, brick-built passageway – Joe could feel the top and bottom and both sides as he inched his way along. In the summer it might not be totally flooded. The question was: did it open out further on, and if so, how much further, and if not, did he have enough breath to make it back the way he'd come? He'd worked his way into some odd corners in the shores in this way in his time and found some decent tosh. This time he had to find something more important than a spoon or two – he had to find a way out for all of them.

There was no good rushing it. You started trying to go too fast in tricky spots like this and you finished up in more trouble, especially with no light. Not that his lantern would have been any use under the water. He could feel his lungs beginning to strain. It was close to decision time now. If he went on much further and didn't find a way out the other end, he was going to drown. It seemed like a stupid way to die too with no hope of tosh of any kind. There were no silver chains or nothing down here. Could be some of those Roman coins the old toshers talked about. The place looked old enough from the outside. Joe stretched his eyes wide under the water, trying to clear his thoughts, and inched forwards. He could feel a roaring beginning in his ears. There were only a few moments left now. He had to go back or he was going to drown down here. He had to—

Then suddenly he was gasping air. The tunnel had opened out, just as he had known – well maybe not quite known – guessed it would. He repeated the three breaths and ducked back the way he'd come. It didn't seem so far going back.

'It's all right,' he gasped, breaking the surface. 'There's a way out. We can go this way.'

This time it was Poundfield who spoke, and it was the first word they had heard him utter since he leaped from the burning house. 'No.'

'It's not that far,' Joe lied. 'Bess, if he won't come, we'll have to leave him.'

'He's a-coming. You're a-coming, aren't you, Mr Poundfield?'

'We ain't got time for this,' insisted Joe.

Bess ignored him; she took hold of the man's arm. 'You don't want to wait for your friends back there to catch up, do you?' She tried to keep her voice light, almost joking.

Poundfield didn't speak again, but when Bess tried to draw him towards the water, he was immovable.

'We ain't got time,' repeated Joe. As he spoke there was an echoing thump in the well shaft above their heads and something ricocheted off the walls, catching Joe a glancing blow on the arm, and crashing past them into the water. Joe let out a stifled cry. A voice came echoing down from above – a voice he knew.

'You down there, Joe Rat?'

'Jack?'

Bess's hand was on Joe's arm, urging him to silence, but it was already too late. Joe shrugged her away. It was Plucky Jack. He was all right.

'Smell you down there, Joe Rat,' came the voice again.

'Watch out, Jack. There's loose bricks up there. Mind you—'

Joe's words were drowned in a thunder of falling bricks. Bess pulled him back against the wall just in time and they crashed into the water below.

'Here!' Jack was shouting at the top of the well. 'They're down here! I've got 'em!'

Joe's mouth tightened. Suddenly it was all too clear: Jack selling on the best pitch in Pound's Field; Jack talking to the Watchman; Jack dropping questions about hidden tosh – Mother had a nose in every house, and in 16 Holywell Court it had been the boy who had claimed to be Joe's friend, Plucky

Jack. Joe took a deep breath and spat once into the well-water at his feet. He didn't kick out or shout the way he had when he'd learned that Billy had been working for Mother all along. There was no time for that.

Now even Poundfield seemed to realize there was no choice. As another hail of bricks crashed down into the well, the three fugitives disappeared under the water, groping blindly into the overflow tunnel. The way had been tight for Joe; for Poundfield it was desperate. But the man didn't panic, allowing Joe to pull him from in front and Bess to push from behind, and finally they all emerged spluttering and treading water into the wider passage beyond.

Bess held onto Poundfield's ragged coat with one hand and swam forwards again into the blackness, trying to follow the sound of Joe's movements ahead of her. She had played in the dark of the coal hole up at the Manor House once or twice when she was little and her father was working there – dirtied her pinafore and got a smack around the head from her mother for it. She remembered the feeling when she couldn't find the way out one terrible afternoon – the rising panic as she lost any sense of which way was forward and which way was back, the relief when the trap door suddenly flew open and her mother's angry voice rang out. Here they were buried yards underground up to the neck in water and with no trap door to open, and before she had swum three strokes she had no idea whether she was going straight ahead or in a circle. She struck the wall of the tunnel, kicking out with her foot. The pain stopped the feeling that she was about to scream. Joe's voice was a relief.

'There's a spill. Can't be more than a few feet down.'

Bess's feet touched hard bottom. Then the water suddenly grew much shallower, and they were crouching where the flow dropped over the edge. From below she could hear moving water, but she couldn't have said whether it was a step down or a plunge of many feet. She was still holding onto Poundfield's coat, and suddenly she was being dragged forward and over the edge. Joe must have jumped and Poundfield had gone with him.

She landed in water no deeper than the little River Hart in summer. That and the fact that there was still not the awful smell she had feared made Bess feel better.

'Underground river.' Joe's voice came out of the darkness. 'Heard tell of it. Never seen it.'

Moving with the current, they followed the course of the underground waterway, feeling the water wash at their knees, hurrying them onward. Around the first bend there was a dim, flickering light in the passage and a confused noise that echoed eerily, and suddenly Joe found himself looking up through a heavy iron grille set into the roof of the tunnel. They were under the Madman's house.

All at once the light was much brighter as a lantern shone down through the grille, and Joe glimpsed a face he knew too well, pressed right up against the bars – hollow eyes, snout-like nose, pock-marked skin – the Watchman! Of course, the fire obviously hadn't reached the lower floors and they were still searching the house for him and Bess. He made a quick gesture to his companions for silence without thinking that the darkness made it useless. Then Poundfield's voice rang out behind him, firm and strong and quite unlike the Madman's rasping tones.

'I know that man!'

The Watchman's eyes swivelled, searching the darkness, and then there were other faces peering down and shouts, as Joe and Bess dragged Poundfield on down the darkening passageway. Behind them they could hear the fading sound of shouted orders. The grating was solid enough, but Joe had no doubt a crowbar would have it out. They would be after them now, and quickly. If he'd been alone he'd have got away easily, but with these two in tow it was anybody's guess.

The passage was pitch dark again now, but steadying herself against the walls, Bess was beginning to find it easier to make progress without falling. Then, at a sharp bend, where the water tugged hard around her legs, she seemed to walk quite suddenly into a different kind of wall. A suffocating, fetid stench filled her head, making her stagger in the water, gasping. It was the same dreadful smell that had reached her nose the first time she encountered Joe, but multiplied a thousand-fold. It was the smell of the London sewers.

Bess bent double, retching against the wall in the darkness: whoever was behind them, she could not take another step forward into that noisome air. She staggered sideways, feeling her head reel, and her feet slipped from under her, sending her plunging over the sheer drop into the sewer.

It wasn't the shallow water which broke her fall; it was a thick, soft layer of rotting vegetables, factory waste, putrefying animal carcasses and human sewage that lined the bottom of the sewer. She staggered to her feet, arms flailing, trying to get her balance in the darkness. She felt a hand holding her and heard Joe's flat, expressionless voice: 'You get used to it. There'll be light further down. Watch the roof.' And with that he was gone.

Retching continuously, Bess followed as best she could, reaching out to the side of the sewer to guide her, recoiling from the vile slime that coated the walls, hearing the sound of splashing feet behind her that indicated Poundfield was still there too. She collided hard with Joe, who had stopped in the darkness in front of her.

'Fork,' he said simply. 'Left or right.' It was not a question.

Bess tried to think, but her mind refused to work in this terrible place. 'Where are we trying to get to? Are we going anywhere?'

'Course we are.' Joe's voice was sharp. 'Keep followin' the flow and we hit the river. I ain't never bin there, but they say there's an outfall.'

'A what?'

'Place where the sewer goes into the Thames. We can get out there.'

'Well, which way is it?' demanded Bess.

'I don't know, do I? This way,' said Joe at random. It was a guess and he knew that if you were going to guess you might as well do it quickly as waste time doing it slowly. He took the right fork.

They went maybe ten yards. It was a mistake. The roof had

collapsed. Feeling with his hands between the fallen rubble and the roof of the tunnel, Joe found a narrow gap. He could get through; Bess would make it too; Poundfield had no chance. He pulled Bess to him, whispering urgently in her ear, 'We've got to leave him! We ain't goin' to make it. They'll have that grille out and they could be close now.'

'Better not waste time a-talking then,' responded Bess quickly. 'We'll try the other way.'

And this time she led the way back down the passage to where they had chosen the right fork. Without waiting for Joe or Poundfield, she plunged into the blackness of the other sewer, oblivious now to the stinking water that washed around her legs, making her sodden clothes cling to her and filling her head with a dizzying stench.

'Get on! I can see 'em.' It was Joe's voice from behind, and looking back, Bess caught a glimpse of a lantern flashing somewhere back, down the narrow drain. She struggled on more quickly, scraping her hands against the rough brickwork, stumbling over unevennesses in the floor, sinking sometimes waist-deep into the sludge and dragging herself out. Once or twice she felt Poundfield's arm helping her. Sometimes she helped him past a spot where the passage grew narrow. The water they waded through was flowing towards them now, and all the time it was getting deeper.

'Water's the wrong way.' Bess stopped suddenly. 'What do we do?'

'It's the tide,' snapped Joe. 'It's comin' in. Keep movin'. Quicker.'

They came to another fork in the tunnel. Joe pushed past to the front, whispering urgently, 'This way!'

'It's not so deep the other way,' returned Bess, unwilling to follow him.

'We got to follow the tide.'

Bess knew it was pointless to argue. She had no idea which way to turn in this nightmarish underground world where the roof might fall at any moment and you were wading waist-deep in filth every step of the way. Poundfield said nothing. The way was harder for him than for either Joe or Bess, but he hadn't spoken since that face at the grille underneath his house.

Joe led the way along a side drain where the brickwork felt newer under his hands. Suddenly a faint light was filtering through from above.

'Light!' cried Bess, and as soon as she'd spoken she knew it was too loud. There was a shout from somewhere back down the sewer. If their pursuers had been uncertain which way to turn, they knew now.

'River Lane!' Joe's voice was a tight whisper more to himself than his companions. He gripped Bess's arm. 'I know this part.' Then his grip tightened. 'Hush now!' he hissed. 'They're on us.'

Down the narrow side drain from which they had just emerged came the sound of voices and clumsy steps, then the flashing of a lantern. Joe's mind sifted options rapidly. They could try to outrun them in the main sewer, but more than likely they wouldn't make it to the river, and if they did they'd be right on their tail when they got to the outfall. That was no good.

'In here!' Joe cut across the main sewer, half swimming in the rising water, and squeezed into the narrow opening of one of the side drains he'd been too scared to try when he was working this area for tosh. It was small, but just big enough even for Poundfield. They hid in the darkness as a group of seven or eight men waded past, too quick for Joe to be sure whether Jack or the Watchman was with them. Whoever the men were, they had missed them, at least for now.

'Have to go on this way,' muttered Joe, and he pressed on down the side drain with no idea where it led. The only hopeful sign was that there was a push of tide water coming in this way too, which meant it wasn't a stunt end, and there was a chance it reached the river by another route.

For perhaps ten minutes they battled on, with the passageway gradually narrowing around them. Progress grew slower and slower as Poundfield fought to get through, and Bess and Joe had to push and pull him along, and all the time the water in the tunnel was getting deeper. Joe had given up trying to guess how long it would be before the place was flooded altogether – another ten minutes, maybe a little more. It was up to his chest now and his head knocked the roof of the drain, which it shouldn't because that could bring on a fall at any moment. But he knew that Bess and Poundfield didn't have the experience to avoid the brickwork, so what was the point of him doing it? They weren't far underground – the rumble of traffic and even voices could be heard from the roadway above – but there were no gratings, no way upwards and no light, so they might as well have been buried in the deepest drain in London.

On they went. The water was at his chin. For the first time it crossed Joe's mind that he might have made a mistake. Should they have gone the other way up the main sewer away from the river? Or got out through the loose grating on River Lane and made a run for it above ground? He was so used to seeing the shores as a place of safety, he hadn't even considered that. He shook his head to dismiss the doubt. Doubting your judgements was a sure way to trouble down here.

It was Bess who felt the first rat.

'Something in the water!' Her voice was a rising cry of fear.

Joe felt one of the creatures' claws on his shoulder as it wriggled quickly past away from the rising tide. Another scrabbled up the side of his face and on up the drain the way they had come. Then he felt a quick, sharp pain on his ankle. A bite.

'Stay still!'

Joe's command barely registered in Bess's terrified mind.

'Rats!' she cried, shaking her head frantically from side to side as if to throw the vermin from her. 'It's rats! They're biting me!' Her voice rose into a scream.

She could feel Poundfield's hand gripping her arm. The man was trembling but he made no sound.

'They ain't biting. Not really! Back against the wall! Stay still!' It was a command again, but Joe laid a hand on her too. His other hand reached out for Poundfield.

The rats were coming faster now. He'd never been caught like this before, but he'd heard the stories and he knew it was only the beginning. The animals were escaping the rising tide and there was going to be a lot of them – hundreds probably. Their only chance was to do absolutely nothing. Keep still. Give them room to pass. That's what all the old toshers said. Question was: could Bess and Poundfield do it? Because if they struck at them or blocked the sharp-toothed creatures' way, the rats would eat through them. Nothing would stop a pack escaping the tide. They'd claw and bite through three people as quick as if they weren't even there. They'd be three more skeletons for the old toshers to yarn about in the gin shops.

Suddenly the main pack was on them, swarming over their heads, sharp little claws digging into skin, teeth nipping at exposed flesh, brushing past their faces as they swam by at eye-level, clawing and scrabbling over each other in their desperation to get away from the rising water.

'Still! Keep still!' Joe tried not even to move his mouth. The grip of his hands tightened on Bess and Poundfield, pressing them back against the wall of the narrow tunnel, willing them to stay where they were. If one of them stepped out into the path of the rats it would mean the end of all of them. The rodents would panic and attack. He felt a peculiar kind of helplessness he had never felt in the shores before. It was no longer just a matter of what he did. It was what they all did that counted. He didn't like the sensation.

Then, just as suddenly as they had come, the rats were gone, and Joe knew they were only minutes from drowning. Heads pressed hard against the roof, struggling and choking for every breath, they waded on against the current, forcing themselves painfully forward, using their arms as levers on the side of the

narrow tunnel. The water washed into their mouths, into their nostrils. The tunnel was flooded. There was no air, only filthy river water and hard brick.

And then they were out, bursting out with a spluttering cry into the widest and deepest sewer Joe had ever seen. They were swimming in deep water, but the roof was high above their heads and there was light, not from above but from a wide opening at the end of the tunnel. Four or five strong strokes and they were clambering, soaked and filthy, onto a low wooden jetty. They had reached the great stinking River Thames itself.

Chapter 20

HELL

Out on the river, boats large and small worked up and down the waterway. Steamers clattered past, belching smoke into the grey sky; long, black coal barges drifted by on the incoming tide, men leaning heavily on their oars. The mist lifted slowly and the opposite bank grew clear with its wharves and warehouses, its cranes and smoking chimney stacks. But for a long time Bess and Joe and Poundfield lay panting for breath on the rickety wooden landing stage, oblivious to their surroundings.

Behind them rose houses on tall, slime-crusted stilts, built right down to and over the water. A set of long wooden steps led up towards a bow-fronted house with a sign on the upper storey reading HARBOUR MASTER. Next door was a public house. The other way the houses were more ramshackle, leaning at odd angles to the river, propped up with wooden beams, looking as if they might collapse at any moment into the soot-black water that heaved and swirled below. A woman leaned out of an upstairs window, emptying a bucket of slops into the river. The three fugitives dragged themselves back into the shadows beneath the stilts of the harbourmaster's house.

Soaked through and filthy, Bess felt herself sink in and out of sleep as the morning wore on. Joe sat staring at the water, apparently unable to move. Finally the girl lifted herself on one arm, keeping her voice low, still wary of being overheard. 'Joe! We need to make a plan.'

'I ain't never bin down this far.' The boy didn't turn to look at her. Arms clamped tight around his knees, shivering constantly, he looked stunned by the sight of the broad river.

Bess craned forward. Away to the right she could see the wide arches of the bridge she had crossed with her mother and Harry Trencher. Across that bridge and a long day's walk south must lie Hartingham and home. But if they were still looking for her, they'd be watching the bridge; and even supposing she got across, there was still the same problem: how was she to find her way back to her father's house?

'Jack!'

Bess turned quickly, believing for a moment they had been discovered. But Joe was talking to himself. 'Joe, we've got to think of where to go next. I reckon—'

But Joe wasn't listening. His face was set hard and he muttered under his breath about 'snitches' and 'spies' as if he was alone. Bess sighed heavily: there was no help to be had from there. She looked sideways at the hunched and silent figure of Poundfield. Might he know the road south?

With the house burning and him shouting for his dead daughter at that upstairs window, there had been no doubt in Bess's mind that she should help the man. But now all the details of that strange and empty child's bedroom and the tomb in the garden came back to her. If she was going to put herself in his hands by asking for help, she wanted to know how Teresa Poundfield had died.

'I need to know about your daughter. About Teresa.' A shudder passed through the man's whole body, as if a terrible pain had travelled the length of his spine. Bess hurried on, her words tumbling over each other. 'We found her coffin in the garden, and we – and I want to know if – whether—' She took a deep breath. 'Was it you that . . . ?'

Suddenly the man's eyes met hers, steady and unblinking, and her words tailed off into silence. 'Yes,' he said. The voice was very quiet and distinct. 'It was I that killed her. I killed my own child, and I buried her with my own hands. She was younger than you.'

Poundfield's gaze never faltered. It was Bess who turned away, unable to meet that piercing, troubled eye. She caught the expression on Joe's face. It said, 'I told you so.'

And yes, it was a confession, but it didn't satisfy Bess. She pressed and probed for details, but the man wouldn't say any more about how his daughter had come to die by his hand. Finally she gave up.

'Do you know the road into Kent – Westerham way?'

'What?' It was Joe who spoke. 'You're going to trust him? A man what killed his own kin?'

Poundfield ignored him. He looked straight at Bess. 'I did once.' There was a short silence, then he added softly, 'You want to be seen on the road, Miss Elizabeth, or not?'

'Not,' said Bess, uncomfortable at the way he looked at her and the name he called her. There was something chilling about its teasing tone, coming from a man who had admitted to killing his ten-year-old child. But his eye was clear and focused in a way it had never been in the house.

'Then we'll wait a while.'

Poundfield lapsed into a brooding silence. Bess shivered as her wet clothes dried on her. She fingered the marks on her body where the rats had bitten her, and thought about her empty stomach. Joe shrugged and turned back to staring at the river and the wide, grey sky above. Boats came and went at the landing stage. They heard voices and the cries of the watermen out on the river, but no one saw them, hidden under the pilings of the harbourmaster's house.

Finally, as the afternoon began to fade, Poundfield stood up abruptly, towering over Bess and Joe. 'Well then, Joe Rat,' he rapped out, 'you showed us your version of hell. I will show you mine.'

And he was off, stalking with long strides across the unsteady wooden staging. Bess quickly got up to follow.

'You a-coming?' she asked, looking down at Joe.

The boy looked up. 'Where to?'

'My home,' said Bess. Then she added, 'I hope.'

'Might as well,' he grunted. 'Ain't got nowhere else to go.'

Joe and Bess followed Poundfield across landing stages that shook under their feet, up wooden stairways and along quiet back streets, avoiding the busy wharves of the riverside. Poundfield turned quickly this way and that without looking back. As far as Bess could tell, every step was taking them further from the bridge, but when she asked how they were going to cross the river, the man just lengthened his stride.

Joe walked mechanically without thinking about where they were going. The first sight of the wide river had frightened him and these unfamiliar streets frightened him too, but at least every step was taking him further away from Mother. He felt helpless in a way he had never done in the sewers and alleys of Pound's Field. He was following a runaway who didn't know where she was going and a madman who had murdered his own child. Maybe *he* was the mad one!

Half an hour through the gathering gloom and they reached a cobbled street, where groups of sailors in white bell-bottomed trousers wandered up and down, and a horse-drawn wagon lumbered towards the quayside loaded with an enormous mast. On the other side of the road stood an oddly shaped building with blackened walls and a pointed glass dome with half the panes missing. Around the end of the building they came to an arched entrance, where a broad set of steps started down into the ground. Poundfield led the way into the place he had called 'hell'.

There were gas lamps as the way grew darker, some of which worked. Furtive men in top hats and shabbily dressed women pushed past them on the seemingly endless stone steps. Voices and footsteps resounded strangely in the cavernous stairwell, so that the air was filled with whispers that seemed to come out of nowhere. A woman with a baby held close was suddenly at Bess's elbow – 'Spare us a penny, will yer! A copper for the infant's sake!' Her voice hissed and echoed from the towering walls. But before Bess could respond, the beggar was gone – a closer look at the filthy girl and her evil-smelling companions and she must have known there was nothing to be had from these three.

The place seemed to give Poundfield a kind of grim satisfaction, but it was hard to tell whether he was talking to them or to himself when he spoke. 'I was here when they opened the place. Speeches and flags and a marching band. And now look at it. This is what *people* do, Miss Elizabeth.' Suddenly his eyes were fixed on Bess and the viciously sarcastic tone was back in his voice. Then his eyes swivelled to Joe, and he finished with a sudden eruption of mirthless laughter, 'Stick to rats, Joe! Rats only bite when they're hungry or scared.'

Joe thought about Plucky Jack and Mother, and the Madman's words made a kind of sense. People *were* more dangerous than rats. Rats didn't make out like they were your friend and then turn on you. And they didn't kill their own children and bury them in a dog's grave. But rats wouldn't have got this man out of his burning house or led a way down into this strange place for that matter.

At the bottom of the stairs two giant horseshoe tunnels – each big enough for a carriage – led away into darkness. Without another word and without inviting them to follow, Poundfield set off down the left-hand one, with Bess and Joe breaking into a trot to keep up. Every few yards there were side passages linking the two main shafts, where shadowy figures lingered under the flickering gas lamps – stallholders with odd bits laid out for sale; a family huddled together, apparently asleep; gaudily dressed women accosting passing men. A glance at the dirty, stick-thin figure of Poundfield, striding stiffly down the centre of the tunnel, and no one approached him. One woman called out sharply as Bess passed, 'I'd keep away from 'im, dearie. You'll end up in the murder museum.' The words ended in a prolonged cackling laugh, joined by several other unseen voices.

Joe hardly noticed the people in the tunnel. It was the place itself that fascinated him. They must be right underneath the great River Thames itself, and the place was dry. Smelled a little damp maybe, and more than a little of horses, but underfoot was a paved roadway. Accustomed as he was to the crumbling underground world of the sewers, to Joe the place seemed like a miracle.

At the end of the long passageway they laboured up another set of the same endless steps and out into the chill of a winter's evening on the south bank of the river. Men were leaving the docks as the trio hurried past brightly lit shops and mean houses that wouldn't have looked out of place in Pound's Field. 'Never known it was so big!' muttered Joe, as the road led on and on past factories and gasworks and railway yards and streets and streets of houses.

Finally the gas lighting ended, the houses began to thin out and the night grew quiet around them. Poundfield led the way, a tall, silent figure stalking on into the darkness, while Joe peered uneasily around him, straining his eyes at the gloom. This was different from the darkness he knew. In Pound's Field the sewers could be pitch black, and there were pools of dark in the back alleys where the gaslight didn't reach and your eyes took time to adjust. But this was a different kind of darkness altogether – as if you were inside the vast, cavern-like drain that had spilled them out into the river, only here there were no walls and the cavern went on and on, stretching out to the very edge of the world.

Joe whirled round. But there was nothing to be seen behind him, any more than there was anything to be seen ahead or to left or to right. He stumbled on the rutted roadway, panting, feeling a rising panic like a burning sensation spreading up through his ankles and his knees and his legs, making it harder and harder to keep moving. Bess was yards in front now. Poundfield was only a dim outline in the dark ahead. And the dark had a rim of red at the edge of Joe's vision now, like the flames licking through the black smoke of the Madman's house.

And then suddenly the whole immense and endless cavern around him was flooded in a ghostly blue light that stretched to the horizon, and it was utterly empty – no horses, no people, no carts or wagons or warehouses. Nothing. No sound. Not a voice or a shout or a rumble of traffic. Just emptiness. Even the air smelled empty, as if there was nothing there at all, as if there was nothing to breathe. No one and nothing to see or to hear or to feel or to breathe.

Joe's eyeballs rolled back in his head and he opened his mouth to scream and no sound came out and he fell to the ground as if the bones in his body had dissolved.

* * *

Bess breathed deeply, feeling her head clear after the smoke of the city. The rain had stopped and a light, chill wind was blowing – easterly or south-easterly, she wasn't sure, but it smelled clean anyway. The night was dark, but not so dark you couldn't see the road. Then the clouds parted and she glanced up to see the moon almost at the full, shining down on a wide expanse of heath, the only landmark a single, ancient tree, shattered by lightning but still standing in the midst of the emptiness. Poundfield was well ahead, striding on, apparently tireless. She turned to check that Joe was keeping up. There was a dark, crumpled heap on the roadway fifty yards back. If it was Joe, he wasn't moving.

With a cry to Poundfield to stop, Bess ran back down the road. Joe was lying on his side. His eyes were open but he didn't move.

'Come on, Joe,' Bess urged him. 'We've got to keep up.' Poundfield was a dim figure, standing on the moonlit road.

'No!'

The single word escaped Joe's mouth, then it clamped tight shut again. His face was rigid. Bess tried to help him to his feet, but his arms and legs were stiff. He lay on his side, staring straight ahead, but he didn't seem to see anything.

Bess's hands were on his shoulders, shaking him. 'Come on, Joe!'

Joe lashed out, catching her a glancing blow on the cheek. She staggered backwards.

'Joe! Joe, what's the matter?'

The noise had brought Poundfield back to join them. Joe

lay still, his arms wrapped around himself. Every now and then a spasm would pass through his body, but his eyes were fixed and he didn't look up. Bess stood over him.

'What's the matter with him?' Bess turned to Poundfield. 'You done something to him?'

Poundfield looked at her. He looked at Joe. 'Never been out of the city. He's afraid.'

Without another word he swept the boy up into his arms and carried him to the side of the road. Bess made as if to stop him; then she remembered the night he had done the same for her, carrying her into his house, bathing her wounded ankle. His hands had been gentle, softer than her father's calloused hands, and yet this man had killed his own child. How could such a thing have happened?

As far as the eye could see there was no sign of shelter on the empty road. Poundfield carried Joe to the tree and laid him inside its hollow trunk. Bess scrambled in quickly, putting herself between Poundfield and the boy, her quick glance an instinctive warning to the man to keep away. Poundfield stepped back. He stood for a moment looking into the hollow of the tree. It was too dark for Bess to distinguish the expression on his face.

'It's all right,' she said quickly. 'I'll look after him now.' Poundfield shrugged and turned away.

The hollow of the tree was filled with dead leaves. They were damp, but less damp than the bare ground. Joe lay curled up, apparently already asleep, while Bess heaped the leaves around him like a nest. When she looked for Poundfield again, he was sitting on the tangle of exposed tree roots at the side of the road, head down between his knees, as motionless as the hollow trunk itself. She lay down next to Joe, listened to his steady breathing for a while, and fell asleep.

Joe woke much later, shifting his arm where Bess had fallen asleep against him. The moon was gone, but in the silence of the night a voice murmured gently, 'Tess . . . Tess . . . Tess . . .' No longer shouting, but soft as the wind soughing through the trees in his own garden, Poundfield repeated his dead daughter's name over and over.

Joe fell back into sleep, but as dawn approached his slumbers grew uneasy. He dreamed he was standing under a towering column of bricks, like one of the supports to the viaduct back in Pound's Field, only much higher, and the arches led away as far as the eye could see, getting smaller until they vanished in the distance. As he watched, line upon line of children, all in their Sunday-best clothes, came marching down the road. They stopped under the huge, vaulting arches, backs pressed up against the brickwork. There were faces Joe half recognized – Plucky Jack was there, and Billy, and several others, but their features were oddly mixed and distorted. And then one by one the children began to disappear, melting away into the bricks of the arch, leaving a line of small, black holes like the entrance to a tunnel. In the dream Joe watched, unable to move, and then suddenly he could feel the bricks soften under his own back and he was sinking, falling, melting into nothingness.

Chapter 21

BLOOD AND SWEETNESS

At the first glimmer of dawn they drank thirstily from little pools of rainwater that had gathered in the hollows among the tree roots. Then they set off again, the ache of hunger in their bellies exaggerated by the cold water. The weather had turned colder in the night, and a heavy mist lay across the ground. But as the light began to grow the mist thinned, and Joe eyed the wide open spaces of the countryside warily. He felt ashamed of what had happened last night, of his own fear and helplessness. He had made a fool of himself fainting like a— he would have said *like a girl*, only he'd never seen Bess act so weak and pathetic. He walked a few paces away from the other two, glaring at each in turn, waiting for Bess to say something about the previous night, but she kept her eyes on the road ahead. Anyway, he made up his mind: if the emptiness of the landscape still frightened him, which it did, he wasn't going to show it again.

At a farmhouse Joe produced the piece of silver chain he'd meant to hide in the Madman's garden, and they exchanged it for bread and milk. Joe knew the chain was silver. Even Mother wouldn't have valued it under two shillings. At the marine stores in Pound's Field he would have haggled until he got what it was worth. But here he felt powerless. Bess had no idea how to bargain, and Poundfield never opened his mouth. In the end the farmer's wife seemed to feel a pang of guilt at robbing such pathetic travellers so completely, and she gave Joe a single copper penny as well as the food and drink.

After breakfast they walked on southwards, leaving the city further behind, staying off the high road. As they crested the brow of a hill, weak winter sunshine lit up the landscape at their feet, casting long shadows across fields and woods. A thin column of smoke rose almost vertically into the still air far away amongst a stand of trees.

They rested for a moment at the top of the hill. Bess hadn't thought about her ankle all the previous day, but the long walk had produced a dull ache in the old wound from Poundfield's animal trap. Still, she was back now in the landscape she knew, the one where she had grown up, the one she had longed to return to. In a matter of hours she would see her father again.

But Bess felt none of the relief she had expected: she had begun to think about what she might find at home. She found herself rehearsing a first conversation with her father back in the low-ceilinged downstairs room in Hartingham. She was telling him about her mother and Harry Trencher; his head drooped; then he took her hand and told her how everything would be all right now it was just the two of them – father and daughter. She shook the fantasy away guiltily when she realized she was enjoying it.

She turned to watch the tall figure of Poundfield, breathing deeply at the clear air. Warmed by the trace of sunshine, his face seemed to have lost some of its deep lines. Even his eyes looked less sunken in his face. He had taken care of her in the house when she was hurt; he had guided them practically all the way back to her home; he'd picked Joe up last night as tenderly as any father. Could this man really have killed his own daughter? But if he hadn't, why did he say he had? She looked at Joe, as if for an answer. He was squatting at the side of the road with his boots off, kneading painfully at his feet. The open skies and the clear light made him look thinner, dirtier, even more stunted than he had in Pound's Field. Suddenly she realized Poundfield was talking to her.

'. . . come down this way many a time, though never on foot, and it's still a good three or four miles.' Bess looked at him blankly. 'Westerham, Miss Elizabeth. I'm saying you won't get there in daylight.'

'Oh.' She nodded her head. She had got used to the name he called her.

'And it's this side or the other you're making for?'

'This side.'

'What's the name of the place?'

'Hartingham.'

'Can't say I've ever heard of it and I know this country a bit. Or I did once . . .'

'Well' – she managed a little laugh – 'it's only a village, you know.'

'Thought you said it was a big place,' put in Joe.

'Oh,' said Bess evasively. 'Well, not big compared to London. Let's get on, shall we?' And she led the way down the hill to join the high road for the last stretch.

The light was fading as they turned off the high road towards Hartingham. Rounding a bend in the steep lane, Joe could see a church and a cluster of houses, each with its smoking chimney. Hartingham didn't look much of a place, but the big house halfway up the other side of the valley was more like it. He could already imagine the food they might produce in a house like that for a daughter come home – and maybe there'd be something for the boy who helped her a bit. Except maybe they wouldn't be so pleased to see her, seeing as how she'd run away and all. Maybe he'd better wait and see what kind of a welcome there was for Bess before he put himself forward.

But the gathering darkness was already stirring some of the terror of last night. With the trees around them he tried telling himself it was just a bigger version of the Madman's garden – not like that terrible open stretch where there was nothing between you and the horizon. All the same it'd be good to be inside four walls before the light went altogether.

'Looks like a palace, Bess.'

'What?'

'Your house.' Joe pointed across the valley. Bess smiled weakly. 'Bigger than your place, Poundfield,' he went on. 'You got servants and all, have you?'

Bess ignored the question. Across a field to their right was a line of low buildings which was the start of Kirby's farm. She peered ahead nervously. At any moment they might run into someone who knew exactly what kind of a house Bess Farleigh lived in. But the only creature on the lane was a small, mangy dog with a torn ear that came scrambling out of the ditch in front of them. It didn't bark. It stopped in the road and then came slowly forward, belly almost scraping in the dirt of the lane. Bess couldn't remember ever having seen it before. Joe picked up a handful of stones and threw one at the animal. It vanished instantly back into the ditch.

'You got a bedroom of your own, I reckon,' he went on, chucking another stone at the place where the dog had disappeared. 'How many rooms altogether then?'

Bess waved an exasperated hand, as if trying to swat away his questions. Instead of answering, she stopped in the lane and turned to Poundfield. She didn't want to go any further with her companions and her home was now just round the next bend, but there was still something bothering her.

'See, what I'm a-wondering,' she said, 'is you say as how you killed your Teresa. But it don't figure. You got her room all clean and tidy like she was still there. You got her dolls on the bed and a fire a-burning. And you yell out her name every night like you was trying to call her back from somewhere—'

'Call her back?' The voice was quiet, calm, regretful. 'You can't call her back, Miss Elizabeth.'

There was a long silence. Nightfall was almost upon them, and the trees, which nearly met over their heads, made this part of the lane darker. A quick rustling in the undergrowth and the harsh alarm call of a bird startled Joe, but Bess and Poundfield didn't seem to notice. The man let out a long, heavy sigh. Then he spoke again. 'I told you I killed her, and it's the truth, and it did me good to tell it. But I didn't kill her with my own hand.'

They stood in the gathering darkness as Poundfield unfolded his story, his voice slow and unwilling, as if memories were forcing their way out of him against his choosing. He had had three children – two boys and then a girl. He had not killed his daughter, but he felt to blame for the deaths of all his off-spring. There had been an outbreak of cholera in the capital one hot summer nearly thirty years ago. Back in those days, when St Saviour's Docks were new, the area around the house was quite different. People had started to move into the district and houses had started to go up, but there was none of the maze of courts and alleys that Joe knew so well, and the air was clean. So when he heard about the sickness away to the west in the city he didn't think it would reach them. Then people started to die.

'They said it was the smell that made folk sick,' Poundfield went on. 'But there was no smell in the air. Except for my factory – Bowman and Poundfield: that had a smell. Smell of blood. Blood in and sweetness out . . .' His voice faded for a moment; then the story continued.

His oldest son, George, had got it first. To begin with they thought it was just a mild fever. Poundfield had washed him with water from the well. People called it a holy well, came from all over to taste the spring that fed it. Then the boy couldn't keep food inside him, and then quite suddenly he was dead.

'And he wasn't even in the ground when young William caught it too. Those are his clothes you're wearing.'

Joe stammered something guiltily, as if he had been caught thieving. But Poundfield had already forgotten about the clothes, as he disappeared once more back into his memories

'My boys!' His voice was a soft, keening lament. 'My beautiful boys! Both dead within a week of each other. We should have left the place then. It was cursed with death. But my wife got sick too, and for a long time they thought she was going to die, and by the time she was better . . . Well, we stayed. There was business.' He spat the word out with disgust. 'And the smell from the river wasn't so bad for years after that. Only I vowed I'd never have children again. Never.'

Again he was silent. The woods and fields around them were silent. No one came or went on the lane. It was as if Poundfield's story had cast a spell across the whole countryside. Finally he went on again. His wife had got better. A couple of years had passed and they had a daughter. They called her Teresa. And then the sickness came again.

'As soon as I heard, we should have run. Come to a place like this maybe and hidden from the evil. But we didn't. We stayed. I filled the house with lavender from the markets. She never went outside, never breathed the foul air. But she caught it just the same. We had half the doctors in London there. Paid them a fortune. And she just lay in her bed while they took blood from her arm day in and day out, and she got weaker and weaker with their purgings and bleedings. And all the time she had this thirst, like a craving, and she wanted water from the spring. From the well, you know? She loved the well; used to spend hours playing with her dolls down amongst the ferns.

219

Only I wouldn't let her have it. Thought the water was cursed, you see. I'd always made her drink from the pump like everyone else. It was only afterwards they started saying it was water that carried the sickness.'

His voice had risen almost to a shout. He went on more quietly, 'The tips of her fingers turned a kind of blue. And her toes. It was beautiful really: face so pale and this blue under the fingernails. I couldn't let them take her, you see? Not my Tess. They would have done like they did with the boys – wrapped them in tarcloth, covered them with lime. It destroys the body. There'd have been nothing left. So I buried her myself. She liked the stone dogs and cats. The family buried their pets there back when there was no sugar and no Bowman and Poundfield. She liked it when the rhododendrons were in flower in the spring. Paper lanterns, she used to call them.'

Joe thought of the flowers in the bushes where he hid his tosh, of how they'd reminded him of the paper lanterns in the market, just as they had Tess Poundfield. For once it didn't set him thinking about his grey cloth bag.

Poundfield told the rest of his story quickly. Not long after, his wife had died too. It wasn't the cholera this time. 'Just tired of life, I reckon.' He stopped going to work, signed over his share of the factory to his partner, turned the servants away, tore the faces of his family out of every painting in the house, let the speculators build their filthy hovels all over the estate. He raised a high wall around what was left, and he never went out in the daylight, and pretty soon he never went out at all. When Joe and Bess came into his house that night, they were the first people to cross the threshold in nearly fifteen years.

'And the Watchman?' Joe's voice was suddenly insistent. 'You recognized him.'

'Who?' Poundfield's face was shadowed with night now. He sounded weary.

'The face at the grille. You said, "I know that man." He used to stand at the dock gates and he'd stare over at the house, and then he was there when they came to get us.'

But Poundfield wasn't looking at him. He was staring into the darkness. And then suddenly he was gone, as if he had dissolved into the surrounding night.

Chapter 22
HOME

Joe followed Bess down the hill in silence. Neither could bring themselves to say anything about Poundfield's terrible story, and Bess had nothing in her mind now except the image of her father. She stopped where the first row of cottages began.

'You'd better go back and find him.'

'What?'

'Mr Poundfield – he must still be about somewhere. You've got a better chance if you stick to him. See, my family may not be so glad to see me come back as all that, and so anyone that's with me, well he might not be that welcome, so' – the words were spilling out of her – 'so you'd better let me go by myself.'

She hurried on down the lane, and for a moment Joe was too surprised to move. He'd already imagined the hot food steaming and the fire burning and maybe a night by the fire, and he hadn't thought beyond that.

'Give them rat bites a good washin',' he called out after her. 'They can turn nasty if you're not accustomed.'

Bess didn't turn round. Joe looked about him. She was

right: Poundfield couldn't have gone far. But whatever she said, he wasn't about to go looking for him. Maybe he hadn't killed his daughter and maybe he didn't seem as crazy as he had back in London, but Joe didn't fancy the idea of meeting up with him again in the dark – not on his own.

He followed Bess's footsteps down the dark lane, hanging back out of sight. Instead of going on through the village and up the hill to the big house, she stopped in front of a doorway in the row of cottages. A narrow shaft of light came through the window shutters, and he could see her turning this way and that. At last she seemed to make up her mind, rapping sharply on the door with her knuckles. Almost at once it opened and a man was stooping in the doorway, peering out into the night. Joe couldn't see his face.

Bess's voice rang out loud and clear. 'I've come home, Father. It's me. Bess.'

Joe couldn't hear if the man spoke. He reached out an arm, folding it around the girl's shoulder, and drew her inside. Joe crept closer. The house was tiny and the thatch over the doorway was falling out in places. Through a crack in the shutter he could see firelight, and the sound of voices was faintly audible. Bess had found her home – not quite the grand place she had told him about in the Madman's garden – but home just the same. Standing in the darkness, Joe formed the word with soundless lips: 'Home.' Then he turned away into the night.

The room was the same as when she left – buckets by the front door, clothes drying on the wooden hoist in the ceiling, copper kettle on its hook, fruit baskets still stacked in the corner, even the same smell of carbolic and wood smoke. Somehow she had expected it to look different, just as she felt different. She waited for her father to say something, but he just stood looking at her, his eyes glistening. Bess had got so used to Poundfield's height that Reuben looked as if he had shrunk. She opened her mouth to speak, trying to remember some of the phrases she had rehearsed on the way: 'You're better off, Father . . . She deceived us both . . .' But before she could say anything another voice filled the room, the last voice Bess had expected ever to hear in that house again.

'Bess, my own dear one! You've come home to us. Thanks be to God!'

Coming down the stairs, arms wide in welcome, was her mother. Bess recoiled from her embrace, backing towards the door, and Jane switched instantly to a tone Bess was more familiar with. 'Now don't start acting about, my girl. You've given us all a deal of worry, you have, and now here you are looking like a tramp and stinking like the dover-house!'

'Now, Jane.' Her father's voice was the same as ever, gentle, conciliatory; but Bess interrupted him fiercely.

'Don't you talk to me like that, Mother. You ain't got no right. And *you* don't know.' She swung round to her father, who held out a hand towards her. 'She – she – she was a-running off with a man.'

Her father's expression didn't falter. 'Bessie, I knows all about it. Your mother has explained about—'

'About Harry Trencher?' demanded Bess. 'About how she

went a-meeting him behind hedges, and riding on carts with him and – and—' Even as she spoke, Bess knew it wasn't coming out right.

'I've confessed my fault.' It was her mother speaking. 'And Reuben, like a good Christian man, has forgiven me. Haven't you, Reuben?'

'Ay. That I have.' Reuben's eyes looked awkwardly to the ground, but when his wife put her arm around him and pressed herself against his side, his face glowed, and he held onto her dress with one hand. Bess couldn't remember seeing her parents like that for years – not since she was a little girl and they used to come and tuck her up in her cot, and she had felt safe in the shadow of their love. Now the sight outraged her. She thought of her mother with Harry Trencher and opened her mouth to speak, but Reuben went on steadily, 'Your mother has promised she'll have no more truck with – Mr Trencher, Bessie. And a promise is a promise. But she's had a deal of worry over you.'

Bess caught the note of reproof in his voice, and was angry at the tears that immediately started to her eyes. She turned to him, ready to defend herself, to tell him more about what had happened in London with Harry Trencher, how her own mother had smeared the horrible blusher on her face and people had laughed at her. But Reuben held up his hand before she could speak.

'Now your mother and I, we came to a decision about you, Bessie. You was to go into service. And then you gets to London and you go a-running off and getting yourself lost, and your mother—'

225

'Days and nights we – I – searched,' broke in Jane. 'Terrible places I went to. Why, I thought you might be dead. And what was you up to all that time, my girl? That's what I wants to know . . .'

But as soon as her mother joined in, Bess stopped listening. She stood dumbly in front of the miserable, smoking fire, feeling the cold in her bones as she hadn't all the long and weary road back to Hartingham, while her mother went on and on about the trouble and the worry she had caused. Bess looked at her father standing at his wife's side, still holding onto her dress, his eyes not quite meeting hers, like – why, he looked for all the world like a child holding onto its mother's apron.

The image shocked her. She had always seen strength in those mild eyes and that gentle voice; now she saw only weakness. For all his country labourer's frame, Reuben suddenly looked weaker even than the boy Joe, who earned his living searching the London sewers for scraps. Joe was afraid of the open countryside and he looked as if a decent autumn gale would blow him over, but Joe was stronger than this man. The thought frightened her, disgusted her even, but at the same time she felt an odd rush of tenderness towards her father. She turned away, struggling with contradictory feelings. It was only when Reuben changed the subject that she began to listen again.

'Now we'll say no more about it, Bessie. But your mother still says – and I agree with her, mind—'

Jane cut in impatiently. 'You're still to go into service in London, Bess. Only this time your father will come along with us, so as to make sure we don't – well, we don't run into no difficulties.'

Bess looked from Jane to Reuben, unable to believe what she was hearing. 'You still want this, Father?'

'Ay, I do.' Bess could hear the uncertainty in her father's voice even as he agreed, but he drew his wife to his side as if for support. 'Your mother thinks – I think you can be the saving of the family, Bessie, even after all that's happened. So you get a good rest now; get out of them clothes and wash yourself a bit maybe, and—'

'And we can be starting in the morning,' Jane interrupted. Reuben looked surprised, and his wife reached up to touch his cheek. 'Won't take long to scrub the dirt out of that dress and do it up nice again. Best to be done with the business, eh, Reuben?'

'Ay,' agreed Reuben. 'Probably best. We'll be a-starting for London in the morning. That's if you're agreeable, Bessie.'

Reuben looked at her, and Bess realized it was up to her to reassure him that he was doing the right thing. This man's voice and his hand and his mere presence had always been a reassurance to her, and now it was the other way around. 'Ay,' she said, taking a long breath and not looking at her mother: this was simply something she had to do for her father. 'If you want it, Father, then I'm agreeable.'

Chapter 23

ALBERT JACKSON

Joe felt his way through the darkness, creeping silently over damp grass, focusing on the darker patches close to him which were trees and bushes. He struggled not to think about the open spaces beyond, which stretched away so empty and so utterly without limit. He tried three doors in the long, low building before he found one that would open. He was guessing it was some kind of outhouse, not a building for people. But even the possibility of coming face to face with an angry stranger who might take him for a housebreaker couldn't persuade Joe to spend another night without a roof to keep out the vast, black sky.

Inside there was a musty smell – a mixture of old sacking and something like the swill the men used in the piggery in Pound's Field. Though he knew it was stupid, Joe still half expected to walk straight into the Madman – he still had trouble thinking of the man by his real name. But no light went on. No creature stirred. Joe edged cautiously into the utter darkness and pushed the door shut.

The smallness of the space made him feel better. Even in

this pitch blackness he could sense walls around him and he felt comfortable for the first time since the moon had shone out the previous night on the wide open spaces of Blackheath. He groped his way around the wooden walls. There were heavy sacks stacked in one area, and in the far corner his feet found straw scattered on the earthen floor. He gathered it together, fashioning a place to lie down.

Almost as soon as he had settled, there was a skittering and scurrying in the darkness that could have been mice or rats or both. The sound comforted him: he could have been back on the shakedown in his airless room in Holywell Court, where the vermin came scampering over your face some nights. He felt himself sinking comfortably towards sleep. Then there was another sound at the door – a faint whining and the sound of claws scratching at wood. The mongrel he'd chucked a stone at on the lane had come back.

Joe slipped out of the straw pile. He crossed silently to the door, eased up the latch and flung the door sharply open. The dog jumped back with a quick yelp as Joe felt quickly in his pocket for a stone. His fingers closed around the bread he'd saved from the morning. He hesitated, shifting his fingers between bread and stone. Then he broke off a scrap of bread and tossed it into the darkness. There was a quick scampering, and he caught a glimpse of the dog's white rump as it darted through the open door before Joe could shut it again. He cursed softly.

Joe settled back down amongst the straw. The dog stayed over by the door. Not that stupid, thought Joe with a little smirk. 'Don't want another stone comin' your way, do yer, boy?' he said aloud. Then he felt a fool for talking to the ragged creature and even more of a fool for giving it food. Never get rid of the thing now! But he didn't bother to try to chase the animal out again. He was too tired.

He closed his eyes and stretched out comfortably. The straw made a softer bed than any shakedown, but sleep was obviously going to be a problem. The sound of the rats scrabbling amongst the sacks might not bother him, but it seemed to drive the dog mad. Before long it was running this way and that in the darkness, yelping and whining and scratching at the door to get out and ignoring altogether Joe's 'Shut your racket!' He tried opening the door. 'Go on then, get out you little brute, if you don't like it!' But the dog didn't seem to know whether it wanted to be inside or out.

The boy gave up trying to get to sleep. There was more than the dog keeping him awake anyway. Bess had lied about Hartingham and her grand home: the tumbledown dump she'd disappeared into didn't look much better than Holywell Court. She'd been making out like she was quality and she wasn't any better than he was – worse if anything, because at least he came from the big city and she was nothing but Jenny Raw up from the country, just like Plucky Jack said. But what was really bothering Joe was why she hadn't let him inside the place, hadn't offered him a scrap of something to eat or a place to sleep. Rich or poor, it just didn't sit right for Bess to turn him away after the Madman had left them flat. There'd have to be a reason why she'd do a thing like that – something more than feeling bad about getting caught out in a lie about how big her house was.

Joe was used to figuring what people might do – people like Mother or Billy or Tyler – whether they'd rob him or beat him or give him food. He'd never seen much point in thinking about *why* they did it. But now, while the rain began to hammer down on the roof of the shed and the rats scurried about and the dog whined over by the door, Joe worried away at it, trying to understand what could have been going on in Bess's mind. He'd given her room on his shakedown; she'd shut him out in the rain. And yet last night she'd made him a place to sleep when he was too scared to get up off the road. Didn't make sense. Finally he gave up: thinking wasn't going to do it; he'd have to go and find out for himself.

Holding a piece of sacking over his head against the rain, Joe left his straw bed and started back across the sodden field towards the lane. The rain was in his eyes, blurring the dark line of the hedgerow, and almost at once he wasn't sure if he was looking at the hedge that ran beside the lane or another one. He tripped on a tussock of grass and fell heavily, cursing himself for an idiot. What was he doing stumbling about in the middle of the night in this awful place, worrying about someone who couldn't have cared less about him? He could feel the panic of last night rising inside him as he turned first left then right, uncertain which direction to take. He was moving quickly now, hands outstretched in front, staggering blindly through the dark and the rain when the shadows in front of him moved.

A huge shape reared up directly in his path, making the ground shudder and letting out a great, bellowing snort. Joe cried out, holding up both hands to defend himself. His fingers touched warmth, and a sharp animal smell reached his nostrils. Whatever the vast, black creature was, it seemed even more alarmed than Joe. It headed off, stamping and snorting across the field. Joe dashed the rain from his eyes. In spite of the shock it had given him, the warmth of the creature's body and its smell had returned him at least partly to his senses. With no idea of which way to turn, he decided to follow it. A dozen steps took him to the edge of the field.

Joe crawled through the hedgerow and found himself standing shakily in the lane. He waited while his breathing steadied and the thudding of his heart subsided; then he turned down the hill towards the row of cottages. A glimpse of white in the darkness showed the dog had followed him every step without his even knowing it. Matching its pace to Joe's, the animal kept back just out of stone-throwing range.

Bess's house was silent, but a faint light still came from the glassless downstairs window. Joe pressed an eye to the crack in the shutter. He could see a pair of large feet sticking out from under a blanket on the floor in front of the fire. Shifting position slightly, he made out a man's face. It wasn't a face Joe knew, but he assumed it was the man who had greeted Bess at the door – the man she had called 'Father'. He craned his neck sideways. Lying under the blanket with the man, fast asleep, her head cradled in his arm, was a woman, her hair hanging loose about her face. Joe looked again, not believing his own eyes. It was the woman who had chased Bess through Pound's Field, the woman he'd seen at Mother's Court, the woman she'd called her aunt.

Joe backed away from the house into the middle of the lane, looking up at the house. There was something terribly wrong here. This wasn't the safe place Bess had been hoping to find. Did she know that? Was that the reason she hadn't wanted him inside?

There was another window in the upper storey not far over his head. A man on horseback could have looked straight into it. There'd been no sign of Bess in the downstairs room, so if she was still in the house, she must be there. He squinted up at the thatch of the roof and the crooked timbers that supported the entrance to the house, none too sure they would hold his weight.

'Bess!'

Joe dared not raise his voice. The only hope was that she was awake upstairs and might hear him while the sleepers downstairs didn't. No movement or sound came from the house. He tried again a little louder, his voice a hoarse whisper.

'Bess!'

Still no answer. He was going to have to climb up there after all. One foot braced against a doorpost and the other feeling for a hold in the rough stonework of the cottage wall, Joe had just got himself off the ground when a big hand suddenly clamped tight across his mouth. An arm around his waist lifted him bodily and marched him kicking and struggling away from the house back up the dark lane. Joe lashed out with his feet, but found only thin air. He bit at the hand, but his teeth could get no purchase. He wrestled and struggled to be free, but the immensely strong arm held him firmly. Finally he found himself set down on the lane in the shelter of the trees where Poundfield had told his story.

'What—? Who—?' he stammered, incoherent with rage.

'Must be close to two a. m., Joe. Who else would it be?'

Joe stared up at the figure of the man, unable to believe what he heard, searching for the horribly familiar features. It was too dark to see the pock-marked face, but the soft, flat voice was familiar from a hundred cold mornings.

'Watchman!' he breathed.

'Tracked you all the way from the river, boy.' The Watchman's level tone never altered.

Joe remembered the last time he'd seen the man, peering down through iron bars into the underground river while Poundfield's house burned above him. 'Come to finish the job, have yer?'

'Think you know Charley Watchman's job, do you, Joe?' There was an unfamiliar trace of irony in his voice – even humour. Then he was all seriousness again. 'I lost track of him.'

'Lost track of who?'

'Mr Poundfield. Where did he say he was going? Back home, was it? Or maybe on to the coast.' There was urgency in the voice now, usually so calm and matter-of-fact.

'He never said. He just went. And he ain't got no money, Watchman, so you leave 'im alone. He knew who you were, didn't he? Knew you was after him.'

'I'm not *after* him.'

'You just said you was. Tracked us from the river, you said. I ain't got no money neither, Watchman. You after my tosh, intcha? I seen you staring at the house. And I seen you come to burn us out too. You was leadin' the whole pack of 'em. Don't say you wasn't.'

'Joe' – The man's voice was soft and calm again – 'I'm not interested in your tosh and I don't mean you or Mr Poundfield any harm. But I need to know where he's gone. Now, do you know?'

'Wouldn't tell yer if I did,' snapped Joe. 'He treated me decent even if he is mad. And he never killed his daughter neither.'

'I know he didn't, Joe.'

'What d'you know about it?'

The man let out a sigh. Then he went on slowly, unwillingly, as if he was saying more than he wanted. 'I was manager on the estate, Joe. Back in old Mr Poundfield's day. Made the old gentleman a promise I'd look after his son, Henry, though he wasn't much younger than me. I reckon I kept my promise too. Albert Jackson's my name. Or it was. Nobody calls me that any more. Now it's just Charley Watchman.'

'He got rid of all the servants,' interrupted Joe, keeping a clear distance between himself and those powerful arms.

'He told you that, did he?' asked Jackson, surprised. 'Yes, he turned us all away. Only I'd made a promise, see? So I hung around. Took the watchman job and a room as near the old house as I could. You know about that, though, don't you?' But the reference to Holywell Court made Joe instantly suspicious again.

'How come you're still hanging around then?' he demanded. 'I still say there's money in it somewhere.'

'Tosh, eh?' asked Jackson sarcastically. 'No, Joe, there's no money involved. There's a promise,' he said simply. 'That's all. Now do you know where he is?'

It sounded a thin story to Joe, and it revived all his ideas about Poundfield having treasure hidden away somewhere. If the Watchman, or Jackson, as he called himself, really had worked for him, he'd know about it. That must be why he'd stuck around Pound's Field when his master went mad. That must be why he was looking for him now. Well, he wasn't going to get any help from Joe. Poundfield had treated him and Bess proper. She'd been right about that much. It wouldn't be Joe that snitched on him.

'No, Watchman, I don't know where he is,' said Joe finally, 'and if I did I wouldn't tell you.' He took a step backwards. 'Now, I'm going back down the lane and I got something to tell Bess, and you'd better not try nothing,' he finished, trying to pick his moment to make a dash for it.

'You leave her with her family, Joe. They'll take care of your Bess.'

'She ain't *my* Bess,' snapped Joe. 'And they ain't her family neither. Leastways that may be her father, but her mother's dead, and there's a woman who could be her aunt or her stepmother, I ain't sure which, but I'm good and sure she's a wrong 'un.'

Albert Jackson suddenly laughed out loud, a hearty guffaw that was startlingly loud in the night. 'Poor old Joe,' he said, 'you are in a muddle, aren't you? You stick to your tosh and leave well alone, my boy. That's my advice. That's her mother and father – her real mother and father, mind,' he added with emphasis. 'I've asked a few questions and heard a good deal of talk, and Albert Jackson knows what's what. They'll do what's best for their child, and there ain't nothing in it for you, Joe Rat. But you help me find Henry Poundfield, and there just might be.'

It was partly the 'Joe Rat' that did it, and it was partly the way the Watchman assumed he was only interested in Bess if there was 'something in it'. Taking a run-up in the darkness Joe swung out with his foot, aiming to catch the man behind the knee. But Joe wasn't a fighter. He missed with his kick and the Watchman reached out a strong arm and had him in a firm grip before he could take another step. Once again Joe was struggling feebly in his powerful grasp, when there was a yapping on the dark lane and a small whitish shape leaped out of the night and fastened its teeth into Albert Jackson's right ankle.

'Get out of it!'

The man lashed out, sending the dog crashing across the road and clear into the ditch, but for an instant his grip on Joe had loosened. It was enough. Twisting quickly in the Watchman's grasp, Joe was crouching in the darkness of the ditch, the dog panting alongside him, before the man could get hold of him again. He heard Jackson cursing. Then there was silence for a moment, before the man spoke softly, as if to himself. 'I've got no more time for this.' He raised his voice slightly. 'You get yourself back to Pound's Field, where you belong, Joe Rat. Make your peace with Mother, and don't go meddling where it doesn't concern you.' And with that he was gone.

The sound of the rain soon covered the Watchman's footsteps, heading back up the lane towards the high road. But Joe waited silent and shivering in the ditch long after he was gone, as the rain fell steadily and the night dragged on through the early hours towards morning.

Chapter 24

A FACE AT THE WINDOW

Bess lay awake a long time alone in the upstairs room, listening to soft voices from below. 'Be nice to be back in your own little bed,' her father had said, as he sent her upstairs. 'Up the wooden hill, Bessie.' But his familiar words hadn't put the old spell of comfort on her – they sounded forced and artificial, as if she was listening to a man who was pretending to be her father. And then there was her mother's *Thanks be to God!* and *I've confessed my fault* . . . The words all rang hollow in Bess's ears. She hadn't felt like these two people's daughter come home; she'd felt like an outsider in the low-ceilinged room downstairs.

She shifted uncomfortably in the cot, wondering if she'd somehow grown taller in the short time she'd been away from the house. Images of the flight through the sewers flashed through her mind – the place where the roof had fallen, the filthy water rising and rising until there were only inches to spare, the rats scratching and biting as they clambered over her. Her fingers felt for the places on her neck and arms where the rats had bitten her. She had washed them the way Joe had said,

239

fetched a bucket from the well in the darkness and scrubbed herself all over with the strong soap they used for the laundry until her skin was raw. But the smell still clung to her. Her mother had used the same water to wash the dress. 'I'll just sit up now and do some mendin' here,' she had said. 'You'll sit with me, Reuben? Soon have you lookin' like the Fair Maid of Kent again, Bess.'

And her father had laughed, and so Bess had felt she had to laugh too, and for a moment she had hated him; hated him for the weakness she saw in everything he said and did now, and for no longer being the man she'd always thought he was.

She sat up on the edge of the cot, pulling a blanket over her shoulders and shivering. She could hear the rain outside. She didn't want to think about her father and her mother any more, and she didn't want to think about the trip back to London tomorrow. She thought about Joe somewhere out in the wet night. She had just left him standing in the lane. She hadn't planned to, but when the moment came she just couldn't take him to the house. Yes, it was partly to do with the stupid lies she had told him about her family and the big house in Hartingham. But it was more to do with everything that had happened in the last weeks – her mother and Harry Trencher and the days and nights in Pound's Field. Bringing Joe into her home would have been like bringing all that back and throwing it on the flagstones in front of her father. She hadn't wanted to do that. She'd wanted to forget what had happened. Her mother would be gone and she and her father would live together as if they'd never heard of Harry Trencher or White

Street and he had never married the beauty of Hartingham. And then she had been there! And he'd forgiven her! Like nothing had happened!

But Bess couldn't forgive. She hadn't forgotten her mother's shoulder rubbing against Harry Trencher's as they drove through the streets of London, or the people looking up at her in the wagon as her own mother put that filthy stuff on her face; and then all her father could say was how she'd been a worry to her mother and—

A sound interrupted Bess's fevered thoughts. A bird on the roof or a mouse in the thatch maybe. There were no voices from downstairs now: inside the house all was silent. But there it was again. A tapping. Someone or something was tapping at the window.

She hurried across the room and pushed open the casement. Joe was whispering urgently before she'd got the stiff window fully open.

'. . . she's downstairs with him, Bess. And if she's there then that fella with the stick ain't far away, I reckon. Now the best thing for you is to make a run for it with me. We can—'

Bess stopped him. 'You'd better come inside, Joe.'

But Joe didn't want to come in. 'I ain't comin' in. There's too many men with strong arms around here for my likin'. I'm off out of it. But you needs to come with me. It ain't safe for you here.'

Suddenly Bess was angry. 'I don't need you a-telling me what to do, boy. You reckon as how you been looking after me, don't you?'

Joe was struck dumb. This wasn't what he'd expected at all.

'Yes, well you haven't,' she went on. 'I don't need you to take care of me, all right? I can look after myself, and I'm a-going to look after my family too.'

'What family?' demanded Joe. 'The one what lives up in the big house or the two sleepin' on the hard floor in this broken-down old gaff?'

Bess took a breath. The slur on her home and her father, even on her mother, stung, but she knew she owed the boy an explanation.

'All right, I'll tell you then,' she whispered angrily. 'Come inside, and keep your voice down for heaven's sake.'

Joe climbed silently through the window, leaving puddles of water on the floorboards. He sat next to her on the cot, and they spoke in whispers, so as not to wake the sleepers downstairs. Bess told him about Reuben losing his job and Jane taking in washing. She told him about the trip to the hiring fair on White Street and how she had run from her mother and Harry Trencher.

'So you ain't got no wicked stepmother?'

'I think I read that in a storybook.'

'Oh, right,' said Joe bitterly, 'and I can't read so all I can manage is the truth. Better off without no schoolin' then, ain't I?'

'Joe, it's nothing to do with—'

'And you don't need me to look after you, is it? Like you didn't need me when we was under in the shores and the rats was all over you, eh?'

Bess tried uneasily to quieten him. She was trying to apologize, but Joe was talking too loudly now and she knew how easily voices carried in this house. Perhaps the best thing was just to get rid of him as quickly as possible. 'I'm a-doing what I think is right, Joe. That's about the size of it. I don't need you to make my mind up for me.'

'So you're goin' to this hirin' place after all?'

'If my father says I must.'

'Well, I don't know much about what goes on there. Ain't never had no call to go as far as White Street. How come you got to dress up like that?'

'Like what?' Bess knew exactly what he meant. It was a question she hadn't wanted to ask herself.

'All that stuff on yer face. And all – low at the front.' Joe made an embarrassed gesture in the general direction of Bess's chest.

'Girls all wear them like that in London,' said Bess quickly.

'Says who?' It had been her mother, but Bess didn't want to say that. When she didn't answer, Joe went on, 'Only girls I seen lookin' like that was a sight older than you. And they was hangin' round the gin shops – sellin' theirselves,' he added awkwardly, not looking directly at her. 'You know what I mean?'

Again, Bess knew exactly what he meant. 'You mean a-selling their bodies for money,' she said bluntly. 'Well, my father wouldn't ask me to do anything like that. He wouldn't never make me do something that wasn't right.' Instinctively she remembered only the old Reuben, not the man downstairs who had held onto his wife's dress. 'You wouldn't know anything about that, would you?'

The words froze on Joe's lips. She didn't need his help, and now she was reminding him she had a mother and a father and he didn't. Pretty soon she'd be calling him Joe Rat and a stinking tosher. Well, serve him right. *Look out for yourself and let others look out for themselves*: that's what Mother said and she was right. And maybe he was better off with the old monster than with a real mother and father if this stupid girl was anything to go by.

'Good luck to you then,' he hissed. 'Just don't come runnin' down my court when they're after you next time.' And he was gone before Bess could think of another word to say.

Joe strode quickly up the lane towards the high road with the dog pattering at his heels, but where he had branched off into the field the night before and found the outhouse, he stopped. 'Bottle-headed baggage,' he muttered. The dog stopped too. 'Some people ain't got the sense of an animal, have they, you flea-bitten mutt?' The dog took a wary step closer. 'What you followin' me around for anyway?' he snarled, and before the dog could jump out of the way he hit it square behind the ear with a stone. 'Serves you right,' called Joe. 'I don't want you around me, you hear?'

The animal scuttled out of sight, but Joe sensed it was still there watching him. He cursed. Part of him wanted to go on up to the high road and start back the way he'd come right this minute, back to the places he knew. But there was the Watchman, Albert Jackson, to think about. He could still be around. The Madman could still be around too. And what would he do if he did get back to Pound's Field? *Make your peace with Mother*, the Watchman had said. But Joe had already decided he was never going back to his old life.

In the end he picked his way over the wet field back to the outhouse, aiming a half-hearted kick at the dog's ribs as it dodged through the door in front of him. He settled back amongst the straw, keeping his boots on. At least he was out of the rain here, and he could be on the road at first light and not bother with Bess Farleigh again. She didn't need his help? All right, maybe she didn't. She could make up her own mind to go to hell if she felt like it, and it wasn't any of his affair if she did.

There was a scurrying and squeaking, and he felt a couple of rats run right past him towards the door. Joe heard the dog scamper out of their way. He swung out an arm blindly but missed it. 'And you ain't nothing but a coward, you lousy mongrel!' he muttered, settling down again to try to sleep the rest of the night away.

For maybe ten minutes it was just like earlier in the night with the dog running backwards and forwards, obviously terrified of the rats. Then quite suddenly the mongrel stopped its whining and scampering, and there was a short bark and a squeak in the darkness. And silence. Then another skittering of clawed feet and another short bark and a squeak. And silence.

'Got a couple then, did yer?' muttered Joe, sinking into sleep. 'Good for you, boy.' The rain still fell on the roof, but inside the outhouse all was quiet.

Chapter 25

THE ROAD NORTH

It was still dark when Joe woke, but not quite the total blackness of night. He could make out the heavy rafters that supported the roof and the line of the door where the grey light of dawn filtered through. He got up stiffly. His feet were sore from the long walk and there was an ache in his bones that he put down to the soaking he'd had the night before: the rain of the countryside seemed different from the water of the London sewers – wetter, colder. He pushed open the door and the dog scuttled through, disappearing into the grass. On the floor where it had been lying lay the partly chewed bodies of two rats.

Joe squinted up at the sky which was gradually lightening over the treetops. The air was chill and heavy with the wetness of the night and a mist lay across the fields, but at least it wasn't raining. Through the mist he could see a house just beyond the trees and a smudge of white smoke rising from its chimney. The low building he'd spent the night in was obviously something to do with the house, and the smoke meant they were awake. It was better to leave before someone came checking.

Ignoring the track that ran down to the house, Joe picked his way through the wet grass back towards the hedgerow. A dozen or so of the big black beasts he had run into in the night stood peacefully in the morning mist, cropping the wet grass. Of course, they were cows. Joe gave a tight little laugh at his own stupidity. It wasn't as if he'd never seen one before: there were dairymen in London, weren't they? He crawled through a gap and out onto the lane.

At the bottom of the hill most of the village was hidden in the low-lying mist, but on the other side of the valley smoke rose from the chimneys of the big house – the one Bess didn't live in. They were early risers round here, but there was no one about yet. He could be away without being spotted if he left now.

A distant barking started up somewhere in the mist, and Joe looked around instinctively for the mongrel with the torn ear. He hadn't been too sure just what had happened in the lane last night, but it seemed like the dog had given the Watchman or Jackson or whatever his name was a decent nip. For that and finishing off a couple of rats he might have given it another scrap of yesterday's bread, especially after he'd gone and chucked a stone at it when he'd really been wanting to chuck one at Bess. But there was no sign of the animal now, so Joe finished what was in his pocket and walked slowly down the lane towards Bess's cottage.

He'd meant to go the other way. When he realized he was walking away from the high road, he stopped and kicked angrily at the rough surface of the lane. But he didn't turn round. Might as well see if the bottle-head really was going back to London.

He was still fifty yards from the first cottage in the row when something moved at the side of the road in the dim early morning light. As if a part of the mist itself had spread wings and taken flight, a great white shape rose into the air, beating heavy wings, coming straight up the lane towards him. Joe threw himself headfirst into the ditch under the hedge, twisting to watch the strange creature pass low over his head. It was a bird of some kind, but it hardly looked real – like one of the Madman's stuffed animals.

Joe shuddered at the apparition. Even in the daylight the place made him long for the familiarity of the soot-crusted walls of Pound's Field. Then the door of Bess's cottage creaked open, and a man came through the door, stooping under the low thatch and putting on an old bowler hat. It was Bess's father – Reuben, she'd called him. If it hadn't been for the bird scaring him like that, he'd have walked right into him.

The man set off down the lane and was soon out of sight. For a quarter of an hour nothing happened except that the mist thinned a little and the day grew a shade lighter. Joe was just getting ready for a quick dash down the lane to take a look through Bess's window, when he heard the heavy tread of a horse and Reuben reappeared out of the mist, coming up the lane with a cart. Immediately the cottage door opened and two female figures hurried out, looking right and left as if they didn't want to be spotted.

They were out of luck. Almost as soon as they were on the

cart, a couple came out of the house next door. Joe could hear raised voices but he couldn't tell what was being said. As if from nowhere, five or six children had gathered as well now, cheering and waving their arms. The horse shied nervously and the man shouted something, which only provoked another ironic cheer. Then they were off, the slow-footed nag pulling more strongly up the hill than Joe had expected for such a poor-looking beast.

As they passed his hiding place, Joe saw Bess perched in the back of the cart. She was all dressed up again with red ribbons all over the place, and her cheeks smeared the same unnaturally bright red as the first time he'd seen her in the alleys of Pound's Field. The rest of her face looked startlingly pale by contrast in the early morning light. Once again Joe was halfway out of the ditch, determined to do something. Then he thought of what she'd said the night before: *I don't need you to take care of me. I can look after myself, and I'm a-going to look after my family too.* She'd made up her mind to do what she was doing, and no one was going to stop her – just like when she made up her mind to go into the room at the top of the Madman's house. There was no stopping her then and there was no stopping her now. He let himself slide back into the ditch.

The couple from next door walked a few yards up the road after the cart, and the boys ran past hollering and throwing stones. Joe waited until they had all disappeared, then he climbed out of the ditch and started up the lane after the cart. If they were heading back to his part of the world, then at least they could show him the way. He had gone perhaps twenty yards when there was a commotion at the side of the road and the dog stuck its head out of the hedge. Joe didn't pause in his stride, but as he went on up the lane he could hear its paws on the lane behind him.

Joe plodded northwards, retracing, as far as he could remember it, the route he had followed with Bess and Poundfield. He half expected to see the Madman on the road, but there was no sign of him. Joe wondered what had become of the man after he walked away into the night on the dark lane outside Hartingham. The Watchman had asked if he'd headed for the coast. Maybe he had, but Joe had no idea what direction that was or how far away.

For a time he managed to keep the horse and cart in sight, but it moved too fast for him, especially with his feet sore from all the walking of the previous day. Without William Poundfield's boots he could never have made the journey at all. There were more people on the road today – market day somewhere about maybe. The dog stuck close, yapping nervously when a horse's hoof or a cart wheel came too near, jumping sideways to avoid the occasional kick aimed by a heavy boot.

Joe reached a crossroads he didn't remember. He eyed the writing on the signpost doubtfully and took a guess – straight on. If he was on the right road and the cart stopped at some point, he still might have a chance of catching up to them. Hurrying down the hill towards another village, he looked anxiously ahead. There was a horse and cart drawn up outside the inn just across the stream, but even at a distance he knew it wasn't the right one.

Joe stopped on the road and closed his eyes for moment. A

profound exhaustion passed through his whole body. He leaned back against the stone parapet of the bridge and let himself sink slowly down at the side of the rutted roadway. There was no sense in hurrying any more: there were miles more of this wearisome, empty countryside yet, and he wasn't even sure he was on the right road. It had been ridiculous to think he could keep up with the cart, and now he might wander round all day on these wretched lanes and be faced with another night in the open. He kicked off his boots and for a long time he was still. The dog lay down on the roadway too, tongue hanging out, watching him.

Gradually a familiar sound seeped in around the edges of Joe's consciousness and he dragged himself upright. Climbing up onto the parapet of the bridge, he found himself peering down into swiftly running water. Swollen by the night's rain, the little river swirled darkly around the bridge's stone supports, twisting and eddying and gurgling. Deep beneath the surface Joe could see his own reflection, silhouetted against the clouded sky.

Joe climbed over the parapet and settled himself precariously on a narrow ledge, feet hanging. Just under the surface a long, green length of streamer weed lashed from side to side with the current. Unconsciously the boy swayed back and forth in time to the movement. Like the spring and the water under Poundfield's house the river below him had no smell.

His mind wandered far away to Pound's Field and Mother and Plucky Jack. He was trying to get back there and he no longer knew why. There was nothing for him to go back to.

Mother would be out for his blood, the nearest thing he'd ever had to a friend had turned out to be her spy, and the girl – Bess – she'd made up her mind on this White Street place and she didn't want him around her.

A gust of wind whipped the surface of the water at his feet and suddenly his balance was gone. The old stonework was crumbly under his hands, and even as he scrabbled for a grip, he wasn't sure why he bothered. If Mother got him, she'd probably have him chucked in the dirty old Thames with an anchor round his legs. This way, when they dragged him out at least he'd come out clean, and he wouldn't have to hear anyone call him a filthy tosher ever again. Then, above the sound of the rushing water and his own chaotic thoughts, there was a shouting voice, a voice he knew from somewhere, and the moment was past. His scrabbling fingers, so used to finding holds in the brickwork of the London sewers, found purchase on the crumbling stone of the bridge, and he scrambled back over the parapet and onto the road.

Outside the inn a man in a stovepipe hat was waving a stick above his head and shouting at another man in a waistcoat and apron. Joe caught something about 'the reckoning' and 'watered beer'. It was the kind of row you heard every hour of the day in Pound's Field, but in this quiet, neat little village it sounded odd. The voice was a London voice too, and suddenly Joe knew where he had heard it before – shouting on the stairs at 16 Holywell Court with Billy and Greasy Tyler, plotting in Mother's over-heated parlour.

The man turned on his heel and strode unsteadily out onto

the road. The landlord took a step after him, shouting at the top of his lungs, 'You owe me money, Harry!'

The man in the stovepipe hat turned quickly, laughing. 'Soon 'ave plenty of money, I will,' he shouted back. 'But blow me tight if you see a penny of it, you barrikin' yokel!'

The face left no doubt at all. This was the man Bess had been running from on Sweetwater Lane. This was Harry Trencher. Or was he her uncle? Perhaps neither story was true. But this man was real and he meant Bess Farleigh no good – that much was certain. And even if she had said she could look after herself and she didn't need his help and whatever she'd said, she had come back for him on that dreadful open road under the full moon and she'd fallen asleep with her arm around him in the hollow tree, and he wasn't going to forget about her just yet a while. He wasn't going into any river, clean or filthy. He was going after this man and he was going to find out just how he planned to get all that money he'd boasted about to the landlord. Something else was certain too: Harry Trencher knew the way back to the big city. It wasn't yet past noon and if Joe followed him he wouldn't have to spend another night in these empty fields.

As the houses grew thicker, the air seemed to thicken too, turning the thin country mist into a freezing, choking blanket of fog, which caught in the throat and set the passers-by coughing. Joe breathed it in with relief. He was tired, but even his feet seemed to hurt less now that the wide open spaces of the countryside were behind him. He kept closer to Harry

Trencher, though it seemed as if he could have walked right alongside him, because the man clearly had no idea he was being followed. Why should he? He'd seen Joe once only for maybe a second in Mother's Court.

On the other hand, for some miles now Joe had had the feeling that there was someone else on the road following him. The dog was still there, of course – seemed like there was no getting rid of the little brute. One scrap of bread and the creature thought he was its best friend! But there was another figure that Joe glimpsed every now and then, hanging back at a bend in the road or fading suddenly into the mist. Now the fog had come down it was impossible to make out any face clearly, but it was a tall man. Could be the Watchman. Could be Poundfield. Now that he was back on his own, Joe wasn't about to trust either of them. If he'd had the time he'd have sneaked down a couple of side alleys and lost him easy enough in the fog. Even here, where he didn't know his way about, he could have done it. But that would have meant losing Harry Trencher and Joe wasn't about to risk that. Somewhere inside he was certain that Trencher would lead him to Bess and just maybe she might turn out to need his help after all.

They crossed London Bridge, and to Joe's relief Trencher skirted Pound's Field. He cut north through narrow, darkening streets where the fog was so thick you could hardly see your feet on the cobblestones, and dirt and rubbish were piled up so high you had to climb over it. Trencher never hesitated. He seemed to know these miserable, stinking courts and alleys as well as Joe knew Pound's Field.

Finally he disappeared into a five-storey house with a rough sign painted on the door. Joe didn't need to be able to read it: the building was obviously a lodging house, and a cheap one at that. On the ground floor there wasn't a single pane of glass in the windows. Screwed-up rags and newspaper filled the gaps. There was even an old hat stuffed into one frame. He waited a few minutes but Trencher didn't come out again. Joe crossed the road: the first thing he had noticed on the street was a cookshop.

A tall boy was standing at the door as Joe approached. 'What you want, stinker?'

'Pie maybe. Cuppa tea.'

'This ain't no charity,' snarled the boy. 'No grease, no grub. That's our motto.'

'I got money,' insisted Joe, producing the penny the farmer's wife had given him the day before. He ducked under the boy's arm and into the shop. A dozen or more people sat at rough wooden tables, hands wrapped around hot mugs of tea or coffee.

'Watch him, chief,' called out the boy at the door. 'Little mudlark on the lift.'

'Ain't no mudlark,' snapped Joe. 'And I got money.'

Behind the counter a red-faced man in a bowler hat was ladling out steaming broth for a customer. 'What's your pleasure then, young master?' he mocked. Some of his customers laughed.

Joe eyed the trays of pies. He caught the scent of the broth. One sniff and he knew there was no point in asking the price:

there was meat in it, and you couldn't get meat broth for a penny.

'I'll take a piece of bread and dripping and a coffee,' said Joe, handing over his last penny. The man held the coin up to the light for a close look, then dropped it into his cash drawer and handed Joe his food and a farthing change. Joe examined the tiny copper coin just like the man, then he wolfed down the greasy slab of bread and took a long, scalding drink at his coffee. It was bitter, but the heat made him feel better.

'You don't taste it like that,' said the man in a friendlier tone. 'You want to savour your food, mudlark.'

'Ain't no mudlark,' replied Joe automatically, folding his hands around the hot mug.

'He's a tosher,' called out one of the customers. 'You can tell by the stink.'

There was a sneer in the voice, but normally Joe would have acknowledged his trade proudly. Only somehow tonight he didn't want to.

'Ain't no tosher neither,' he muttered.

'No offence,' said the cookshop owner reasonably. 'Only you smell like one.'

One or two of the customers laughed at this too, but the cookshop owner gave them a sharp look and they were quiet. Joe took no notice. He finished his coffee, wiped his mouth with the back of his sleeve and looked up at the man.

'You know a man named Harry Trencher?'

The man looked at him quickly. 'Who wants to know?'

'Nobody.'

'You want my advice, mudlark, you'll stay away from Trencher. He ain't a man to trifle with.' The man was laughing, but there was something else in his manner. He was hiding it in front of his customers, but Joe's quick eyes had spotted the expression that flitted across the cookshop owner's face at the first mention of Harry Trencher – frightened might be putting it too strong, but uneasy certainly. 'You're sellin', are you?' he went on.

Selling? Joe's mind turned immediately to tosh, but he'd said nothing about selling anything and he had nothing to sell. He followed the man's eyes, which were directed past him towards the door. He looked round. The tall boy was still standing at the door. What had he got to do with selling? Then Joe looked down. Sitting on the step outside the cookshop, one ear pricked, the other drooping raggedly, nose twitching at the smells that came through the door, was the little white mongrel that had followed him all the way from Hartingham.

'Sellin'?' replied Joe, catching on. 'Yeah. Maybe.'

'Sportin' animal, is he?'

Joe was lost again.

'A ratter,' explained the cookshop owner impatiently.

'What? Yeah. A ratter,' agreed Joe quickly.

'Don't look like much,' said the man, moving to the door to examine the animal. The dog backed away, belly flattened to the ground. 'Looks scared of his own shadow. Rats'd probably eat him!' The man laughed uproariously, and the boy at the door joined in.

'He's a fighter!' insisted Joe. 'A real terror!'

'A terror of a terrier, eh?' laughed the man. 'If you say so, mudlark. Oh, no, sorry, you ain't no mudlark, are you? Same as this little mongrel ain't no terrier, I reckon.' Another burst of laughter from the tall boy. Half the customers in the shop joined in this time, enjoying the free show. 'Still,' finished the man, turning back to his food counter, 'if you're hopin' to sell him to Harry Trencher, he'll be at Nimms's tonight down on Flower Street. Only they won't let you in stinkin' like that!'

The sound of laughter ringing in his ears, Joe ducked out of the cookshop and back towards the main road. Following Harry Trencher he'd noticed a substantial building with a tall chimney set back a little from the busy street. Joe knew what it was, though he'd never been inside one.

He approached the elaborately carved entrance warily, shoulders hunched so high he looked as if he was trying to make his head disappear. The front door was open. He peered in at the shiny green and white tiles, sniffing at the sharp, unfamiliar odour of disinfectant. The cookshop owner was right: he'd never get into Nimms's looking the way he did. Besides, this was like unfinished business – unfinished since the Saturday night when Bess had surprised him at the enamel sink in the Madman's basement. Joe took a deep breath, wished he hadn't as the sharp smell caught in his throat, wished one last time that it was the darkest, dirtiest sewer in Pound's Field he was stepping into, then he walked through the door of the Public Bath House.

Chapter 26
Hot Water

A man sat behind a high wooden table in the entrance hall to the Bath House. He wore a cap and a coat with brass buttons that looked a bit like a policeman's uniform. There were white towels piled at one end of the table, little pale-coloured squares of soap arranged in neat rows at the other. The uniformed man wrinkled his nose and his eyes bulged at the first glimpse of Joe, but before he could speak Joe burst out with, 'Course I stink. That's why I'm here, ain't it? I want a . . .' Joe hesitated. 'I want a bath. With soap,' he added quickly.

'A towel too, perhaps?' asked the man, raising both eyebrows ironically.

'And I needs to wash me togs.'

'You certainly do,' said the man. 'How old are you?'

'What difference does that make?' demanded Joe. 'I'm old enough to take a bath, ain't I?'

'You certainly are,' said the man. 'That'll be a penny then. Including towel.'

'I got a fadge and that's it.'

'A farthing?' The man looked disgusted. 'I can't let you in for a farthing.'

'Yes, you can. Just give me the towel.'

The man shrugged. He took Joe's farthing, handed him a tiny square of soap and the smallest, thinnest towel he could find, and let him through.

The corridors in the place all had echoing stone floors and the same green and white tiles. The smell was stronger in here, a pungent, stinging kind of a smell that got inside Joe's nose and down his throat and made him cough worse than the fog had. In the waiting room he found a crowd of men on wooden benches. One or two looked up as Joe came through the door, taking in the state of his clothes and the thick crust of dirt that clung to his boots and covered his face and arms. A man in overalls started complaining loudly to his neighbour about the kind of persons they were letting in here these days. Joe took no notice: half the men in the room were tramps anyway. They weren't planning on washing; they were just looking for a warm place to sit out the evening until the workhouse opened up for the night.

He was right that many of the men weren't there for a bath, because it was Joe's turn much sooner than he expected. An attendant with the same shiny brass buttons as the man at the door showed him into a stone-floored cubicle. There was a narrow wooden bench on one side and an enormous, white, enamelled bath, already almost full with steaming water. Joe stripped off William Poundfield's clothes and folded them carefully in a pile on the bench. They were nearly as filthy as his old togs had been, but at least they didn't fall apart in your hands.

The edge of the bath was icy to his touch. His hand left a black stain on the enamel, which he tried to wipe away, looking guiltily around and making the mess worse. He gave up, dipped a cautious toe into the steaming water and recoiled with a sharp cry at the unbelievable heat. There were no taps on the bath. Perhaps he was supposed to fetch cold water himself. Joe looked around for a bucket, but there was no sign of one.

'It's too hot!' he called out, his voice echoing from the tiles.

A voice came from somewhere outside the cubicle – 'Cold water coming!' – and a great spout of water came gushing out of the fill-pipe at one end of the bath.

'Blimey!'

Whoever was operating the water must have taken Joe's exclamation as a signal to stop, because that was the end of the cold water. He tried calling again, but there seemed to be no chance of any more water, hot or cold.

Gripping the sides of the bath, Joe lowered himself inch by inch into the scalding water. As the first shock began to wear off, he shifted his limbs cautiously, feeling the warmth around him, watching dirt begin to lift off his skin and cloud the bath. The water in the sewers could be warm in summer, but this was something different altogether. In fact to call this steaming liquid and what flowed through the Flower Street drain both by the name of water seemed to make no sense. Joe lay back in the enormous bath: even stretching with his toes he couldn't reach the other end. Vague memories stirred inside him of high, whitewashed walls and barred windows. There was a face in the memories too, a woman's face, but it wasn't clear and he didn't want it to be clear. Joe knew where those memories led and he didn't want to follow.

He ran an experimental finger along the line of his arm, leaving a long whitish mark, and another dark stain began to spread through the water. Joe sniffed cautiously at the soap, which had no smell of any kind as far as he could tell. He rubbed it against his arm, then the other arm, then he started on his legs, and as he rubbed, the water around him all began to turn as black as sewer water and his skin took on the colour of under-cooked ham. Joe watched the transformation, fascinated and just a shade revolted.

Towel wrapped around him, Joe stood shivering at a long line of sinks in the next room. His skin felt cold and strange on him as he worked at his clothes with what was left of the soap. A couple of weeks of Joe wearing them had already taken their toll on William Poundfield's jacket and breeches. But with the dirt scrubbed out of them, they still looked a decent set of clothes. The man who showed him how to use a flat iron and where to hang his things to dry didn't sneer about 'tosher's rags'. He was polite, helpful, even lent him a fine-tooth comb, which Joe tried unsuccessfully to force through his matted hair. Finally the attendant took a pair of scissors and cut out some of the worst of the knots. He also gave Joe a bottle of liquid 'to kill the nits' without asking for money. But Joe didn't like the smell of the stuff and in the end he poured it down the sink when the man wasn't looking.

Two hours after entering the Bath House Joe re-emerged

into the foggy evening air, his clothes still damp against his skin. The man at the entrance had to look twice, but the dog recognized him all right. It was waiting on the step outside, chewing at a scrap of bone it had found somewhere and making little growling noises. As soon as it saw Joe, it got quickly to its feet and followed him down the road, the bone clamped in its jaws.

Joe walked down the foggy main road in the direction of Pound's Field. The street was full of people, and most of the shops were open even though it was Sunday evening. The taverns and gin shops that lined the thoroughfare were doing a roaring trade.

He had noticed it in the market that Saturday night with Bess, but he noticed it even more now that he was alone. It was not that people looked at him differently with his clean clothes and scrubbed face; it was that they didn't look at him at all. No one stopped to stare at the state of his clothes; no one stepped out of his way with a '*Stinking tosher!*' or, worse still, '*Mudlark!*' It was as if he had become invisible.

He stopped in front of a brightly lit shop window full of pastries and cakes and coloured sweets piled into enormous glowing pyramids, but for once Joe wasn't looking at the food. The dog stopped too, settling to its bone again, as Joe lifted his hand slowly to his face, watching the unfamiliar reflection do the same thing. He felt weightless, as if he had left a part of himself with the filth in the bath water. The boots were already dirty again from the roadway, but from his ankles up he was someone else. He wasn't a tosher. He wasn't Joe Rat. Maybe he was young William Poundfield who'd died of the cholera twenty years back. One thing was sure – and Joe clenched his fists into balls of determination as he made himself the promise – he wasn't going down the sewers again. Not ever.

Outside Nimms's gin shop, Joe hung back amongst the loiterers, keeping out of the gaslight. With the fog so thick there had been little chance of anyone spotting him as he made his way through the familiar streets of Pound's Field and the uncanny feeling of invisibility had still not left him, but he didn't want to take any chances. He thought of his grey cloth bag. He could nip down River Street and see what was left of the Madman's house. Maybe he could get into the garden and retrieve his hidden hoard – if it was still there. But he feared watching eyes, and anyway he had come looking for Harry Trencher. He was going to find out once and for all what kind of a man he was and what business he had with Bess Farleigh.

Men and women were pushing their way into the tavern while Nimms himself collected a shilling entrance money at the door. Nimms questioned anyone he didn't know, and turned away some he did, even if they had the shilling. This one Sunday night in the month he had enough customers to refuse entry to the drunks and troublemakers that made up most of his usual clientele. Joe spotted the rat-catcher he'd seen down the Flower Street sewer going in with two enormous cages. He didn't have to pay. Several men went in leading dogs, and the onlookers moved back, pointing and commenting: 'There's a sportsman!' 'Fancy little tyke!' An enormous white bulldog waddled in behind an equally bow-legged man. 'What a beauty!' commented an awed voice in the crowd. 'A real rum buffer!' Nimms gave the man a particularly hearty greeting. None of the dog owners seemed to be paying either.

Trying to adopt the swagger of the man with the bulldog, Joe stepped under the flaring gaslights and walked purposefully towards the plate-glass doors of the public house. Nimms stuck out an arm, but Joe was relieved to see that he showed no sign of recognizing him. The boy had never been inside the gin shop, but he'd had a kick or two aimed at his backside in passing by Nimms and his waiters.

'I'm lookin' for Harry Trencher,' announced Joe in as big a voice as he could muster. 'I got a sportin' dog for 'im.'

'Oh, yes?' Nimms sounded less than convinced. 'Where?'

Joe looked around quickly. For once the wretched little mongrel was nowhere to be seen. Then he spotted it, skulking in the shadows with the remains of its bone.

'There he is!' said Joe, heading for the door once more. 'Come on, boy. That's his name,' he added for the man's benefit. 'Boy.'

'Is it?' said Nimms sarcastically. 'Thought it up all by yourself, did yer?'

'He's a real fighter,' said Joe, puffing out his chest. 'A real rum buffer,' he added, remembering a phrase he'd just heard. 'Killed twenty rats just last night. Didn't you, Boy? Come on!'

The dog flattened his belly to the pavement, eyeing Joe warily.

'Looks more like the rats'd eat him,' laughed the man. It was the same joke Joe had heard in the cookshop. He felt sick inside. This wasn't going to work. The animal wouldn't even come to him. And why should he, considering he'd chucked a stone the first time he saw him? He tried again, making his voice as encouraging as he could.

'Come on, Boy.'

Slowly, without raising his belly off the floor, the dog crawled forwards through the dirt towards Joe. The loiterers gathered round, forming a kind of alleyway. 'A tanner says he doesn't make it,' shouted out one voice. 'Half a sov it bites him!' called out another.

It seemed to take for ever, but at last the dog reached Joe's feet, the remains of his bone still held tight in his jaws, his beady little black eyes studying Joe without blinking. The boy bent down. The dog gave a low, warning growl.

'Come on then, Boy,' said Joe as casually as he could manage, and reached out to pick up the dog.

The growl transformed itself into as fierce a noise as the small dog could manage. His body went rigid as Joe's hands reached under its belly. He twisted sharply, almost loosening his grasp, stretching his head for his right hand. If his jaws hadn't been occupied with the bone, Joe was sure he would have bitten him. But he didn't. Instead, after a second convulsive attempt at escape, the dog seemed to change his mind and lay perfectly still in the boy's hands. Joe transferred the animal under one arm.

'Go on then,' said Nimms with a shrug. 'Only Harry

Trencher's more likely to have that mutt roasted for his supper than he is to buy it.'

The downstairs of Nimms's gin shop was a low-ceilinged room with a couple of tarnished mirrors behind the bar and row upon row of bottles lined up on shelves. Around the walls hung pictures of dogs, old dog collars, stuffed dogs in glass cases, but the place had none of the brightly coloured glass and fancy chandeliers of the gin palaces up on the Whitechapel Road. Most nights of the week the customers at Nimms's place came in to get drunk as fast as they could, and they didn't care much about the decor, just that the gin was strong and cheap.

But tonight was different. Tonight the place was packed to overflowing with men, women and children – soldiers in uniform, gentlemen in fancy waistcoats, costermongers and shopkeepers, mothers with children, gaudily dressed girls hanging on the men's arms. Perhaps twenty or so of the people in the room had dogs with them, either tied on a lead or clamped in their arms. An excited barking mixed with the racket of voices all talking at once about dogs and bets and rats, and over everything hung a thick haze of tobacco smoke and the powerful smell of hot gin.

Through the crowd, moving from group to group, examining each animal in turn by squeezing its paws or peering into its eyes or ears, went Harry Trencher, stovepipe hat still firmly clamped to his head. Joe stayed close to the door, jostled by each newcomer. He had no idea what was going to happen next. He'd heard tell of the ratting at Nimms's but he'd never asked exactly what went on. Trencher was coming towards him now. What was he going to say to the man? He was going to be exposed as a fraud straight away and thrown out.

But just before Trencher reached Joe, Nimms climbed onto the bar with both hands raised for silence and Harry Trencher forgot about Joe and his dog. 'Gentlemen,' said Nimms solemnly, 'the door is locked.' And he made a great show of sending a waiter over to close the front entrance. 'Let sport commence!'

Chapter 27

BOY

The crowd of people that filled Nimms's downstairs bar surged towards the staircase at the back, carrying Joe with them. Upstairs he found himself in a big room with bare walls and floorboards. A large white square had been painted in the middle of the floor with a waist-high wooden barrier around it to form a kind of arena. Overhead a branched gas lamp hung low, making the white paint glare in the light. On three sides benches and tables had been arranged for the onlookers, but Joe joined the group of men with dogs who had an area set aside on the fourth side of the arena. The rest of the crowd jostled for a vantage point, while the dogs yapped excitedly. Tucked under Joe's right arm, the ragged mongrel that he had just named 'Boy' was the only silent animal in the place. Wide-eyed, trembling slightly, he stared round at the other dogs and the seventy or eighty people crowded into the room as if he had never seen anything like it in his life which, Joe reckoned, he almost certainly hadn't.

'Ladies and gentlemen! The main event of the evening will

be a grand match in which up to one hundred rodents will be slain by the winning dog!'

Nimms was enjoying his role as master of ceremonies, though it was Harry Trencher himself who was pulling rats from the rat-catcher's cage, lifting them quickly by their tails, avoiding their sharp teeth. 'But first,' went on Nimms, 'for your entertainment and to rouse your sporting blood' – the crowd raised a cheer at this – 'an invitation event in which our champion, the world-famous Captain, will take on all comers!'

At this there was a tremendous outburst of cheering and stamping, which made the dogs bark even more frantically. The bow-legged man stepped forward just next to Joe, holding the white bulldog named Captain high above his head for the crowd to admire. Joe could see silver and gold coins changing hands, as Nimms moved amongst his customers, collecting bets and recording them in a book. Meanwhile Trencher had picked out a dozen rats and loosed them into the ring. Some scuttled around the white floor, searching desperately for a way out, others sat up on their hind legs, cleaning their faces with their paws, apparently oblivious to the noise.

The first challenger was a little terrier. It looked excited enough when it saw the rats, barking and struggling in its owner's arms. But once the man put it down in the arena it wouldn't go anywhere near them and started trying to climb out again. Nimms held his watch in the air, keeping a check on the time, while the crowd jeered and booed. The owner leaped over the barrier, stamping and clapping his hands and screaming encouragement at the top of his voice. Finally the dog rushed blindly at one of the rats and the animal reared up in its face, sending the terrier leaping back, terrified. At this point the owner gave up and took the dog out of the ring. The booing got louder.

The second challenger seized a rat by the neck, but the rodent twisted round and bit it on the nose, sending the owner into a panic. 'Poisoned!' he cried out. 'Rat bites is poisonous, you know!' This time the crowd roared with laughter.

In between the challengers Captain wreaked carnage amongst the rats. As soon as he was put into the arena, they started to climb on top of each other, forming great mounds of scrabbling, squeaking fur and tails, trying to burrow their way through the wooden barrier. Foaming at the mouth, howling and gasping, Captain strained at his leash, desperate to be amongst them. His bow-legged owner slipped the leash with a cry of 'At 'em, Captain!' and the dog flew at the pile of rats. One after another he dragged them out of the heap, lashing them against the side of the arena, and in less than a minute on Nimms's watch the white boards were spattered with blood and a dozen rats lay dead on the floor or twitching in their death agony.

As Captain put an end to his fourth batch of victims, another cheer went up from the crowd and Nimms circulated quickly, settling bets. No one was betting against Captain. The wagers were about how many rats each challenger might kill or how long it would take Captain to dispose of his dozen this time. Harry Trencher had bought one challenger who'd done well in the ring. He'd also been betting heavily, and from the grim expression on his face he'd been losing. Captain's owner turned to Joe, who was still clutching Boy under his arm.

'He don't look like much, do he? Keepin' 'im out of the ring, are yer?'

'Course not,' responded Joe quickly. Then before the man could say anything else, the boy went on, trying to talk the way Plucky Jack might have done. 'Looks like the rats'd eat him, don't he?' The man laughed. 'You shoulda seed him last night though. Laid out his dozen 'fore you could blink your eye.'

'Where's that then?' asked the man doubtfully. 'Ain't no rattin' round 'ere on a Saturday.'

'Weren't round here, was it? Down south.' Joe waved his arm vaguely. 'In the country. But he's a rum buffer, he is!'

'Come on then,' responded the man. 'Let's see your Johnny Raw against my Captain. I'll lay you five to one he don't kill more than three.'

'I ain't got no money,' said Joe. 'But he's on for it. Ain't yer, Boy?'

Joe gave the dog an encouraging pat, and the animal shook his head, making the bow-legged man laugh again. 'Here you are, Nimms. We got one more challenger. He's a fierce one from out in the country, or so I'm told.' Then he turned to Joe, slapping him on the back. 'Tell you what, sonny: forget the bet. I'll give you a tanner for every one your mutt kills more than eight. How's that then?'

The announcement provoked a cheer and another round of furious betting amongst the crowd. Joe watched Trencher having a long conversation with Nimms and pressing money into his hand. The publican didn't look happy, but he took the bet. Then Joe climbed into the pit.

Trencher was still counting the rats out of their cage, but one that was already on the floor quickly found Joe's foot and scrambled up the leg of his breeches. Joe shook the rat off – 'Get out of it!' – and for the first time since the boy had picked the dog up, the animal seemed to come to life, whining softly and stretching its neck towards the rat. Finally all the bets were taken and Nimms raised his watch dramatically into the air. This was the signal. The room went quiet, except for the yapping of the other dogs.

Joe put Boy gently down onto the painted floor. The dog shook himself. Then he sat down and began to scratch his torn ear. The crowd erupted in laughter, with Harry Trencher leading the way. 'Go on, Boy!' Joe urged. The dog looked at him. He looked at the rats which were all searching desperately for a way out of the pit. Then he began to scratch his other ear. Another burst of laughter came from the onlookers.

'On 'em, Boy,' whispered Joe, unable to bring himself to the kind of war cries the other owners had been using.

Harry Trencher's voice rang out. 'Look! What did I tell yer? One of the rats is goin' for 'im!'

And, to Joe's horror, it seemed to be true. The biggest of the rats, nose twitching at the air, had advanced to within a pace of the dog. Boy sprang to his feet, legs outstretched and rigid, eyes wide, tail quivering. Joe remembered the whimpering in the corner of the outhouse as the animal had cowered from the barn rats, and these sewer rats were much nastier specimens than any barn rat. But not a sound escaped the dog now.

Suddenly with a spring so quick the rat didn't have time to move, Boy had it in his mouth. For a moment the dog didn't seem to know what to do with the creature. Then he shook his head from side to side with a quick movement, and the rat hung limp, its neck broken.

The dog seemed almost as surprised as Joe. Then Nimms shouted out, 'Dead 'un. Drop it!' Boy looked up at the man. He looked at Joe. Then he dropped the dead rat, and chased across the white boards, looking for the next one. Joe thumped the side of the ring, beating it like a drum and shouting for all he was worth, 'Hi, Boy! Good dog! Go on now, Boy!'

The dog seized his second rat and smashed it so hard against the side of the arena that its head came off, spattering blood across the floor. Some of the crowd who had taken the long odds and bet on this unlikely challenger began to join in with Joe, cheering Boy on. Harry Trencher's face was set and grim.

By the time Nimms raised his arm once again with a shout of 'Time!' all but one of the dozen rats lay still on the floor, and the last one was shivering in its own blood right in the centre of the ring. Nimms climbed over the barricade, bent down to examine the rat, and lifted it ceremoniously by its tail for all to see.

'Dead 'un!' he cried. 'All twelve killed in two minutes flat!'

Even many of those who had lost money managed a cheer. A shower of ha'pennies landed in the arena, sending Joe scrabbling around the floor to collect them. On all sides dog owners and watchers alike were congratulating him.

'Sixpence a head over eight was what I said, and sixpence a head is what I'll do,' said the bow-legged man, to the approval of all the other dog owners. And Joe found himself grasping two silver shilling pieces along with his handful of coppers.

As Nimms selected a dozen more rats from the cage for Captain, Joe spotted Harry Trencher coming towards him. He walked straight across the white square, stepping easily over the barrier, and stopped right in front of Joe. Boy was on the floor at his feet. He had nothing to tie the dog up with, but the animal showed no sign of wanting to get away. He looked exhausted. Everyone else in the room was busy watching Captain killing more rats as Trencher, with a swift movement, scooped Boy up by the scruff of the neck, holding him in front of his face with one hand, turning the animal slowly, examining him from every angle. Finally he spoke. His voice was thick with gin and hoarse from shouting at the dogs.

'Sellin', are you, young fella?'

'Might be.' Joe tried to keep his voice neutral. He hadn't thought about really selling the dog. What kind of money was the man going to offer? Suddenly Trencher threw Boy into the corner of the room, and Joe felt his right wrist gripped and twisted. His fingers opened and the coins he had been holding fell into Trencher's open palm.

'Make up for some of my losings,' he rasped.

Keeping hold of his wrist, Trencher pulled Joe almost off his feet, lifting him until he was eyeball to eyeball with the boy. 'You bring in a dog from no one knows where, and try to put the bite on me, boy? You ain't sellin' nothin' to Harry Trencher.'

He pressed his nose against Joe's. The boy could feel the roughness of his face and smell the strong liquor on his breath. 'But Harry Trencher might be able to sell you. Take you down White Street. I know a gentleman or two who might not be averse. If'n you wasn't so thin and ugly!'

With a sharp movement he threw Joe to the floor and turned back to the arena, pocketing the coins he had taken. Holding his raw wrist, Joe looked quickly around for the dog, and made for the door. He'd lost maybe half a crown in money, but he wasn't thinking about that. He was thinking about what Harry Trencher had said. White Street. And he'd talked about selling him. What did that mean exactly? And if White Street was where Bess was being taken, then just what was Trencher planning for her?

Back on foggy Flower Street, Joe watched the door of the gin shop and waited. The dog lay next to him, panting heavily. At last men and women began to spill out of Nimms's. Harry Trencher was among the first. Hidden by the night and the enveloping fog, Joe tracked the man back to his lodgings.

It was very late and the street was deserted now. In the doorway next to the cookshop, he settled down to wait out another night. The air grew chill. Trembling with cold, the dog slunk forward on his belly, pressing against his side. Joe didn't push him away.

Chapter 28

WHITE STREET

The fog made all the streets look the same, blanketing road signs, reducing the entire city to the few feet of pavement in front of them, but her mother seemed to know where she was going. Jane walked ahead, while Bess and Reuben followed, the girl taking her father's arm as they skirted another puddle of stagnant water. Bess lifted the hem of her dress away from the dirt. With all its ribbons and flounces Bess hated that dress now. She tried not to think about what Joe had said, about how it made her look like one of the women who sold their bodies for money. You just dressed up special for a hiring. That was all. And anyway, whatever she thought of the dress, she didn't want to arrive covered in mud.

At the corner ahead her mother stopped, squinting at a sign high up on the house wall. 'Should be here,' she said doubtfully.

Bess read out the road sign for her. 'It says White Street, Mother.'

As far as the eye could see that dim morning the cobble-stoned side road was lined with identical two-storey houses, each with a little yard in front piled high with rubbish. The drainage channel down the centre of the road was blocked with more rubbish, and they would have to edge their way round yet another pool of stinking water if they were going to go down this way.

'P'raps we should be asking someone, my dear,' offered Reuben timidly. 'This don't look like a place for an 'iring fair.'

'Says White Street, don't it?' snapped Jane. 'Come on. And mind the dress, Bess,' she added for about the hundredth time since yesterday.

'I'll be glad to see the back part of this job,' muttered Reuben miserably to himself.

Bess thought he'd probably said that a hundred times too. She pressed his arm to her, and looked up into her father's haggard face, trying to smile encouragement, but he wouldn't meet her gaze.

Halfway down, White Street was cut in two by the sharp line of the railway viaduct. The upper part of a massive brick arch hung over the road, apparently suspended in the air, its supports shrouded in fog. On this side the chimneys pressed close to the arch. On the other side, where White Street continued, several houses had been demolished. As they got closer Bess could see tatters of wallpaper hanging from an exposed wall where the demolition men had sliced through the terrace. Great heaps of rubble lay scattered across the open ground.

Bess and her parents stood in the shadow of the railway arch. Then they stood over on the rubble-strewn waste ground. Back on the main road there had been people around even this early, but here the street was deserted. There was no sign of a hiring fair. 'Just hold still where you are,' insisted Jane. 'This is the place.'

No one had mentioned the name Harry Trencher, but it was there unspoken in the air. Clearly he had told Jane where to go. It was as if he was still with them, guiding them for good or ill.

Bess spotted the women coming first. Out of the fog, stumbling along the foul, uneven street they came – four of them. One didn't look much older than Bess; the other three could have been any age between fifteen and fifty. They were all muffled up against the weather, and each carried a ragged bundle, wrapped up as tightly as themselves. From one of the bundles came a sickly, keening crying that set the nerves on edge. The women stopped by the arch, ignoring Bess and her family altogether.

Other people began to arrive from both directions: more men and women with infants; girls, some younger even than Bess, dressed up bright and showy like she was; children in pathetic rags, shivering in the chill of morning. A policeman in a crisp blue uniform with perfectly white, starched gloves appeared from the other end of White Street. He positioned himself by the railway arch, swinging his truncheon by its leather strap, watching the crowd impassively.

There was no signal given, but the arrival of a number of gentlemen in heavy coats with mufflers wrapped around their faces started a movement amongst the crowd. Gradually the children began lining up under the railway arch, some leaning against the blackened brickwork, apparently half asleep, some standing up as straight as they could with forced smiles and chins sticking out. Jane nodded to Bess. She gave her father's arm a final squeeze and disengaged herself carefully. His own arm was clamped to hers, unwilling or unable to let go. She pushed him away gently but firmly.

'I'll be going now, Father,' she said softly. 'You'll be a-hearing from me soon, you hear.'

Reuben didn't seem to hear anything. He stared dumbly from his daughter to his wife. His mouth opened and closed a couple of times but no sound came out. When he finally spoke, his voice was gruff. 'You do us proud with these 'ere foreigners, Bessie,' he said.

Bess managed a quick smile which she hoped was reassuring, but she couldn't answer. She crossed the road to join the line under the railway arch. The ragged kids were at one end. She edged in amongst a group of other girls with the same unnaturally red cheeks as herself. People, some prosperous looking, some apparently beggars, were starting to walk up and down, examining the boys and girls. She braced herself for their approach, ignoring the unfriendly stares of the girls on either side.

There was quite a crowd of folk on White Street by the time Joe arrived. He was alone: there had been no sign of the dog when he woke in the doorway at first light. Maybe he'd had enough after the rats at Nimms's. You couldn't blame the animal for clearing off. Perhaps he'd found someone who'd feed him.

Dodging through the crowd, Joe lost sight of the familiar stovepipe hat. He peered over shoulders; he tried ducking down to get a sight of the man between people's legs, but Trencher was nowhere to be seen. Down by the railway arch the crowd was at its thickest. There were tradesmen looking for delivery boys and women wanting cheap maids to look after their children or clean their houses. Joe overheard a steady chatter about business and prices and how you couldn't get decent lads or lasses to work for wages these days. But there were other sorts of people doing business on White Street that morning

An old woman marched down the middle of the street pushing an enormous pram straight through the filthy puddles, forcing the crowd to part in front of her. As she reached the railway arch, one of the women with a baby approached her. The old woman pulled back the corner of the bundle, glancing quickly at the infant inside. A few words were exchanged. Then Joe saw the mother pocket some coins and the ragged parcel was transferred to the old woman's pram. She pushed on into the crowd, approaching each of the mothers in turn and making the same transaction. Finally the youngest of the women, the one Bess had thought looked no older than her, almost ran to the old woman, thrusting her bundle into the now heavily laden pram. She took her payment and escaped quickly into the crowd. The sound of wailing from the pram joined the hubbub of voices.

Joe worked his way though the crowd, stopping in the shelter of the railway arch, trying to see and not be seen. Bargains were being struck now. Beggars picked out the most

ragged and pathetic looking children. Joe knew that dodge – a beggar with a half-starved kid alongside him could reckon on doubling his take. The gentlemen in coats and mufflers stood in a loose group, not speaking to each other or to anyone else, hardly appearing interested in what was going on around them. Then in ones and twos they wandered casually over towards the railway arch, keeping their faces hidden, making for the centre of the line where the brightly dressed girls stood.

Joe groped in his mind for something that felt like a memory. He had never been to White Street before, and yet what he was looking at was oddly familiar: those pale-faced children pressed against the blackened bricks, disappearing one by one as they were led away . . .

Suddenly there was a voice at his ear.

'Smell you comin', Joe Rat.'

Joe jumped as if he had been stung. Plucky Jack was standing at his elbow. Joe was too surprised to speak or move.

''Cept you're all figged out like one of them fancy gents over there, ain't you, Joe boy?' went on Jack easily. 'Now whatever 'appened to Mother's favourite little tosher, eh?'

'You snitched on me, Jack,' Joe blurted out finally. 'You was Mother's nose all along, wasn't you, and you snitched on me and the girl.'

'I never!' Jack's voice was all outraged innocence. 'What a thing to accuse a comrade of! You gotta trust your friends, Joe Rat. I got you away from Billy, I did; give you the apples right outa my basket . . .'

'Yeah, and you chucked bricks at me down a well and all! I seen you, Jack. I know it was you.'

'I was tryin' to stop 'em, Joe. Honest I was. It was Billy and Charley Watchman. You seen him, didn'tcha? He's the nose, not me.'

'I don't believe you, Jack. You – you betrayed me, you did!'

'Ooh, that's a big word, Joe Rat. You bin listenin' to fairy-stories again, you have.'

Joe turned away, ignoring Jack, trying to see past the people in front of him, to find out whether Bess was there or not, whether Harry Trencher was there. If Jack was around then Billy and the rest could be too and it would end in a beating more than like, but he wasn't going to run for it until he knew what was going on. The old woman pushed past, heading back up White Street with eight or nine little parcels packed neatly side by side in her pram.

'Now that's a nice little game,' murmured Jack admiringly. 'Like to get me a dodge like that one of these days, Joe Rat. Needs a bit of capital, that's all. That old witch has just paid five shilling a head for them cubs. Say forty shillings in all. She has a nice respectable-looking party who goes and insures their little lives at five guineas a piece. Then it's a couple of months of not too much tuck for bonny baby; eight paupers' funerals sets you back maybe six pound; and forty shillings has turned into more than thirty guineas. Beats toshin', eh, Joe?'

'Look,' said Joe impatiently, 'I know why you're here, all right, Jack? If you and Billy want to kick my face out the back of my neck, you go on and do it, only I come here to see some-one and—'

Jack was laughing. 'I ain't interested in you right now, Joe Rat. Mother's got other matters on hand apart from your stink-ing little pile of tosh, ain't she? I'm here because of *her*!' The crowd in front of them had parted for moment, and Jack pointed over at the line under the railway arch. 'Fresh as milk.' A smile twisted the corners of the boy's mouth. 'She should fetch a nice price.'

Joe realized he had looked all along the row without recognizing the girl he had come to find. Jack was pointing straight at Bess Farleigh, and at that moment Joe remembered where he had seen the railway arch and the lines of children before. It wasn't a memory at all. It had been that night in the terrifying wide open spaces of the heath as they fled the city and he lay in a hollow tree with Bess, trembling at his own dreams.

'What does Mother want with—?'

He looked around quickly for Jack, but the boy was gone. Something was coming – Joe could sense it – something bad. He raised his hand, trying to catch Bess's attention, but the girl was too far away. One of the muffled-up gents handed a wad of paper money to a man and led away the girl immediately on Bess's left. She looked too young for housemaid's work. What was going on here? He looked again for Jack – he would know – and then he spotted him over on the other side of the railway arch, doing something Joe had never expected to see as long as he lived. Plucky Jack was talking as polite as you like to a crusher. The tall policeman bent his head to listen, nodding at whatever it was Jack was saying.

One after another the men stopped to stare at her. Bess looked straight ahead, eyes focused dumbly on a succession of heavy overcoats, counting the buttons. Sometimes she looked down at a pair of shining boots, splashed with the mud of the city, but she never looked up to meet the eyes that examined her so minutely.

'Turn around, would you be so kind?' This man's voice was soft, deceptively gentle. Bess turned slowly all the way around, feeling the man's eyes on her. But when she was facing front again he was gone. She told herself it was all part of the hiring process, but a horror was growing inside her at being inspected like an animal at market. No one asked where she came from or what she could do – all the questions she'd prepared answers for – they just stared.

She stole a glance down the line. More men in top hats were coming. The girls to left and right had both been chosen already and led away. Somehow she knew this time it was her turn. She clenched her teeth, fighting the impulse to run, holding down a rising nausea.

Joe forgot about Plucky Jack as he looked on, increasingly horrified at what was happening. *Take you down White Street. Harry Trencher might be able to sell you!* He could hear the man's rasping voice, smell the gin on his breath. He scanned the crowd, but there was no sign of Trencher. Bess's father and the woman she now called her mother were standing no more than a dozen yards away, watching Bess. If they were there, that meant it must be all right, didn't it? *They'll do what's best for their child, and there ain't nothing in it for you.* That's what the Watchman had said. But Harry Trencher's words still echoed in Joe's head: . . . *might be able to sell you. I know a gentleman or two who might not be averse.* That was what was going on here. These fine-looking gentlemen with their top hats and their faces all hidden – they were buying kids off the street. Cash down!

The man stopped in front of her for what felt like an eternity. He didn't speak, but he was so close Bess could hear him breathing quite distinctly. He bent to study her face, but Bess kept her eyes down, not meeting his gaze. Then he turned away. Another one that didn't want her. Bess felt an odd mixture of relief and disappointment. Then he was back, and her father and mother were with him.

Money was changing hands. Joe could see that quite clearly. The tall man in the heavy black coat was counting out bank notes and pressing them into Bess's father's hands. Reuben looked stunned, as if he hardly knew what was happening. One of the notes fell to the dirty roadway and the woman pounced on it.

Bess was leaving. The tall man had hold of her by the arm. They were going to pass close to where Joe was standing. He could reach out and touch the man, grab a hold of Bess, drag her away, explain to her that the man wasn't looking for a maid, that he'd bought her for cash to use any filthy way he wanted. They could run through these streets as they had run through the alleys of Pound's Field and escape.

But Joe didn't know his way around here the way he knew his way round Pound's Field, and he was filled with an absolute certainty that they would not get away. There were too many people here. There was Jack and a crusher, and like as not Billy and the rest of the boys, and Bess's mother and father and the tall man.

'Bess!' Joe called out. People turned to look at him, but though the girl was quite close she didn't seem to hear. He tried again – louder this time.

'Bess!'

This time she heard him. Joe saw the man's grip tighten on her arm. Her face showed scarcely a trace of surprise as she recognized Joe. 'Don't follow me, Joe!' she called out. 'I know what I'm doing.' And then she was gone, disappearing into the throng.

Joe pushed desperately through the crowd, which was already beginning to disperse. The man had led Bess away under the arch and on down the continuation of White Street, but Joe could see no sign of them now. He might already have her in a cab and be driving her away. *I know what I'm doing*, she'd said. He didn't believe it.

Across the waste ground Joe could see Bess's mother hurrying her husband away where the houses had been demolished. Why were they going that way? There was no road through there. Then things happened quickly.

As Jane and Reuben disappeared behind a mound of rubble, Joe spied a heavy-set figure looming out of the fog behind them. As soon as he saw the battered stovepipe hat Joe knew who it was, but Bess's father never saw Harry Trencher coming. He never saw the stick either. With a single crushing blow Trencher brought the heavy cane down on Reuben Farleigh's head, and he collapsed without a sound. As he hit the ground, his wife leaped on him, rifling through his pockets, extracting the wad of banknotes the tall man had given them.

For a moment Joe didn't know what to do. Bess was gone. If he didn't try to follow now, there was no chance of ever catching up with her. But this man was her father, and it seemed as if no one else had seen the attack.

He sprinted across to where Reuben lay unconscious on the ground. Trencher and the woman were heading off across the waste ground along the line of the viaduct. There was a back alley there after all, even though the houses were gone. Trencher had planned his escape well. Joe bent quickly to examine the man on the ground. Reuben was breathing, but blood seeped steadily from an ugly wound in his head. Joe cast around for something to stop the bleeding. That was when he spotted the scrap of paper clutched in the man's right fist.

Prising the fingers open, Joe lifted the paper up in the light. There was writing on it and a number. He knew that much. But what it said, he had no idea. He looked up despairingly for help. The policeman was coming straight for him.

Joe knew exactly what was going to happen next. The policeman had seen him bending over a bleeding man; he'd soon find out money was missing. Joe could already feel a heavy hand on his shoulder. It was too late to run. But the hand never came. To Joe's astonishment the policeman ran straight past him. He was after Harry Trencher.

Trencher must have heard the heavy tread behind him because he turned sharply, raising his stick with a snarl. But the sight of the policeman seemed to change his mind. Instead of staying to fight he threw Jane to one side and made a run for it, dodging across the waste ground, slipping and stumbling, scrambling over a heap of rubble. The policeman had hold of Jane Farleigh now, but it looked as if Trencher might escape after all. Then, as he reached the top of the great pile of rubble, a burly figure loomed out of the fog, blocking his path. Even at this distance Joe knew who it was. He had seen him often enough throwing troublemakers three or four at a time out of St Saviour's Docks. He had woken up in the darkness to his pock-marked face more times than he could remember. It was the Watchman.

Trencher raised his stick to strike, but the Watchman was too quick. Side-stepping, he caught the man off balance and sent him staggering with a blow across the back of the neck. Trencher let out a cry as he fell, tumbling over and over down the hill of dust and broken bricks he had climbed. At the bottom he lay still.

Joe didn't wait to see whether Harry Trencher was alive or dead. He raced up the hill of rubble to where the Watchman was still standing.

'Watchman! Jackson!' The man turned slowly. 'What does this say?' He thrust the piece of paper into the Watchman's hand. Jackson looked at it. He looked at Joe. He said nothing. 'What does it say?!' Joe demanded again.

At last the Watchman spoke. 'It says Number One, River Street.'

'What? But that's – that's—' He snatched the piece of paper from the Watchman's hand, staring at it as if it might tell him something else, something different.

'It's all right, Joe.'

'All right?' Joe's voice was a rising scream of disbelief. 'All right?'

He backed away from Jackson, slipping on the loose rubble. Number One, River Street was the Madman's house.

'I found Mr Poundfield,' said the Watchman slowly. 'We made a plan.'

'What kind of a plan?' demanded Joe frantically. Was it Jackson and the Madman who were selling Bess to some dirty toff? 'I know what this place is,' he stammered. 'Those men in their top hats and coats – they ain't hirin' servants. They're buyin' kids!'

Jackson reached out a hand but Joe sprang away. The big man was trying to get hold of him – just as he'd grabbed him outside Bess's house in Hartingham. He'd tried to tell him it was all right then too, tried to persuade him Bess's mother and father knew what was best for her, and now look what had happened to the girl.

'You're all in on it!' he shouted. 'You and the Madman and that dirty toff!'

All Joe's long memories of the garden and the voice that shouted in the night and the silent tombs in the long grass returned. The man in the heavy coat must be taking Bess to the Madman's house, or what was left of it. Anything could happen to her there. Poundfield had spun them a yarn about how his daughter died and the Watchman had spun him a yarn too, but at that moment Joe didn't believe a word of any of it. They'd all told him a pack of lies – Bess too. But he wasn't going to leave her to the Madman or to some toff who thought he could buy kids off the street. He thought of the way Poundfield had stared at her, how he had reached out for her when he found them in that strange room at the top of the house. Clearest of all he could see again the Madman bending over her as she lay helpless on the couch that first night in the house.

Without a word Joe was off at a run, slipping and sliding down the hill of rubble, and then on down White Street, heading back towards familiar territory, back to Pound's Field.

Chapter 29

POUND'S FIELD

On Flower Street it could have been any Monday morning. Nimms's gin shop was quiet after the weekend. Smoke belched from the chimneys of the soap factory. Joe's stomach gave its customary empty lurch as he caught the smells coming out of the cookshop. River Street was its usual busy self too, except there was no Plucky Jack at his pitch on the corner. But men were heading down the road towards the docks as usual and the costermongers were setting out with barrows laden with goods. Joe tried not to run, not to attract the attention of any watching eyes. He knew it was useless. As soon as he turned the corner onto Flower Street word would have been on its way to Mother that her Joseph had returned.

It wasn't until he got further down towards the docks that the road didn't look quite right. The warehouses were there; the entrance to St Saviour's was the same except for the new man at the gate. Then, with a shock that stopped him on the crowded pavement, Joe realized what was missing. The high wooden gables of the old house that had dominated the street and the whole neighbourhood for so many years were gone. The front wall was standing. The spiked railings along the top that had deterred intruders for so long still looked as if they could protect Poundfield's home from any attack. But the timbers of the gate had been smashed, and through the jagged gap Joe could see that scarcely anything was left of the Madman's house. The shattered remnants of two brick chimney stacks rose into the foggy sky. At one end part of the oak frame stood like a charred skeleton amidst the ruins. The rest of the house was ash and a tangle of blackened timbers.

Joe picked his way through the weeds that still flourished in the broad gravel drive. He spotted a couple of pigs rooting amongst the scorched bushes close to where the front door had been, but there was no sign of human life. Anywhere else in Pound's Field there would have been ragged folk scavenging for what the flames hadn't consumed, chipping bricks from the chimneys, dragging out scorched timbers that could be used for building elsewhere or broken up for firewood. But even with the Madman gone, the gates wide open and the house destroyed, people would think twice before coming in here.

One look at the place and Joe was certain Bess couldn't be there. But why had Reuben had the address in his hand then? Should he go back to White Street and try to find the man? Joe stood a moment, hesitating in front of the ruins, but he already knew what he was going to do. Bess might not be here, but there was something else that could be, something he had never quite stopped thinking about all the way through the sewers as they fled their pursuers, all the way down the long road to

Hartingham and back again – the small, grey cloth bag, and the silver teaspoons, the pewter tankard and the silver signet ring that lay inside.

He circled the wreckage of the house, heading for the far corner of the garden. Away from the ruined building the place was oddly unchanged. He found another pig searching amongst the brambles and weeds but otherwise everything was the same – the trees stood patiently, their bare branches shrouded in fog; ahead of him were the big evergreen bushes, and beyond that . . . Joe pushed quickly through the foliage, fearing what he would find on the other side.

The tombs were unchanged too. The great mastiff still lay silent, sleeping his stone sleep. The cat curled its head under its tail. The weather-worn terrier rested his nose on his paws, eyes closed to the world. But instead of setting straight to work, searching his old hiding places, Joe stood looking at the line of statues. Rather than making him think only of his hidden hoard, they had got him thinking again about the mangy dog that had followed him to London. That morning he'd told himself the animal had probably cleared off on his own, maybe found someone who wouldn't chuck stones at him. But Joe knew that wasn't really the most likely explanation for Boy's disappearance. Gangs of dog thieves roamed the streets looking for strays. If they'd got him, he might get sold for ratting if he was lucky, but more likely he'd be a trayful of penny pies before nightfall. These pampered pets had grand tombs and carvings and Boy was going to end up as bow-wow mutton.

Joe shrugged quickly. Finally he had the chance to search for his hidden tosh and here he was wasting time moping over a scruffy mutt. Then, just as suddenly as it had surprised him on White Street, the same familiar voice startled him here.

'Hi, Joe. Lookin' for somethin', are we?'

'Jack!'

'Keep bumpin' into each other today, don't we? Funny that.'

'I was lookin' for the girl, Jack,' Joe improvised quickly. 'Thought she might be here.'

'Dead, is she?'

'What?'

'Only it's mostly dead animals down here, ain't it, Joe? Or is there somethin' else that Plucky Jack don't know about?'

'I thought the man from White Street might have brought her here.'

'Why would he do that?'

It was a genuine question. If the man who had Bess was in with Poundfield, Jack obviously didn't know about it. Joe steered the conversation another way.

'I seen you talkin' to a crusher, Jack. Didn't think I'd ever see Plucky Jack talkin' to a crusher 'less he'd pinched you for somethin'.'

Jack laughed loudly. 'Good that, weren't it? Crushers doin' Mother's dirty work. I told him what Harry Trencher was plannin', see?' Jack sounded very pleased with himself. 'Course, Mother knew about friend Harry's little money-makin' scheme. Only Harry thought he'd hoof it with the whole wad. Now he's goin' down for a five-year stretch instead. And that woman with him.'

So Jane Farleigh had been arrested. Serve her right. Joe tried to edge away from the tombs, back through the surrounding bushes, drawing Jack with him. 'Still, Mother won't get the money now, will she?' he said. 'I mean, not if the crushers have got it.'

'You're right, Joe Rat. And it's good of you to worry about your Mother like that. Only, see, it's more important to the dear old soul for people to see what happens to those who try to bubble her out of her whack than it is for her to get the money itself. And speakin' of people who try to bubble her out of her whack—' Jack placed a hand on Joe's shoulder, pressing down heavily. 'Now I'm the closest you got to a friend, Joe Rat, and I got a piece of friendly advice for you. You dig out the tosh you got hidden double quick and hand it over to Mother and she just might persuade Billy not to tie you up in a sack and drop you off of London Bridge.'

'It's good advice, Joseph.'

Joe knew the voice, and there was only one person who ever called him Joseph. But it couldn't be her. Not here. Not away from that blazing coal fire and the four-poster bed. The voice came again.

'You owe me money, Joseph!'

This time there was steel in the voice and Joe was certain. He turned slowly, instinctively stooping at the waist to make a smaller target.

Billy was there, shirtsleeves rolled up tight as ever. Eight or ten of his gang of mug-hunters were already ranged in a semi-circle around Joe. Three more were pushing through the bushes with the wall of Holywell Court behind them. They moved slowly, circling him. But Joe didn't turn to look for an escape route as he might usually have done, because next to Billy, one hand gripping his arm, the other reaching up to a tall man's shoulder for support, stood Mother. It was the first time Joe had ever seen her upright, and the sight of this great mountain of a woman, standing there, quivering slightly with the effort of holding herself up, held him transfixed.

Behind her, as still more of Billy's mob emerged from the bushes, Joe could see a big hole gashed in the back of the 'cow sheds' on Holywell Court. The fire hadn't spread and there was no other damage to the buildings; it looked as if Mother had simply walked through the old wall, pushing aside lathe and plaster like one of the curtains around her bed. Joe stared stupidly, wondering if those white mice had come too, if one was about to poke its nose out of a fold in the layers and layers of clothing that covered the woman. Mother obviously misinterpreted his expression.

'Don't you recognize your poor old Mother, Joseph?' she queried, her voice suddenly frail and querulous. Then, abruptly, it was back to a harsh bark: 'Seems like you forgot what you owed her for long enough!' Then she smiled, exposing a mouth full of blackened teeth. 'Come here and give your poor old Mother a hug, Joseph.'

Joe couldn't move.

'Come on.' Swaying slightly, she let go of Billy's arm, extending a pudgy hand towards him, one trembling finger beckoning. Joe watched, fascinated, still rooted to the spot, still

waiting to see if a white mouse would emerge from somewhere.
'Come here!'

The command startled Joe into life. He moved warily
forward, keeping close to the ground, eyes shifting left and
right. As he came within arm's reach of her, Mother suddenly
gripped his shoulder with a strength he wouldn't have believed
possible in her quivering frame. She bore down on him with
her whole weight, while Joe braced himself, not wanting to
show the effort of supporting her massive bulk.

He looked straight up into her narrow eyes almost lost in
the folds of skin on her pale face. There was a line of sweat on
her upper lip, and the smell that came from her reminded Joe
of that stuffy room, of nights stretched out on a shakedown by
the fire when he was much younger. All at once he remembered
quite clearly Mother reading to him from a big, leather-bound
book, when he was so small he had to climb down backwards
from her bed.

She had read him the same story over and over again, said it
was her favourite. It was about a poor man whose wife died and
then he and his next wife decided they had to get rid of their
children, and they took them out into a forest, and – and that
was why Bess's story, the one she told him in the Madman's
garden that first night, had sounded so familiar. It was Mother's
story. Bess had told him a storybook tale, because she was too
ashamed of the truth. She was dressed up all fine and fancy
and she talked pretty big, but her mother had wanted to
get rid of her, to sell her to a stranger for cash and spend
it with a bully-boy like Harry Trencher. Thinking of Bess

steadied him, and he met Mother's gaze without blinking.

Mother seemed to sense the change in the boy. 'Well, Joseph,' she purred, 'seems like you've been growing up, my dear. And finally some nice clothes too.' Her fingers dug harder into Joe's shoulder, but the boy didn't flinch. 'Now you've helped a little runaway that Mother wanted and you've cost the poor old soul money,' she went on in a deceptively even tone, 'but all you've got to do is to give Mother all that tosh she knows you've been hiding so cleverly, and then we'll be friends again, won't we?'

Billy let out an evil little laugh at her shoulder, and Mother's head snapped round. 'Shut it!' Billy's face fell, and he was silent.

Joe's eyes shifted, looking for a way out he knew wasn't there. He could feel his legs beginning to buckle under Mother's weight. She bent very close, almost whispering, 'Such a clever little fellow. Mother never knew what a clever little fellow she'd found. And a brave one too. Not scared of the bogey man in the big house. Comes and hides his tosh all by himself. Only now the bogey man's gone, ain't he?' Mother raised her voice for the benefit of Billy and the gang, and Joe realized how difficult it might have been to persuade them into the garden even now.

She turned back to Joe, kneading his shoulder painfully, working on the same spot over and over. 'And now, my clever and brave little Joseph, now it's time to share with Mother!'

The hoarse shout turned into an open-mouthed laugh and then a terrible hacking cough. She brought up a mouthful of phlegm and spat straight at Joe. Billy laughed again. So did the rest of the gang. This time Mother didn't stop them.

Joe felt the spittle dripping down his face, but he made no move to wipe it away. He looked deep into Mother's tiny, piggy eyes. This old monster had robbed and cheated him for years. She had read him fairy-tales and given him a place to sleep and it had mixed him up inside until he didn't know whether he was supposed to fear her or love her. But now he knew. His head was quite clear all of a sudden and he knew that he hated this terrible old woman as much as he hated the life he had led in the sewers. She was going to rob him again, take all he'd saved from three years of toshing, but it didn't matter, because the only power she had over him was the power of Billy and his mug-hunters. There was nothing else. Inside he was free.

'I'll get it.' Joe spat out the three words and began his search. Billy took a step forward, but Mother held up a hand to stop him.

They stood in a ring around him while Joe scrabbled at the foot of the first stone plinth. There were twelve tombs in all, and Joe had hiding places in four of them. He tried those first, oddly certain that he would find nothing. Sure enough, all the familiar spots were empty. Someone had got up the nerve to break open the tombs and they'd cleared out his tosh down to the last copper coin. But Joe didn't waste time regretting what he'd lost. With Mother standing there watching, it was lost to him anyway. The point was that if he came up with nothing, he was lost too.

He searched the other tombs more slowly, playing for time

without knowing what he was waiting for. He could make a break for the hole in the wall or back towards River Lane, but glancing up at the silent figures standing round, he could see no way through the line. There were too many of them.

The last tomb had an elaborately carved canopy. There was no stone animal resting on the plinth of this one, just a stone seat with a shawl made to look as if it was falling off the side. Joe knew what lay behind its iron doors and it wasn't his grey cloth bag; it was a coffin containing the remains of ten-year-old Teresa Poundfield, twenty years dead. But shouldn't the doors have been open? Bess had levered them open; they'd pulled the coffin out, seen the inscription on the top. Yet now they were solid and immovable, as if they had been locked shut for twenty years and no one had ever dared disturb the grisly secret they concealed.

Crouched in front of the tomb, Joe looked over his shoulder. Billy was standing right behind him. There was a smile on his face, a smile Joe knew only too well. He looked around for Mother. She stood impassively, watching, waiting for him to open the last tomb and produce what he owed her.

'It's his daughter,' said Joe.

'What is, Joseph?'

'The Madman's daughter is buried in there.'

Mother's face didn't move, but out of the corner of his eye Joe caught a flicker at the corner of Billy's mouth. His eyes shifted quickly around the rest of the gang. In the fog it was hard to make out expressions even this close, but he could see one or two shifting uneasily from one foot to the other and looking around them. He went on, raising his voice, saying whatever he thought they would least like to hear: 'Tess, her name was. He murdered her and buried her here. That's what drove him mad.'

Mother's voice cut through, hard and certain. 'Open it. We ain't afraid of no bogey man, are we, boys?' She looked around the gang and they seemed to take courage from her, murmuring agreement.

'Open it, Joe Rat!' snarled Billy.

'Open it, Joe Rat!' came another voice.

'Joe Rat! Joe Rat!' They were all joining in now. It was almost a chant. Joe had no choice. He slid his fingers into the thin gap in the doors and braced himself to lever the tomb open.

'It's no use! It won't budge!'

His voice was drowned as the gang advanced, still chanting his name. They were only yards from him now and still the metal doors wouldn't budge, and if they did it wouldn't save him, because the tosh wasn't there.

Billy was the first to reach him. A hand touched the top of his head, softly, almost caressingly, and at the same moment a high, raw voice cried out above the gang's shouts, echoing from the garden's mossy walls, out into the foggy courts and alleyways of Pound's Field, across the docks and down to the river.

'*Tess!!*'

Billy's hand didn't move. The gang fell instantly silent. Joe felt the hairs on the back of his neck stir. There was a hush on the whole garden as if the day had come to a halt. Then it came again.

'*Tess!!*'

As one, Billy, Mother, the whole group wheeled round towards the ruins of the house. Joe looked up with the rest. Through a gap in the surrounding bushes, the broken remains of the Madman's house rose in the swirling fog – the skeleton of half a wall, two broken chimney stacks pointing into the filthy air. And on the very top of the tallest of those two piles of charred bricks, arms outstretched towards the heavens, covered from head to toe in a coat of white ash that made his outline blur with the fog around him as if he was a thing of the air, not the earth, stood the unmistakable figure of the Madman himself, Henry Poundfield.

A sound ran round the watching group – something between a groan and a whimper. Joe's eyes went at once to Mother. For a moment she didn't budge, still leaning heavily for support on the man next to her. Then he took an involuntary step backwards and she was forced to follow. The gang seemed to sense her movement. Every face turned away from the ghostly shape atop the blackened remains of the house and back towards the hole in the wall and Holywell Court. And as they turned, Joe himself leaped back with a cry of horror, because the metal doors he had been straining on without success had suddenly swung open, and, crouched like an animal in its lair, a ghastly figure was emerging from Teresa Poundfield's tomb.

She was dressed in a long, white gown, stained with earth

and damp, and her blonde hair hung loose and dishevelled on her shoulders. Her eyes were dark smudges in a face pale as the fog, and over all lay a thick coat of the same ashes that covered the Madman. As slow as a dream, she lifted one hand, wrist uppermost, limp and heavy, as if the effort was almost more than she could manage. Then the wrist turned, still in slow motion, and the hand extended like an invitation, a greeting towards Joe.

The boy stood rooted to the spot, unable to look away. But amongst the rest of the group Billy was the first to move. With a terrible shriek he ran straight for the gaping hole in the wall. The rest of the gang was at his heels in a moment. Out of the corner of his eye Joe saw the whole group tearing at the bushes, scattering leaves and twigs in their desperation to escape, Mother pushing with the rest.

'Joe.' At first the voice didn't register. Mother and Billy and the gang were gone, and he was alone with – 'Joe!' – he was left alone with – 'Joe, it's me.'

Finally the familiar tones penetrated his consciousness and Joe's eyes focused properly for the first time on who was in front of him. The mouth was smiling. The hands were rubbing with a handkerchief at the eyes, removing smudges of black soot.

It was Bess.

Joe gasped in disbelief. He turned back towards the house. The awful figure on the broken chimney stack was scrambling down from the burned house, smoothing his tousled hair, shaking a cloud of ash from his heavy black coat. It was Poundfield. But as he replaced his top hat and tied a muffler around his throat, Joe realized with a shock that it was also the prosperous-looking gentleman who had bought Bess at White Street. The muffled stranger moving down the line of children had been Poundfield himself.

Joe turned back to Bess, stammering questions, feeling his heart still pounding from the horror of seeing those iron doors creak open and that figure emerge.

'It was Bess's idea, Joe.' Poundfield had reached them now. 'We came straight here in a hansom cab from White Street, and she dreamed up the whole scheme on the way.' His voice was steady. The great height was still there, the face was still thin and drawn, but Henry Poundfield was transformed from the man who had gone mad with grief in a house full of dead animals.

Poundfield was still talking. Joe tried to concentrate on what he was saying, but the words didn't seem to make sense. Bess had made a plan. That's what he was saying. When she realized it was Poundfield who'd bought her, she had made a plan to save him from Mother and Billy and the gang.

'I knew you'd follow me if I told you not to, you see.' Seeing his confusion, Bess had joined in the explanations. 'And I thought that terrible woman might be here a-looking for your tosh.' Bess's voice broke into a giggle. 'So me and Mr Poundfield here, we cooked up a little play-acting to give them a scare. I just had time to get in the tomb afore you arrived. Wouldn't have fancied sticking in there much longer, mind.'

'So it was you what followed me?' Joe asked Poundfield. 'I knew there was somebody all the way back from Hartingham.'

'Me and someone else, Joe,' said Poundfield. 'Someone Bess and I have both got a lot to thank for.'

'Just doing my job, Mr Poundfield, sir,' came a voice. 'Even if there's been no sign of wages these last few years.'

Out of the murk stepped Albert Jackson. He was smiling – something Joe had never seen him do – and he was helping to support the unsteady figure of Reuben Farleigh, who had a thick bandage wrapped around his head. Bess ran to her father's side, putting herself gently but firmly between him and Jackson, taking over the support of her father as if she was the adult now and he the child. Jackson stepped aside. But he was still smiling.

'I caught up with Mr Poundfield after that little dog of yours let go of my ankle, Joe,' he said. 'Brought him back to the city. I knew Harry Trencher had something planned for Bess here, so we just made sure it was the right man bought her this morning.'

Bess didn't leave her father, but her face was glowing. 'Thank you, Mr Jackson,' she said. 'Seems like you been a-looking out for all of us.'

'I've got something of yours too, Joe,' the big man went on. 'Charley Watchman been keeping an eye on it for you while you were away in the country.'

Everyone except Joe managed a laugh at that as Jackson pulled out a small, grey cloth bag from the recesses of his coat. Joe took it from him quickly, pulling open the drawstring, checking its contents, frowning at the laughter that grew louder at this. Seemed like everybody had been spying on his 'secret' hiding place.

'Don't worry, Joe,' said Jackson. 'It's all there down to the last groat. Thought it might be safer with me, with the gate down and all.' Then he advanced towards the boy. 'Mr Poundfield is coming with me, Joe. My home town's not far past Colchester way, and he's got a hankering for a new life, away from' – he hesitated delicately, glancing across at Poundfield, who stood solemn and silent now – 'well, away from old memories. You'd be welcome to share my roof too. Ain't a grand place, but there'd be a bed for you.'

Joe looked into the pock-marked face he knew so well – or thought he had known. He felt a fool. For years he had feared this man, suspected him of being Mother's spy, and now he didn't know what to say to him. The Watchman had been looking out for Henry Poundfield all along – keeping the promise he made his father, just like he'd said on the lane in Hartingham. He didn't care about a few miserable bits a tosher had managed to save. Suddenly a dozen little incidents flashed back into Joe's mind – the Watchman delaying Billy's boys as they chased him up River Lane, the Watchman offering to lend him money, the Watchman trying to steer him and Bess to a safe place for the night. Yes, he'd been a fool every way.

Joe looked down, not knowing what to say. It was Bess who spoke.

'It was Mr Jackson left the coal and the oil in the shed behind the house. Done it secret-like for years with his own money. Remember how it never seemed to run out?'

Jackson smiled. 'That's right, Joe. I had a key to the door in the gate. The one you didn't use . . .' He laughed at the expression of astonishment on Joe's face. 'Oh, yes, I seen you slipping in and out. Had to be careful no one spotted me though. Mr Poundfield didn't want any of the old servants around the house, did you, sir?'

'I was not myself, Albert,' said Poundfield humbly. 'I apologize and I thank you again.'

Bess thought Jackson looked more pleased at the use of his first name than he did at Poundfield's thanks. She hadn't joined in the laughter at Joe's surprise. As the boy still didn't say anything, now she spoke up again. 'Wouldn't be as grand with us, Joe,' she said softly. 'But I'll be a-taking Father back home and we'd be mighty glad if you was to come with us. Wouldn't we, Father?'

Reuben didn't seem able to say anything. But he clung tightly to his daughter and nodded agreement. Bess went on, 'You can't stay here now. Won't be safe for you in the long run. 'Sides,' she went on with a smile, 'you won't never survive without me.'

'What you talkin' about?' This was too much. Finally Joe was roused from his stunned silence. 'You wouldn't never have survived without me!'

There was more laughter. Joe joined in this time. He looked from Poundfield and Jackson to Bess and her father. These people were all offering him a home. He'd given them nothing and they wanted to give him that. He searched for words but none came. Finally he managed a stammered, 'Thanks. Thank you.' Then his head cleared, and he knew what he wanted to say. 'Reckon I'd better stick to my own part of the world though. Didn't take to the country too well.' He gave a tight little laugh. 'Anyway, I'm rich now.' He remembered a phrase of Plucky Jack's. 'I got capital. Maybe find a better trade than toshing – somewhere away from Pound's Field.'

Poundfield and Jackson were the first to leave. Poundfield stood for a while in front of his daughter's tomb. Then he closed the doors carefully, took a last look around and allowed his old servant to lead him quietly away across the garden towards River Lane. Reuben Farleigh had still not spoken. As Bess and Joe faced each other amongst the old stone tombs he stood at a slight distance, staring dumbly in front of him as if his mind was far away.

'I'll be a-seeing you then,' said Bess at last.

'Likely not,' said Joe.

'No. Likely not,' the girl agreed. She turned away, walking over to her father, taking him gently by the arm and steering him in the direction Poundfield and Jackson had gone. Then she turned, framed by the bushes with the ruins of the Madman's house behind her. She lifted a hand. Joe lifted his.

'It was me as looked after you though,' she called.

Joe shrugged. 'Bit of both maybe.'

'Ay. Bit of both.' And she was gone.

Joe waited a moment to let them get properly away. He didn't want to risk running into Bess again out on River Lane. Maybe he'd be changing his mind and following her back to her world and living a life he couldn't see himself living. Then he glanced back at the bushes where Mother and Billy had disappeared. It wouldn't do to leave it too long. You never knew whether someone might get their courage up enough to come back through that hole in the wall and see what had become of him.

Joe slung the grey cloth bag over his shoulder. Then he changed his mind and tucked it inside William Poundfield's jacket. He went quickly over to the stone mastiff and gave him a pat on the head for luck. Then he skirted round the side of the garden, keeping to the tracks Poundfield had worn amongst the brambles and weeds, taking the long route back to River Lane. By the line of trees he hesitated, and instead of heading straight on past the house and away up the road, he turned aside.

Even at a distance it was obvious the brick structure above the well had been destroyed. There was nothing left but a shallow depression in the ground, and coming closer, Joe could see bricks and rubbish had been dropped in until there was no sign that the well had ever existed. But the sound was still there, the sound that had drawn Joe now just as it always did, the sound of running water.

As he approached, the choking, grey fog that still blanketed the garden lifted and lightened a shade, and the silver dusting of a hundred cobwebs shone faintly amongst the dewy grass. Joe squinted up at the blurred outline of a glowing, silver shilling that hung suspended in the air above him. For a moment he couldn't understand what he was looking at. He looked down again, still following the sound of water. And then he spotted him.

Down in the deep gulley, nothing but the white tip of his tail visible amongst the weeds and ferns, the little mongrel was drinking greedily from the spring, while the water splashed clear and bright in the dim London sun.